Two Little Boys

Two Little Boys

Ted Darling crime series

'A topical, dark and disturbing crime thriller'

L. M. Krier

TWO LITTLE BOYS
Second Edition

ISBN 978-2-901773-03-0

Contents

About the Author

L M Krier is the pen name of former journalist (court reporter) and freelance copywriter, Lesley Tither, who also writes travel memoirs under the name Tottie Limejuice. Lesley also worked as a case tracker for the Crown Prosecution Service.

The Ted Darling series of crime novels comprises: *The First Time Ever, Baby's Got Blue Eyes, Two Little Boys, When I'm Old and Grey, Shut Up and Drive, Only the Lonely, Wild Thing, Walk on By, Preacher Man.*

All books in the series are available in Kindle and paperback format and are also available to read free with Kindle Unlimited.

Contact Details

If you would like to get in touch, please do so at:

tottielimejuice@gmail.com

facebook.com/LMKrier

facebook.com/groups/1450797141836111/

https://twitter.com/tottielimejuice

For a light-hearted look at Ted and the other characters, please consider joining the We Love Ted Darling group on Facebook.

Discover the DI Ted Darling series

If you've enjoyed meeting Ted Darling, you may like to discover the other books in the series:

The First Time Ever
Baby's Got Blue Eyes
Two Little Boys
When I'm Old and Grey
Shut Up and Drive
Only the Lonely
Wild Thing
Walk on By
Preacher Man

Acknowledgements

Thanks to all those who helped with this second book in the DI Ted Darling series, Jill Pennington – my Alpha beta reader who encourages me to continue, beta readers Emma Heath, Kate Pill, Mikki Ashe, Chas Stewart., additional editing Alex Potter.

I have also talked to a lot of people in researching this book, abuse victims, police officers, social workers, journalists, teachers and youth workers. Thanks to all of them for their input and help.

To Alex

a survivor

Chapter One

'Ted! Ted!' the insistent voice was accompanied by a repeated tugging at the back of Ted's judo jacket.

Ted turned and saw a small boy with a fiercely determined expression standing there. He knew the boy was eleven years old but he looked younger. His light chestnut hair was always fighting to flop over his brown, spaniel eyes, despite his best efforts with the gel.

Ted was not tall. He didn't have far to bend down to be at eye level with the boy.

'Yes, Flip,' he said. 'What can I do for you?'

'You're a copper, right?' the boy asked.

'I'm a Detective Inspector,' he replied. 'Can I help you with something?'

'I want to talk to you about summat,' the boy said. 'Just me and you, on us own.'

'I'm sorry, Flip, that's not allowed,' Ted told him. 'I'm happy to talk to you, but we can't do it alone, it's against all the rules. What we can do though, if you like, is go and sit over there on those benches at the far end of the gym, while the seniors are warming up. Then everyone can see us but no one will be able to hear what you say to me.'

The boy looked hesitant. Ted turned to his partner, Trevor, and made an apologetic face. He and Trev ran a self-defence class for youngsters at their local martial arts club. It was proving a big help in combating bullying. The juniors had just finished their session. Ted, Trev and the other senior members should now be warming up for their own judo practice.

1

Trev nodded his understanding and made his way to the matted area without his partner.

'Best I can offer you for now, Flip. Any good to you?' Ted asked the boy.

Reluctantly the boy nodded in turn and the two of them walked the length of the large gymnasium so they were out of earshot of anyone on the mats. They sat down side by side on a low gym bench.

'What can I help you with?' Ted asked.

'I'm worried about me mate, Aiden,' the boy said. 'He's gone missing. We were in the kids' home together, then I got fostered. I've not heard nowt from Aide for a while so I went to the home to ask but they wouldn't tell me nothing.'

'Perhaps he's just been fostered in a different area?' Ted suggested. 'How do you usually keep in touch, does he phone you or text you?'

The boy shook his head and said defensively, 'I ain't got a mobile. Me foster mum says she'll get me one for my birthday. But me and Aide always keep in touch. And I'm worried about where he's been hanging out.'

Ted's ears pricked up immediately. He knew the staggering statistics for youngsters in care running away and the fate that could befall them. He'd done a lot of work with the uniform branch, trying to return missing young people to places of safety before they got themselves into serious trouble.

'Do you want to tell me about that?' he asked.

'A bunch of us hang around near some taxi ranks in town sometimes,' the boy began. 'The drivers hand out fags and drink and stuff. I'm not into any of that. I want to do judo like you an' Trev so I want to stay fit. Sometimes the drivers ask kids to go with them and tell them they can make a bit of money if they do.'

Ted felt his blood run cold as the boy said that. He had a horrible feeling he knew what was coming next and it was the worst possible news for his patch.

'I'm guessing Aide went with them a few times?' he asked. 'Did you ever go too?'

'Yeah, I went once, to see what it was like,' the boy told him. 'First time Aide went, he came back with a load of dosh and I fancied a bit of that.'

'Are you happy to talk about it?' Ted prompted gently.

'Yeah, but only to you, then you can do summat about it,' the boy replied. 'When I went, we got taken to this big posh house. There was a load of blokes there, old blokes. They were all drinking, they gave us stuff to drink, strong alcohol, like, but I didn't touch mine.

'One dirty old bastard came over to me. He had his stiffy in his hand and he tried to shove his hand down me kecks. I kicked him right where you and Trev showed us to and I legged it out of there and never went back. But Aide kept on going, for the money. That's why I'm worried about him.'

'Thanks for telling me this, Flip, I know it can't be easy to talk about and I appreciate your honesty,' Ted said. 'What I need to do now is to make this all official. That means I'd like to come round to your foster home, with another officer, and go over this in detail, get some notes. Would that be all right with you?'

'Will they kick me out of me foster place and back to the home, if they think I've been up to stuff like that?' the boy asked anxiously. 'It was before I went to live with them and they're nice, they treat me nice.'

'I'll have a word,' Ted promised. 'Try not to worry about that or about your friend. What's his full name, Aiden what?'

'Bradshaw,' Flip told him. 'Aiden Bradshaw. I call him Aide or Aidie.'

'You did the right thing talking to me, I'll take it from here. Have we got your foster home details on your membership form here, so I can get in touch?'

The boy nodded, automatically flicking back his rebellious hair, damp with sweat after his enthusiastic session of self-defence. They both stood up and Ted shook the boy's hand in thanks, the only physical contact he dared make, even in full view of everyone, although he would have liked to give him a reassuring pat on the shoulder.

Flip headed off to the changing rooms while Ted made his way over to the mat. He was wearing his judo black belt, although he held them in several different martial arts.

Trev was waiting for him at the side of the mat. They were partners in life as well as in martial arts. Trev was a lot taller, eleven years younger and stunningly good looking, with curly black hair and vivid blue eyes. Ted was short, slight and dirty blonde. They made an unlikely, though blissfully happy, couple.

'You all right?' Trev asked anxiously, seeing the tense muscles along Ted's jawline and the darkening of his usually warm hazel eyes.

Ted bowed before stepping on to the mat next to his partner. 'Possible paedo ring operating on my patch,' he growled between clenched teeth. 'And a possible missing kid.'

'Do you want to go?' Trev asked. They were speaking quietly, out of respect to the other members who had already started their warm-up. Senior coach Bernard was looking at them, gauging from a distance the tension in Ted. He knew from previous experience that things could get a little exciting in practice sessions when Ted was under pressure from work.

Ted shook his head. 'I need to burn off a bit of tension,' he said. 'Do you mind if it gets a bit rough?'

Trev, the only person in the dojo capable of sparring with Ted when he was in a mood like that, smiled a long-suffering smile.

'Do I ever?' he asked.

Chapter Two

Ted tapped lightly at the door of the Detective Chief Inspector's office and went in without waiting to be invited. He and DCI Jim Baker went back a long time and were friends as well as colleagues. A recent case had put their friendship to the test but it had survived intact.

But now their relationship was about to change. After striving hard for his promotion, the DCI had finally been made up to Detective Superintendent, and was due to be transferred at any time to another division. Ted was still waiting anxiously to hear who his replacement was to be.

'Morning, Jim,' Ted greeted him, taking a seat, also without waiting to be asked. 'Got a sniff of something on our patch that you're not going to like.'

'Tell me,' the DCI said. 'Then in return I can offer you good news or bad news.'

Ted grimaced. 'I think mine is bad enough,' he said. 'I've not checked any of it out yet but it looks as if we may have a paedo ring on the patch, grooming kids. Some of them are in care, at least one of them may have gone missing. Can you top that?'

'Christ, that's bad,' the DCI growled. 'I know there are some sick perverts about but let's kick their arses off our patch and into prison where they belong as soon as possible. Right, work with Uniform on this, run your own operation between the two of you and let me know how it develops. And let's hope the poor kid turns up safe and sound somewhere. How did you hear of it?'

'A lad at the self-defence club Trev and I run,' Ted told him. 'Nothing concrete yet, but I didn't like any of what he told me and I don't know why he would make it up. I only know him through the club, but he seems a good kid, very dedicated and mad keen on martial arts.'

'So, which do you want first? Good or bad news?' the DCI asked him. Ted shrugged, so he carried on. 'Good news, I've got my transfer through. Moving to South Manchester, nice and handy for home. Bad news … now don't shoot the messenger, Ted. I know who your new boss will be.'

'I'm sensing this is not what I want to hear right now,' Ted said ironically.

'You're getting Superintendent Caldwell,' the DCI said in a tone grave enough for announcing a death sentence. 'The Ice Queen cometh. I take it you know her?'

Ted groaned theatrically. 'I know her all right. I've shot against her in competitions.'

Ted had been a firearms officer years ago. He gave up the role when he and Trevor settled down together as Trev worried about him too much. He still kept his skills up, with regular refreshers. He knew the Superintendent was probably the finest female marksman in the force, certainly leagues ahead of many her male counterparts. He knew too that she, like him, was no longer active but still kept up her qualifications.

'Well, I hope you never beat her,' the DCI said dryly. 'She's enough of a stickler for form without holding a grudge against you for something.'

'Why are they putting a uniform in charge of CID, though?' Ted asked. 'Part of the new reforms? Role-merging? All in together, girls and boys?'

'She'll be in overall charge of everyone in the station, and becomes Assistant Divisional Commander as well,' the DCI told him. 'Formidable roles for a formidable lady.'

'What will it take for you not to go?' Ted asked, tongue very much in cheek. 'What if I promise to go straight and marry a woman?'

Jim Baker looked uncomfortable. As much as he liked and admired Ted, he was never comfortable talking about his sexuality, especially when Ted made jokes about it as he often did. He quickly changed the subject.

'Right, this paedo enquiry. I don't need to tell you to tread very carefully. If these bastards get wind that you're on to them, they'll just drop out of sight and start up somewhere else. Keep me posted at all times, then make sure you brief the Ice Queen on Monday.'

'So soon?' Ted asked in surprise. 'The top brass don't hang about. My team's an officer down, don't forget. Can you do anything about that before you go?'

The DCI shook his head. 'All staffing matters are out of my hands now. In fact my role is strictly keeping this seat warm for the Ice Queen. But you know where I live, Ted. Keep in touch. If ever you need me for anything, don't hesitate to ask. I owe you a lot for what you've done for me in the past.'

Ted stood up and laughed. 'I'm going now before you either start to cry or decide to kiss me.'

He went out into the main office where his team members were at their desks, waiting for their regular briefing at the start of the day. He had a good solid team, a detective sergeant, four detective constables and the youngest member, a temporary detective constable. Every one of them thought the world of Ted as he treated them all with respect and was known as a fair boss, relaxed with his team.

'Right team, listen up,' he said, with his customary call to order. 'Last night I got wind of something very nasty. It's just rumour at the moment but we're going to treat it as true until we find out otherwise, if we do.'

He briefly outlined what Flip had told him the previous evening, particularly the involvement of taxi drivers seemingly grooming children. He saw the looks of distaste which appeared on the faces of all of his team members as he spoke.

7

'You all know as well as I do that this stuff happens. It's all over everywhere, it's in the news depressingly frequently. So you also know that these are clever and potentially dangerous people who may have friends in high places. The slightest sniff that we may be on to them and they'll just disappear off the radar. So, I need total discretion from all of you, at all times. That goes without saying.'

DC Maurice Brown was always the team member who could be relied on to say the wrong thing. After a messy divorce, he fought a constant battle with his two addictions, cigarettes and sticky buns. He hadn't brought in his usual bag of cakes this morning so Ted guessed the fags were currently winning.

'If I get my hands on any nonce bastards … ' then even he, insensitive as he could be, ground to a halt in the face of the hard stares he was getting from both Ted and the DS.

'Maurice,' Ted said icily, 'I know that's just talk but for the record, you will do nothing, and I do mean nothing, which could in any way jeopardise our chances of a conviction in the future.' Then in a more gentle tone, he continued, 'We all feel that way, we just need to keep a tight lid on it or we could blow the whole operation.

'Steve,' he turned to the youngest member of the team who was only just learning not to go red and squirm whenever the DI spoke to him. 'I'll give you contact details for the boy's foster home. Philip, his name is, but everyone calls him Flip. Set up a meeting with him, this evening after school if possible, then you come with me to see him. He'll talk to me, he knows me, you take notes, please.'

'Sir,' DC Abisali Ahmed spoke up. 'I have a cousin who's a taxi driver. I know you can never tell but I'd put money on him being on the level. I could talk to him, see if he's heard anything from any of the other drivers?'

'Excellent, do it. Mike,' he turned to his DS, Mike Hallam. 'You liaise with Uniform on missing youngsters. I suspect we're probably looking at younger boys in particular, but we'll get more confirmation of that as we go along. I want to know where every young missing kid is on the entire patch. Let's find them, make them safe. Maurice, you can do the checking on any names the DS gives you. That will keep you safely occupied.

'Right, Rob,' he turned to another team member, DC Rob O'Connell. 'Take a Uniform officer with you and go round to this children's home where the two boys were in care. I want to know exactly where this Aiden is. Aiden Bradshaw. If he's simply been fostered, I want to know where. Make sure they know that if they start all the confidentiality malarkey I will get a warrant to see all of their records. Some of these private homes are not as squeaky clean as they might be.

'Virgil,' Ted looked at DC Dennis Tibbs, nicknamed Virgil by everyone, which he didn't mind in the least. He preferred it to Dennis. 'You've got good street contacts. Use them. Get out there, ask around, see if anyone knows or even suspects anyone or anything. Someone knows something, and we need to know it too.

'Mike, sort out what else is ongoing at the moment and share it out but I want this to take priority over anything it can. We've had to deal with some nasty stuff recently but a paedophile ring operating on our patch is about as bad as it gets and I want it sorting, fast.'

Chapter Three

Trevor was not a morning person. He was seldom awake, let alone up and about, when Ted was getting ready for work. Even on the rare occasions Ted made any noise, Trev usually carried on sleeping. He always slept spread-eagled across the bed, buried under their seven cats, leaving little room for Ted to sleep.

That Monday morning however, he made an effort to stir, opening one bright blue, sleepy eye and saying, 'I feel as if you're going off to a new school with an ultra-strict headmistress awaiting you. Like I should get up and make you an extra special packed lunch.'

Ted smiled. 'Ultra-strict is about right. I'll have to call her ma'am every other word and there'll be no cosy morning chats over coffee like I used to have with Jim.'

Trev sat up, redistributing cats to make it easier to do so. 'Seriously, do you want me to get up and make your breakfast while you take a shower? I know today won't be easy, with all this stuff with Flip. That kind of case is bound to be deeply troubling, especially for you.'

Ted lent across to kiss him lightly. 'That's a kind thought, thank you, but don't worry, I'll be fine. You get your beauty sleep. I'll see you this evening – if the new headmistress doesn't keep me in after school.'

As ever, Ted was in work and at his desk early, before any of his team appeared. He had barely sat down when the phone on his desk rang. He had known he would be summoned by the Ice Queen once she was installed. He just hadn't expected it to be so soon.

'Inspector Darling? Can you come down to my office please, unless you have anything pressing to do immediately?' The way she said it made it clear that he was not really being given a choice.

Ted replied with a curt, 'Ma'am', then headed down the stairs. The new Super had been given an office on the ground floor, with a bit of a reshuffle of existing Uniform officers to accommodate her. Ted's opposite number in uniform, Inspector Kevin Turner, now had an office so small it made Ted's broom cupboard, as he affectionately called it, seem positively spacious.

Ted knocked on the door and waited for a moment until he heard, 'Come in.' At least his new boss was not one of the pretentious ones who simply said, 'Come.'

The new Superintendent was dealing with some paperwork. Her uniform was so immaculate it looked brand new. She left him standing quite a few moments until she looked up. He wasn't sure if she was being meticulous or making a point.

'Good morning, Inspector,' she said formally. 'I just wanted the chance to touch base with you first thing and to lay out my expectations for you.'

Ted groaned inwardly. Superintendent Caldwell came with a formidable reputation. Ted strongly suspected that even her poor husband, a lowly inspector in traffic, had to call her ma'am most of the time.

'I know that you come with an excellent record, Inspector, and have been offered commendations, which you have refused for reasons of your own, which I respect.' Ted sensed a big 'but' coming. 'However, I do expect officers under my command to adhere to the dress code laid down for plain clothes.'

She looked him up and down in evident distaste, her glance taking in Ted's customary polo neck, dark jeans and Doc Marten's boots.

'Ma'am, with respect ...' was as far as Ted got before the

Ice Queen held up an imperious hand to stop him in his tracks.

'Inspector, as soon as someone says that to me, I know that respect is the last thing on their mind,' she said. 'I'm sure you are going to tell me that how you dress has absolutely no bearing on your performance rates and that might well be true. However, rules are there for a reason and you know the guidelines as well as I do. Your current attire would be acceptable if you were working under cover. Are you working under cover at this precise moment, Inspector?'

Ted ground his teeth. He was feeling particularly irritated that she had not yet allowed him to sit down but had him standing in front of her desk so that he really did feel he was in the headmistress's study.

'No, ma'am.'

'Then please, tomorrow, report for duty correctly dressed in suit and tie. Set a good example to your team and make sure they also sharpen up. And not, please, the crumpled safari suit look which I know you favour for court appearances,' she added.

Ted made one last valiant effort. 'Ma'am, when you're my size, it's not exactly easy to find formal clothes to fit off the peg.'

She waved a dismissive hand and said, 'I believe the Trafford Centre is open until ten most evenings. I'm sure you will find something suitable there in that time. Otherwise do your best and order something altered to fit. Now please sit down and brief me on what you are currently working on.'

Still seething, Ted sat down and explained where they were up to with the information from Flip and their enquiries into the whereabouts of Aiden, which had shown up only that he was indeed missing. The home he was in had admitted he had disappeared and had not been seen for several days.

He also took the opportunity to ask for an additional officer to bring his team up to full strength to handle a potentially difficult enquiry.

The Ice Queen was nothing if not brisk efficiency. 'I have the perfect officer for you, I'll arrange to have her seconded. She's Uniform, but frequently works with plain clothes. She's a sergeant with a lot of valuable experience for this enquiry in her speciality of child protection.' She was making notes as she spoke. 'I'll get her here as soon as possible, she'll be a valuable addition to the team. In fact, in many ways, she may well be more suitable to head up this particular enquiry than you are.'

Despite himself, Ted immediately felt his hackles going up. 'Ma'am, are you suggesting that because I'm gay, I'm not suitable to be heading an enquiry into potential sexual abuse of young boys?'

The Ice Queen's eyes flashed angrily. 'Don't be ridiculous, Inspector,' she retorted. 'I am merely saying that an officer with specific training in all areas of child protection and a lot of experience in this type of offence may well be better placed to steer the enquiry. And don't you ever again dare to accuse me of discrimination of any sort unless you have very good grounds for doing so.'

It took all of the self-control Ted had learned over the years through his martial arts for him to bring his temper back from tipping point. The Ice Queen had hit a raw nerve. He was so accustomed to being discriminated against because of his sexuality he tended to see prejudice where perhaps none existed.

'Ma'am, I apologise unreservedly. I was out of order. I made an assumption,' he said, once he was sure he had his voice back under control.

The Ice Queen's eyes thawed somewhat too. 'I accept your apology, Inspector. A simple misunderstanding. I am not your enemy. I would like you to be clear on that from the outset. I'll arrange for Sergeant Reynolds to join your team as soon as she can. Jan Reynolds, a very good officer, I'm confident she'll fit in and be a great asset to you.

'Now I'm sure you have a lot to do. Please feel free to

leave a little earlier this evening to go on your shopping trip. Thank you for your time. That will be all.'

As Ted left the office, it took a lot more self-control not to slam the door behind him. It was only his first day without his old friend Jim Baker and his easy-going ways and already he was missing him enormously.

He went back up to the sanctuary of his own office and headed straight for the kettle. He was in urgent need of green tea to restore his equilibrium.

Whilst he waited for the kettle to boil, he reached for his mobile to phone Trev at work. Despite having an impressive array of A-levels and speaking several languages fluently, Trev's big passion was motorbikes. He'd decided against university, opting instead to work in a bike dealership where he was blissfully happy. There was absolutely no problem about him taking calls in work time since his boss thought he could do no wrong.

'How do you fancy taking me clothes shopping after work?' he asked as soon as Trev answered.

There was a pause, then Trev laughed. 'Who are you and what have you done with my Ted?'

'The Ice Queen has issued an edict that I must appear suited and booted unless working under cover,' Ted told him. 'She has generously given me until tomorrow morning to get a new wardrobe as she has already forbidden what she unkindly calls my safari suit,' referring to his usual compromise attire of softly crumpled cotton chino jacket and trousers, which he wore for court appearances.

Trev was laughing loudly now. 'I like the Ice Queen already!' he said. 'You know it's my dream, clothes shopping for you, but you always put up such a fight when I suggest it.'

'I'll come and pick you up after work,' Ted said. 'Leave the bike there, I'll take you out for a meal afterwards as a thank you. That way you can have a glass or two of wine. I'll sort you out a taxi in to work for the morning, just in case I get an early call-out.'

Then he added, 'You're really loving this, aren't you?'

'Oh yes,' said Trev. 'The Ice Queen is very definitely going on my Christmas card list.'

Chapter Four

Ted's team gaped at him in astonishment when he appeared for the morning briefing. He was totally transformed in an impeccable light grey suit, striped shirt and tie. Gone were the Docs, replaced by stylish brogues with a hint of a heel which just compensated for the slightly too long trouser length.

He glared at his team, daring them to say a word. They all sensed that even their normally easy-going boss was not going to tolerate any comments on his new appearance.

'Where are we up to?' he asked, perching on the edge of a desk, instinctively reaching up to undo his top button and slightly loosen the hated tie. He felt as if he were being strangled. 'Anybody got anything new to report?'

'I talked to my cousin, boss,' Abisali, known to everyone as Sal, told him. 'He's asked around carefully among the other drivers. He told me there's one who's hinted at knowing something but seems very afraid. My cousin's trying to work on him, see if he would agree to talk to me somewhere on neutral territory. That way if anyone saw us I could be just a cousin of one driver meeting another driver for a cup of tea and a chat.'

'Good work, but be careful,' Ted told him. 'What else?'

The phone was ringing in Ted's office but he ignored it as he listened to feedback on where the team were up to. Then the DS's phone rang.

Mike Hallam answered it and said, 'Yes, he's here,' then handed the phone to Ted saying, 'It's the front desk for you, boss.'

Ted took the phone. 'It's Bill, Ted,' the desk sergeant's voice said.' We just got a shout. A kid's body has been found in a skip. A young lad.'

'Shit,' Ted said. 'Thanks Bill, on my way,' and he handed the phone back to the DS to hang up.

'Right everyone, it may not be connected to this, but we've just had a call about a young lad's body found in a skip. It's bad enough, whoever it is, but let's hope it's not Aiden. I'm on my way there now. Mike, you and Rob come with me. The rest of you, crack on with what you've got so far.'

They took two cars and Ted was on the scene before the other two, having had his foot down hard. The skip was in a yard behind a row of shops in a busy suburban area on the edge of town. A skip lorry was parked nearby. It had presumably come to collect the skip, which was full, and the driver had made the gruesome discovery.

Uniform branch officers were already on site, Scenes of Crime Officers were there and just setting up. Someone had put a ladder up against the skip and Ted could see that the police surgeon, Tim Elliott, was just coming down it.

His face mask was pulled down, showing that his complexion was quite white. He was, as usual, sneezing violently. As it often did, it crossed Ted's mind to wonder what it was about the doctor's job to which he was clearly allergic.

Ted felt in the pocket of the unfamiliar suit jacket, highly relieved that he had thought to transfer from his usual leather jacket his essential packet of Fisherman's Friend. Sucking on the menthol lozenges was his own way of dealing with the distressing parts of his job.

'Morning, Ted,' Tim Elliott greeted him. 'This is a bad business, a very bad business. Do you want to see him before I get him moved?'

'I never want to see them, Tim,' Ted told him pointedly. 'But I need to, with this one as much as any. What can you tell me first?' He was busy putting a couple of Fisherman's Friends into his mouth to prepare for the ordeal to come.

'Poor little lad looks about twelve, I'd say. Probably been there since last night some time. Partially clothed. His trousers and pants are down round his ankles. There are signs of violent sexual activity, although that's not my field, just my initial observation, and he appears to have been strangled. I've notified the coroner, he's arranging for a pathologist to come out to the scene before he's moved. What kind of sick people would do that sort of thing to a little boy, Ted?' he asked in bewilderment.

'I really don't know the answer to that,' Ted told him. 'But you can be sure my team and I are going to do everything we possibly can to make sure we catch the perverts responsible.'

He tried to prepare himself mentally as he climbed up the short ladder. No matter how many deaths he saw, they were never easy to deal with, and the deaths of children were always the worst part of his job.

A small foot in a trainer was what he saw first. Not a bad trainer, although just a cheap market knock-off of a better brand. Then his eyes came level with the other foot and he saw stained pants and trousers crumpled up around the ankles.

Bare, skinny legs, bony buttocks, streaked with blood. A T-shirt and sweat-shirt hoody, partly pulled up to reveal a thinnish body, with protruding ribs and signs of recent bruising. The face, turned to the side, in amongst old cardboard boxes, was discoloured, the tongue protruding between blueish lips. There was a cord wound around the thin neck and pulled tight. Ted couldn't be sure without getting closer but it looked like the cord out of the hoody.

Ted had put on gloves and covers over his new shoes but still didn't venture any closer so as not to contaminate the scene. He took a moment to look at the boy and in his mind he promised him justice before he climbed back down the ladder and went to find Rob and Maurice.

'Rob, get on to the home. You've already had contact with

them. I want an ID on this boy as soon as possible. If it is Aiden, they should know. Wait for the pathologist to arrive here and find out how soon someone can view the body for identification purposes,' he told him. 'Maurice, ask around the scene. Talk to the skip driver, find out what he knows. You know what to do. Let's find these bastards as soon as we can, before there are any more kids in skips.'

The pathologist was just arriving as Ted turned to head back to his elderly Renault. The coroner had sent out the senior Home Office pathologist for what was likely to be a difficult and complicated case. She was relatively new in the post and she and Ted were still getting to know one another, still at the formal stage.

Professor Nelson was short, even shorter than Ted, well built, with a weather-beaten complexion which spoke of a love of the great outdoors. She wore an unfashionable tweed skirt and lace-up shoes and looked as if she should be striding across the family estate, trailed by Labradors and spaniels. She was brusque and extremely efficient, with a good reputation.

'Morning, Professor,' Ted greeted her with a handshake. 'Not a very pleasant one at all, this.'

'Good morning, Inspector,' she responded. 'I'm just going to take a preliminary look at the scene first, then get this poor young boy removed from here as soon as I can. Do we have any ID as yet?'

'Not so far,' Ted told her, 'but my team are working on it and we hope to have someone who might be able to ID the body as soon as you can make that possible, preferably today.'

'I'll do what I can for you, Inspector,' she promised as she started up the ladder.

Ted headed back to the station to bring the Ice Queen up to speed. The meeting was brief but frostily cordial on both sides. On his way back upstairs, he stopped by to talk to his opposite number in uniform, Inspector Kevin Turner.

'Morning, Kev,' Ted said as he went into his office.

'How's life in Narnia?'

'Ha-bloody-ha,' Kevin responded, nodding to Ted to take a seat. 'I suppose that's some smart-arse reference to the Ice Queen, is it? Well, I see she's already brought you to heel. Love the threads, Ted. What's the news from the scene?'

'Poor little sod,' Ted said with feeling. 'Kid of about twelve, looks like he's been raped and strangled. I'm hoping it's not this missing lad Aiden but I'm betting it is.'

Kevin swore comprehensively. 'Just let me know how many of my officers you need and for what. I imagine even the Ice Queen will be willing to run to overtime on this one.'

Ted got the call late afternoon confirming his worst fears. The boy was Flip's missing friend Aiden Bradshaw, positively identified by someone from the home from which he had earlier disappeared. Ted had another meeting, three-way this time, with the Ice Queen and Kevin Turner, to discuss strategy, now the case had officially gone from a possible paedophile investigation to a child sexual assault and murder. It was agreed that officers from Uniform branch would go and talk further to Flip the following day, to see if he could identify the house where he had gone with Aiden, or anything else that might be of help.

On an impulse, Ted left slightly earlier than usual telling his team he had to be somewhere, and would be contactable on his mobile should they need him.

He headed back to Flip's foster home near Davenport, where he had previously been with Steve, the young TDC. Ted decided he would like to be the one to break the news to the boy of what had happened to Aiden, if his foster mother agreed.

The house was a small, neat semi-detached in a respectable-looking area. Flip's foster mother came to the door, a tea towel over her shoulder, soap suds on her hands.

'Sorry to trouble you again, Mrs Atkinson, I'm Inspector Darling, you may remember,' Ted began.

'Yes, I know who you are,' she said, her tone so neutral he had difficulty deciphering any hidden meaning behind her words.

'I'm afraid I have bad news about Flip's friend, Aiden. The worst kind,' Ted told her. 'He's been found dead. I wondered if you wanted me to tell him, or do it yourself. I also wondered if I could see him in any case?'

She looked at him for a moment then said, 'He's in the kitchen, doing his homework. You'd better come in.'

Flip looked up and beamed when he saw Ted. 'Have you found Aide?' he asked hopefully.

Ted looked towards the boy's foster mother and she nodded briefly, clearly telling him to break the news.

'Flip, I'm really sorry to have to tell you this, but I'm afraid Aiden has been found dead,' Ted said, as gently as he could.

The boy stared hard at him for a long moment. Then, to Ted's surprise, Flip jumped up from his chair, knocking it over backwards, and flung himself at him, locking his arms around his waist and sobbing against him.

Ted threw an apologetic glance at Flip's foster mother, who was looking disapproving. He risked one gentle pat on the boy's back then carefully extricated himself from his embrace. Flip ran out of the kitchen and disappeared noisily up the stairs.

'He's never hugged me or my husband and he's been here a good few weeks now,' she said in a slightly accusatory tone.

Ted felt acutely uncomfortable. 'I'm sorry, he's never done anything like that with me before either,' he said awkwardly. 'I just wanted to tell him myself because I'd promised to find his friend.'

Still tight-lipped, the woman led the way to the door to show him out. As he was leaving, Ted turned and said, 'Please don't take this the wrong way, Mrs Atkinson. I know how interested Flip is in martial arts and I wondered if I could give him a judo outfit for his birthday? It wouldn't be new, just one to get him started. Through the various martial arts clubs I'm involved with, I can easily get a good second hand one, if that would be all right?'

'I really don't think that would be at all appropriate, but thank you for the offer,' she said coldly, and shut the door firmly in his face.

Chapter Five

Brave spring sunshine was still making its presence felt when Ted arrived home that evening, earlier than usual. Trev's beloved red Triumph Bonneville motorbike was already safely locked away in the garage when he opened it up to put his Renault away.

As Ted went into the house, he could see the back door from the kitchen was wide open. He went out to the patio and found Trev, still half in his leathers, sprawled in a steamer chair, making the most of the weak sun. The cats were spread out around him, lying on the warm flag-stones, soaking up what heat had been accumulated during the day.

'You're home early,' Trev commented as he looked up. 'Hard day?'

Ted sank wearily into the other chair and turned his face up towards the sun, eyes closed.

'The worst,' he said. 'That young friend of Flip, Aiden, was found dead today, in a skip. Raped and strangled, from the early look of things.'

Trev sat up immediately and reached out to put a hand on his arm. 'I'm so sorry,' he said. 'That must have been dreadful for you. I haven't started to cook yet, did you want to go out to eat?'

'What I want,' Ted said, 'is to crawl into a fort made of blankets and chairs and stay there with my colouring books until the madness has passed.'

Trev smiled gently. 'You can do that if you want to,' he said. 'I'll cook something, so you don't have to go anywhere.

This must be so hard for you. Are you all right?'

Ted patted his hand reassuringly. 'I will be,' he said. 'Except tomorrow I will have to come out of my blanket fort and be a grown up policeman again, and probably have to go to this young boy's post-mortem. Oh, and I think I may have done something rather stupid.'

'Do you want to talk about it?' Trev asked.

Ted opened his eyes and sat up.

'I thought I'd go and tell Flip myself, on my way home,' he began. 'His foster mother was there. She was a bit reserved from the start. Then when I told Flip, he suddenly flung his arms round me and hugged me. The foster mother looked at me as if I was a child molester.'

'But she was with you all the time, she could see what was done and said?' Trev asked. 'Just like in the dojo when you were talking to Flip, we could all see you. You've never been alone with him anywhere?'

'Even I am not that stupid,' Ted said with a rueful grin. 'It was just the way she looked at me. It was very unexpected, the way Flip behaved. Then I made it worse. As I was leaving, I asked if I could get Flip a judogi for his birthday. He's so keen on martial arts and he was so upset. But if it was ever the right thing to do, it was certainly the wrong time to do it.'

'You know the kids at the club all look up to you. I suppose it was that, the way Flip reacted and knowing that you're a policeman. I'm sure the foster mother just saw it as a kind, if misplaced, gesture.'

Although Ted hardly ever spoke about his work at home, Trev asked, 'Do you want to talk about the case?'

Ted shook his head emphatically. 'I don't even want to think about the case unless I have to. Shall we go out somewhere? Take the bike, go for a bit of a walk, blow away the cobwebs, then have a meal out?'

'Is this going to be one of your cheap dates?' Trev asked smiling. 'A walk up a country lane and a bag of chips?'

Ted gave a small laugh. Trev always succeeded in raising his spirits, no matter how grim things were at work. 'Come on, we can be in the High Peak in twenty minutes,' he said persuasively. 'Do us both good. Just let me get out of these clothes and put something comfortable on.'

He fairly sprinted up the stairs to get back into casual clothes, while Trev herded cats into the kitchen and got himself back into his leathers. Trev handed Ted his helmet when he came back down and said, 'I've had a brilliant idea. We'll head 'em off at the pass!'

This time Ted's laugh was spontaneous and genuine as he finished off Trev's quote from his favourite film, Blazing Saddles. 'Head 'em off at the pass? I hate that cliché,' he said, and mimed shooting Trev in the foot.

Trev knew how intensely personally Ted took each and every murder on his patch, so much more so when the victim was a child. He also knew this one would be especially tough for him, involving child sexual abuse, which was going to unleash dark demons from the past.

As the big bike roared out towards Hope and Castleton, Ted asked through the helmet intercom, 'So where are we headed?'

'I thought you were a detective,' Trev joked. 'We're heading for the High Peak and I mentioned a pass. Isn't that enough of a clue for you?'

'Winnats Pass?' Ted asked. 'Just what I need to relax, the scene of a historic double murder.'

'God, Ted, I'm sorry,' Trev said apologetically. 'Do you want to go somewhere else?'

'Don't be daft, it's fine,' Ted reassured him, 'that was three hundred years ago. Come on, open the throttle a bit, there's no policemen watching you, honest.'

Trev needed no encouragement to let the big bike have its head so they were in the Peaks in no time. They were soon peeling off helmets and breathing in clean country air, away from the town.

As well as the martial arts club where they had first met, hill walking had always been their thing. Their relationship had developed on long walks and leisurely picnics in hills and mountains. They'd shared their first hesitant kiss in the High Peak.

It was always out in the hills that Ted felt able to open up and talk about himself other than in his usual joking, self-deprecating way. He seemed to feel safe outdoors, talking about himself in a way he never did at home, even in the intimacy of the bedroom. With each hill walked and each mountain climbed, he opened up a little more until Trev felt he knew almost all about him. Ted told him things he had never told anyone else, but Trev suspected there were still dark secrets in hidden corners of his mind that his complex partner was not yet ready to let go of.

They walked until the light went, then headed to the nearest pub which was serving food. Their choices from the impressive menu spoke volumes about their different personalities. Traditional to the point of old-fashioned, Ted went straight for the steak and ale pie, Trev for the seared swordfish with courgette tagliatelle.

A non-drinker, Ted offered to ride the bike home so Trev could enjoy a glass or two of decent wine and sit in Ted's usual place on the back. Ted could handle the bike well enough and borrowed it on rare occasions, though he had none of the flair and natural ease of Trev. To his surprise, Trev agreed and ordered half a bottle of a good French white wine.

The image of the little boy in the skip was never far from Ted's mind but good food and excellent company were going a long way towards healing the hurt of the day.

'Would you mind if I had a cognac to finish off?' Trev asked him.

Ted shook his head. He was delighted to see his partner so obviously enjoying himself. Living with a copper was never easy on the social front and Trev was hugely sociable. A lot of their evenings out centred on their martial arts.

Trev went over to the bar in search of his drink as there was no sign of a waiter. Ted watched him through the open archway that separated the bar from the dining room. There were two women sitting on bar stools, drinking cocktails. Ted smiled to himself as they both immediately started talking to Trev who was soon laughing and joking with them.

When Trev came back with his brandy, he told Ted, 'Get your coat, you've pulled. The older one at the bar thinks you look cute. She was quite disappointed when I said I did too and you were with me.'

It felt strange, on the short ride back, to have Trev sitting behind him, arms lightly around his waist, as Ted handled the big bike competently but rather conservatively.

Trev seemed very happy. 'This evening has been really nice,' he said. 'We should make time to do it more often, although I know it's not easy with your hours.'

Ted felt his batteries had been recharged. He still faced probably the toughest case of his career so far but at least he felt better able to handle the challenges of the days ahead.

'You're right,' he replied, 'and we shouldn't wait for another poor kid to finish up dead in a skip before we do.'

Chapter Six

Ted was not the only one in unfamiliar dress the following morning. He was first in, as usual, but Sal was not far behind him, dressed in black shalwar kameez. It was the first time Ted had seen him in traditional dress and he felt a pang of envy – it certainly looked a lot more comfortable than his hated suit and tie.

'My cousin's set up a meeting today with this taxi driver, boss,' Sal said by way of explanation. 'Khalid, my cousin, says he's as jumpy as a kitten, he's not even sure he'll turn up, but even if he does, he doesn't think he'll tell us very much until he's more confident.'

'We desperately need intelligence, Sal, but not desperately enough for you to panic him at the first meeting,' Ted told him. 'I take it he has no clue that you're a copper?'

'None at all, boss. In fact,' he hesitated as if unsure whether what he said would meet with approval, 'Khalid hinted that I was a driver after work and looking for a way to make a bit more money on the side than just doing airport runs.'

'It's your shout entirely on this one, Sal. Whatever you decide I'll back you, you know that,' Ted reassured him. 'We need information and we can't afford to be all that fussy about how we get it. Just be very careful. If this really is an organised paedophile ring, they will be on the lookout for leaks and they will be ruthless in how they deal with them. Don't put yourself at risk.'

The rest of the team members were starting to drift in now. Maurice Brown was last, as usual, though still on time. No bag of sticky buns once more, but his clothing smelt strongly of cigarettes. Ted had a mental bet with himself as to how long it would be before tactless Maurice made a crack about Sal's dress. When he did, it raised a laugh from all of them, Ted included.

'Blimey, boss, I reckon you should wear some of that get-up, you look a lot less comfy than Sal does.'

'Sal's out under cover today, as you probably all guessed, trying to find a way to talk to taxi drivers, after the information we got from Flip – Philip,' Ted told them. 'I need as many of you out there as possible today. We need to know where Aiden Bradshaw was in the hours before his death. But it's very important you stay well away from taxi ranks and drivers. If any of you go sniffing round there while Sal is trying to talk to a possible key witness, it could all go pear-shaped on us.

'First off, Sex Offenders' Register. I want every single name in our area and a bit beyond checked on and accounted for on the day Aiden was killed. Steve, you're the one for computer stuff, get lists, pass them to the DS. If you have any way at all of finding names who aren't on the register yet but should be, give him those as well. Even if it's only rumour. We need any lead we can get.

'Mike, can you split the team up as you see fit, make as many available to work on this case as possible, without neglecting anything else that's urgent. I'm planning on leaving questioning other kids at the home where Aiden was until our new team member, Sgt Reynolds, joins us. She's the one with the child protection experience, she would be best suited to that role.

'Sal, when are you setting off?'

'Soon as I can,' Sal replied. 'I've arranged to meet Khalid about a mile away and I'm going there on foot, just in case. Don't want to take any risk of anyone seeing me meeting up with him too close to the nick. I'll go out the back way and walk a less direct route to the meet-up. I'm leaving my warrant card here, and I plan to keep my mobile phone switched off all the time, in full sight, so he knows I'm not trying to record him or anything.'

'Good thinking,' Ted nodded. 'Right, get going, good luck, and check in as soon as you can.'

Sal left the station and walked briskly to where he'd arranged to meet his cousin. Khalid was going to come in his taxi to pick him up, then drive across to the other side of town to a café favoured by many of the drivers in the area. Sal didn't have more than a few moments to wait. Khalid was on time and greeted his younger cousin warmly.

'I'm not sure this driver's going to turn up,' he warned him. 'He's clearly very afraid. He's been working a night shift, he'll be going to the café for breakfast in the next hour or so, if he shows up. If he does, he won't acknowledge me at all when he first sees me. He really is scared. He told me he wants to make sure there is no chance of anyone he knows seeing him there talking to me when I'm with someone else.'

The café was quite busy doing breakfasts. Khalid went to order cups of tea while Sal picked a table close to the entrance. From force of habit, Sal took a seat where he had a view of the entire room, leaving Khalid a chair facing the door so he could see who came in. There was room for the other driver to sit down with them, if he arrived.

They had a long wait, chatting about family affairs and getting to their third cup of tea each before Khalid said very quietly, 'He's just come in and is heading to the counter.'

Without appearing to watch, Sal carefully noted the newcomer as he went to order breakfast. He was small and thin, with an anxious face and dark eyes which darted ceaselessly round the café as he waited for his food. Like all the other drivers in the café, he was wearing western clothing, a dark suit. Only Sal and the off-duty drivers were in shalwar kameez.

Once his food was ready, he headed over towards the front

of the café, studiously ignoring Khalid, who looked up and greeted him casually.

'Would you like to join us? There's a spare seat here. This is my cousin, Abisali, and this is my friend, Mohnid.'

The man hesitated a moment, his eyes still sliding right and left, from one diner to another. Sal stood up and greeted him politely in Urdu, shaking his hand, then the three men sat down.

They talked all round the houses for what seemed to Sal an interminably long time before there was any chance of steering the conversation in the direction he wanted it to go. He forced himself to be patient as it was clear from the way he reacted every time the door opened that the man was extremely jumpy.

Finally Khalid saw an opportunity and said, 'My young cousin is looking for driving work at the moment. There's nothing where I am, but I wondered if you knew of any openings for a keen young man with a clean licence?'

Sal kept his face impassive as the man's dark eyes scrutinised him at length. As he'd said at the morning briefing, he had deliberately put his mobile in full view on the table, switched off.

He smiled in what he hoped was a reassuring way and said, 'I find myself in the unfortunate position of owing rather a lot of money to some people who are not at all patient. I'm prepared to work long hours to clear my debts but I fear that might not be enough to get me out of my current predicament.'

After a long pause, the man said evasively, 'I have heard there are ways of making extra money.'

'How could I make contact with people who might show me how it's possible? Sal asked, trying not to sound too eager.

''It's stupid to be so impatient,' the man said scornfully. 'You don't contact these people, they make contact with you, but only when they have observed you for long enough to know that you can be trusted. They are very dangerous people. You are going to cause trouble if you ask things like that. You will make danger for yourself and for others. You must go now and leave me alone.'

Khalid tried to smooth things over, but the man was adamant and refused to talk any more. Sal felt like kicking himself for pressing on too quickly and blowing possibly his best lead to date.

As they walked back to the car, his cousin tried to console him. 'I told you he was very nervous,' he said. 'I'll talk to him again, you may not have blown it. I'll explain you too are involved with dangerous people, chasing you for money, so you were a little hasty. Don't worry about it, it may still be possible to move forward.'

Ted said more or less the same thing when Sal got back to the station and reported on his meeting. Knowing how keen the DI was on encouraging his team with positive feedback, Sal wasn't sure whether he meant it, or was just saying it.

'If I could just get in there under cover, boss, get a job driving and start asking for more and more shifts,' Sal began.

Ted shook his head emphatically. 'Out of the question at this stage,' he said. 'We don't know who we're dealing with, or how dangerous they really are. I'm not sending anyone in under cover until we do, and the Superintendent would never allow it even if I suggested it.

'You did well, you made initial contact, we have more intelligence than we had before your meeting. Don't beat yourself up about it, it's a start and a start is what we needed.'

Chapter Seven

Ted's desk phone was ringing as he walked through his office door the next morning. As soon as he answered it, a woman's voice began speaking as if he should know who she was.

'Ah, Inspector, I'm sorry I haven't done anything yet with this young boy of yours, we have been rather busy. I wonder if tomorrow morning would suit you? I like to start at about eight o'clock, if that is convenient to you?'

'Thank you, Professor.' Ted hadn't immediately recognised the new senior pathologist's voice on the phone, but deduced who it was from the content of her conversation. 'That's fine by me, I'll be there.'

'Jolly good,' she said brusquely, as if he had just accepted an invitation to afternoon tea, then hung up.

Ted went back out into the main office, ready for his team arriving. The door opened and a young woman appeared, stepping hesitantly in and looking round her. She had a fresh complexion and a smiling face, framed by wavy blonde hair. The first word that came to Ted's mind about her appearance was 'friendly'.

'DI Darling?' she asked him, moving forward with a hand outstretched. 'I'm Jancis.'

Ted was puzzled for a moment, as she could see from his face. She laughed and said, ' Sorry, sir, I'd heard this was an informal team. I'm your new team member, Sgt Jancis Reynolds.'

Ted smiled in reply and shook her hand. 'Sorry, I stupidly saw Jan and thought Janet.'

'Everyone does,' she said. 'My parents loved books. Precious Bane, Mary Webb? Jancis was the main character.'

'I'm not all that much of a reader,' Ted said apologetically. 'The rest of the team will be here any minute, we usually start the day with a bit of a briefing. I assume the Super has filled you in on what we have going on?'

'Yes sir,' she said. 'Nasty business. Happy to help in any way I can.'

'We're going to have to interview a lot of children in care homes, that's where I hope you can take the lead,' Ted told her.

Ted's phone started to ring again. 'Sorry, I'd better take that,' he said apologetically, and went back into his office.

This time it was Kevin Turner, from downstairs. His call was brief and left no time for Ted to speak.

'Ted? Kev. Come down can you, now.'

'I'm sorry to abandon you, I have to go downstairs,' Ted told the new sergeant. 'Make yourself at home until the others get here. There's a spare desk there. I'll hopefully be back shortly.

As a formality, he tapped lightly on Inspector Turner's door before he went in. Kevin was not looking his usual good-natured self. His tirade began almost before Ted had taken a seat.

'Ted, you're a nice bloke. I sometimes think you're too nice to be a copper, yet you manage to be a bloody good one, most of the time,' he began. 'But just sometimes, you can be a complete and utter twat.'

'Suppose you pause in hurling insults at me and tell me what this is all about'' Ted suggested calmly, although he had a bad feeling he probably already knew.

'I sent two of my lads round yesterday to talk to this boy of yours, this Flip or whatever he's called,' Kevin continued, his voice still raised. 'What do you think it looked like when the boy tells my officers he doesn't want to talk to anyone except you because you're kind to him and you hug him? Then when my lads are leaving, the foster mother asks if you're some kind of a nonce because you asked her if you can buy presents for the lad. For fuck's sake, Ted, what do you think the Ice Queen would say if she got to hear about this?'

'Do you want me to tell her?' Ted asked, half rising.

'Are you out of your mind?' Kevin almost shouted. 'She'll have your bollocks for earrings.'

Just at that moment, the door opened without a knock and the Ice Queen stood framed in the doorway. Both men immediately leapt guiltily to their feet. She was tall and statuesque and made Ted feel uncomfortably like a naughty schoolboy once again.

'Gentlemen,' she said. 'I heard raised voices from my office. Not dissent in the ranks, I hope?'

'No ma'am,' Kevin replied, almost too quickly, glaring at Ted to keep his mouth shut. 'Just a healthy difference of opinion and lively debate on procedural issues. Sorry if we were too loud, ma'am.'

She looked long and hard from one to the other, clearly not believing a word of it. 'I'm sure I don't need to remind either of you that we have a particularly nasty murder on our hands and no signs of any real progress on the case. This is no time for debate, we need action,' she told them severely, and left the office.

The two men remained standing for a moment then grinned at one another as they sat back down.

'You really want to throw yourself on the mercy of that cold bitch?' Kevin asked, in a quieter tone. 'Look, Ted, I know you didn't mean any harm, but you must see what it looked like. Luckily for you, for some reason every copper in this nick has nothing but respect for you. My lads told me about it, of course, but they won't say anything to anyone else. It's best, though, if you keep well away from that boy while this case is ongoing.'

'Tricky that, I teach him at the self-defence club Trev and I run,' Ted told him.

'Well, for Christ's sake don't ever be alone with him anywhere, and don't lay a finger on him, even with witnesses,' Kevin advised him. 'Shit, I knew Jim Baker had to keep you on a lead a lot of the time, but I never realised how much you needed him to stop you making a prick of yourself.'

'Thanks for the vote of confidence,' Ted said dryly. 'Most of it was deserved, though. I consider myself told off. I've got this new child protection officer just started today, I'll get her to go and talk to Flip, perhaps with one of your lads who went yesterday. Is he off school?'

'His foster mum kept him home yesterday because he was understandably upset,' Kevin told him, 'but the lads said she was keen for him to go back as soon as possible, perhaps today. Get your new sergeant to phone up and find out when they can go, then liaise with my lads. You keep right out of it from now on, would be my best advice to you.

'And seriously, Ted, the Ice Queen does not need to know. God knows how, but you are a good copper. You committing career suicide right now is not what this case needs. Just promise me you'll borrow a brain from somewhere.'

Ted was known for being mild-tempered and good-natured. His extensive martial arts training helped him keep control most of the time, apart from the occasional karate kick at his office door. He knew he deserved the bollocking, and he took Kevin's tirade without a murmur. Even he could not explain why he had behaved as he had.

'In other news,' he said, defusing the tension of the situation, 'it looks as if taxi drivers are our link. I've got an officer trying to get an opening on that. We'll see if any of the other kids, Flip or any of the ones from the home, can give us even an approximate idea of where the drivers are taking the kids that go with them. If we could just pin down, even roughly, where Aiden was killed, that would move us forward.'

'Are you putting someone in on the taxis?' Kevin asked.

Ted shook his head. 'Too soon,' he said. 'We don't really know who we're dealing with yet and it may be dangerous. There's still a possibility the driver my officer talked to today may come back to him with some more information. But he was really scared, which suggests we are dealing with some very nasty types.'

'Goes without saying, Ted,' Kevin agreed. 'What worries me is, if this really is a paedo ring, how high up does it go and to what extent are these people protected?'

'Protected or not, I'm going after them,' Ted told him. 'I hope you're with me, Kev.'

Chapter Eight

Ted arrived in good time at the hospital the next morning and made his way to the autopsy suite. He put on coveralls and went in to join Professor Nelson, who was just making her preparations.

Ted had attended many post-mortem examinations, though this was his first with the new pathologist. Frequency didn't make them any easier to deal with. The sight of the young boy's naked body, too small for the table he lay on, tore at his heart and churned his stomach.

'Good morning, Inspector,' the Professor greeted him breezily. 'Now, before we begin, are you a puker?'

Despite the solemnity of the occasion, Ted had to smile at her brusque manner. He wondered if all pathologists were somewhat eccentric, whether it was their way of dealing with the horrors of their job.

'Not usually, but I have had my moments,' he said honestly. 'I have my own secret weapon though, which works most of the time.' He took out his ever-present packet of Fisherman's Friend sweets and offered one to Professor Nelson, which she accepted with evident delight.

'Next question. We have quite some time to spend in one another's company. Do you prefer Inspector, or something a little less formal? If so, what?' she asked.

'Ted is fine,' he told her.

'And I'm Elizabeth,' she replied. 'Ted? Is that short for Edward?'

'It will utterly destroy what street cred I possess if I tell you,' Ted smiled. 'Actually, only my partner knows this, but it's Edwin. My father was a great reader, a lover of Dickens.'

'Since you have trusted me with that information, you may call me Bizzie, which is reserved for family and friends,' she said. 'I know you have good reason to distrust those in my profession. But I assure you, Ted, I will do everything I can to help you get justice for this poor little boy.'

She was ready to make the first incision, always the part Ted found the hardest to watch. He reached instinctively for another lozenge, although he had not yet finished the first. The Professor was talking into her voice recorder, giving the details of her first observations.

'What can you tell me about this young lad, Ted?' she asked, as she worked quickly and efficiently.

'Abandoned as a baby, in care all his life, occasionally with a foster family although more usually in a children's home,' Ted told her. 'Considered difficult to place because of behavioural issues. He absconded from the home a couple of weeks ago. Would you routinely test for blood-alcohol levels in a case like this?'

'Not usually, for a child,' she told him. 'I would always do toxicology tests but I will certainly test blood-alcohol levels if you think that may be relevant.'

'Our intelligence so far points towards the possibility of grooming and a paedophile ring. We've been told taxi drivers may have been luring young boys with cigarettes and alcohol then taking them on somewhere with drink freely available,' Ted told her.

She shook her head in bewilderment. 'What kind of dreadful society do we live in that does things like this to children? In a way I hope he did have alcohol, and hopefully spiked with something, to ease his passing, poor little sod.'

She carried on working efficiently in silence then said, 'He has certainly been sexually assaulted quite savagely, poor thing. I'll take samples everywhere, of course, but I wouldn't get your hopes up too high for DNA. It's not something I know very much about at all, thankfully, but I imagine people are so well aware of DNA now that condoms would be *de rigueur* for this sort of activity.'

'Did you know that more than five hundred in care under-eighteens go missing in a year, just in Greater Manchester?' Ted asked her. 'That's an awful lot of vulnerable kids out there, easy prey for child abusers. Yet who knows about it? Who cares?'

The Professor gave him a reproachful look. 'Some of us care, Ted, very deeply,' she said and went back to her work.

After some time she said, 'I can tell you that the cause of death was asphyxia due to strangulation. The killer used what looks like the cord taken from the hooded sweatshirt he was wearing. What I cannot tell you is whether this was done as part of some deviant sexual thrill-seeking or simply because the wee lad might have been able to identify his abusers.

'That concludes my preliminary findings for now. The rest requires detailed analysis and lab work. I'll let you have all those results as soon as I possibly can.'

She took off her gloves and shook Ted's hand. 'Thank you for caring about this little boy, Ted. Do you have children?'

'No, we have cats,' Ted smiled. 'Thank you, Bizzie. I won't say I've enjoyed it, I never do, but you have been a delight to work with.'

The post-mortem had been bad enough. Now Ted was heading back to the station and would have to brief the Ice Queen on the findings and bring her up to speed with the case in general. There was precious little progress and Ted was dreading her reaction.

As he headed for her office, he hitched his tie up to disguise the fact that his top button was undone, as usual. He felt strangled in his new outfit, not at all as comfortable and ready for action as in his chosen dress code of polo neck and jeans.

He knocked at the door and waited for her invitation to enter. At least this time she didn't leave him standing like a spare part before telling him to sit down. He told her everything he had to report. He was careful with the way in which he presented how Sal had got on trying to talk to the taxi driver.

Ted always made sure to protect his team from any criticism from above. If they made mistakes, he dealt with it, but to get them to work well for him, he needed to watch their backs for them. When he mentioned his decision not to put Sal in under cover until he knew more about who they were facing, he was surprised by the Ice Queen's reaction.

'I totally concur with your reasoning and decision, Inspector,' she told him. 'No point putting one of our officers at risk until we have a clearer picture of who we're up against. We need to be very sure of our ground before we take any action. Going off half-cocked could put officers' lives at risk and certainly won't help us round up all of the people involved.

'Now, while you're here, I'll see if Inspector Turner can join us. There's something I want to say to both of you.'

Ted had an anxious moment, while she phoned through to Kevin to request that he join them, wondering if he had done something else stupid that she had got wind of.

Kevin came in and he and Ted nodded to one another as he took a seat.

'Gentlemen,' the Ice Queen began. 'What I am about to tell you is highly confidential, just to keep you in the loop. It goes no further than this office. Is that clear?'

'Ma'am,' they replied in unison.

'I've been talking to officers in Cheshire. They are carrying out a raid on a rock star's house in Wilmslow, within the next day or two,' she told them. 'The reason that they are liaising with us is that they've heard about the murder of this young boy and they think there is a possible link between the cases.

41

'They intercepted some serious child porn images from this singer, posted online, and they think there's a chance that some of these were filmed in our area, based on intelligence they have. The singer is away on tour out of the country and warrants are being sorted. It is therefore, of course, vital that no word gets out. They're very keen to get in there and seize all computers and other material before any of it can be removed or destroyed.

'If there is a tie-in with our case, it's of great concern because of the scale it indicates. But it does mean that with two forces working together, we can bring considerable resources to bear to crack this case.

'But if this were to leak out before the raid had been successfully completed, the implications would be disastrous. That's why I must stress once again, no mention of this is to be made outside the walls of this office. Thank you, gentlemen.'

Chapter Nine

Sgt Jancis Reynolds had centre stage for the team briefing the following morning. Ted had asked her to feed back to the team on what she had found out from talking to children at the home where Aiden had lived. He'd also asked her to outline anything else she thought would help them, since she was the one with experience in the field. She was relaxed and confident and clearly knew what she was talking about.

'I thought it might be helpful if I just outlined a bit about the kind of child abuse we may be up against here, for those of you lucky enough not to have experience in this area. Some of what I tell you may surprise or even shock you, but I assure you there are statistics to confirm everything I say.

'It's important at the outset to realise that this kind of violent sexual abuse of children, as in Aiden's case is mercifully quite rare. What is far more common is the abuse of children by people they know, often people within their own family circle. If not by family members, then by someone within the periphery, a trusted family friend, or even someone given charge of the children, a school teacher, someone running a club, perhaps.'

Ted felt a rising anger within himself as past memories, buried deep, started to resurface. He was conscious of the muscles in his jaw and at his temples becoming tight, and his hands were forming fists, whitening his knuckles. He tugged at his tie to loosen his collar a bit more and struggled to regulate his breathing.

'The thing to remember about paedophiles grooming

children who don't know them is that they can appear to a child to be kind, generous and even loving. To a young boy like Aiden, who had probably never been shown much affection, that side of things as much as the money would keep him coming back.'

She looked round at the faces of the team members, many of them expressing disbelief. Finally it was Maurice Brown who broke the silence.

'Bloody hell, Sarge,' he said. 'Are you saying the kids might actually like what happens to them?'

Maurice was the father of ten-year-old twin girls and he doted on them. They lived with their mother since the divorce but he was allowed unlimited access to them. Apparently bad parenting was not one of his many faults. Mike Hallam, also a father of two, was looking horrified.

Jancis Reynolds shook her head. 'Not like it, Maurice, exactly,' she told him, 'but it's important to realise that there is a world of difference between how these people operate when grooming children, and the brutal rape of a child by either a stranger, or someone unexpected.'

Ted felt as if he was choking. His memory conjured up the smell of chlorine, invading his nostrils, smothering him, and burning the back of his throat. His hand went instinctively to his pocket for a Fisherman's Friend to disguise the vivid smell and taste. He noticed that the hand was shaking badly as he put a lozenge in his mouth, and quickly put it back in his pocket.

'What I'm saying is that sometimes children will have a confused idea about these people, not quite the straightforward fear and loathing you might expect. They will know them by their first names, although, of course, not necessarily their real ones. They won't always see them simply as the Bogey Man.

'Now, from talking to Flip and some of the others, the children are often taken to private houses but Flip had no real idea where he was taken the only time he went. We're going to arrange to drive him around a bit just to see if anywhere jogs his memory. Both he and some of the others said that Aiden boasted of going to what he called posh hotels.

'We have no way of knowing what was true and what he was embellishing, but he seems to have told the same or similar stories to everyone, so there may be a grain of truth in it. We're talking small, probably private hotels, not the big cheap and cheerful chains or motels. He mentioned a ballroom on more than one occasion, but I must stress some of this may just have been him trying to make himself look more important.

'That's about all I have for now, boss,' she said, looking towards Ted.

Ted stood up, glad of the chance to be doing something. He headed to the white-board and picked up markers to start logging what they had. Gripping a pen helped him regain control over the shakes. Aiden's name was already written at the top of the board. So far there was nothing else.

Sal had given him the name of the taxi firm where the driver he had tried to talk to worked. He wrote it at the side, linked with a line and several question marks. On the other side of the board he wrote 'small hotels' and linked that to the boy's name.

'Steve, another computer job for you,' Ted said. 'Pull up a list of all the small and medium-sized private hotels on our patch. They may be listed as guest houses as well. It might even be worth looking at bigger B&Bs, although I'm not sure where the ballroom story would fit in with them. How have you got on with sex offenders?'

'I've given the DS the list of anyone within the patch who's on the register, sir. I'm still searching for anyone under suspicion but not yet convicted,' he replied.

Now there was a growing assurance about the way he answered and spoke up, compared to how he had been when he first joined the team.

Ted stood back and looked at the board. 'What we need,' he said aloud, half to himself, 'is something linking the taxi firm with one or more of these hotels. That might help narrow things down a bit.'

Virgil Tibbs, always the joker of the team, piped up quickly. 'Boss, if I can put it on expenses, I'll take the missus out to dinner in all of them and ask for a taxi home, then see which firm they suggest.'

It raised a small laugh from all of them, despite the serious nature of the discussion. 'Nice try, but I can't see the new Superintendent agreeing to that, Virgil,' Ted said. 'But I do think you've hit on something. Once Steve produces the list, you and Rob, separately, can go round them all and see what cards for taxi firms they have on the reception desk. While you're at it, check out which of them have function rooms with a dance floor, anything which a young lad like Aiden might have called a ballroom. Try saying you're looking for a venue for a party or something, pick up some brochures.'

Ted noticed that Rob O'Connell was not looking his usual self. He seemed distant, uncomfortable. He would normally have chipped in with a few ideas but he was unusually quiet.

'I know this case is a hard one, for all of us,' Ted told his team. 'If anyone is finding it particularly difficult for whatever reason, don't forget you can come and talk to me, in confidence. There are other cases we still need to work on. If anyone is struggling, there's no shame in asking to be reassigned.

'In the meantime, why don't we all have a quick drink together this evening after work, my shout? Jan, more often than this lot would have you believe, I've been known to put my hand in my pocket for a round at The Grapes. You're welcome, as our newest team member, unless you have family commitments to hurry back for?'

'I have two small children, sir, but I'm lucky enough to have a husband who works from home and can take care of them, so I'd love to join you,' she said. 'Without sounding too pushy, being the newbie, could I just say that I've had a lot of experience in this sort of enquiry. If anybody wanted to come and talk to me, in private, I would be happy to listen and advise.'

Ted looked appreciatively at his newly-seconded officer. Perhaps the Ice Queen had a good side after all, despite her formality and adherence to rules. She had certainly been right in her choice of Jan Reynolds to make up his team's numbers.

Chapter Ten

Sal was in his own clothes once more. He told Ted that his cousin had heard further from the other driver and they were going to meet him again, to see if they could get any more out of him.

'This time he wants to meet at a service station on the motorway,' he said. 'He's certainly acting scared and clearly trying to make sure no one is watching him.'

'Be careful, Sal,' Ted told him. 'His behaviour suggests whoever he is working for is dangerous and cautious. Do not under any circumstances put yourself at risk. If you get the least sign that things are not right, you walk away. We'll find a way to get these people, but I don't want you or any of the team put in avoidable danger.'

As before, Sal walked to the place he had arranged to meet his cousin, this time a different place and a different approach route. Even without the DI's warning, he was not taking any chances of being seen anywhere near the police station before heading off to meet the driver.

The service station was crowded, as usual. It was a good place to meet with some degree of anonymity, easier to blend into a crowd. Sal's cousin was off duty and he too was wearing shalwar kameez. Although they were no more than a couple of miles from where Sal lived, he didn't spot a single face he recognised, which was encouraging.

This time they had an even longer wait until the other man showed up. They'd found themselves a quiet corner where they could watch the frequent comings and goings in the busy place, but there was still no sign of their contact.

'How long do we give him until we decide he's not coming?' Sal asked his cousin.

'As long as it takes,' Khalid replied. 'I think he will come. It's possible it was not him who picked up the little boy who died, but he might know something about who did. He told me he would talk to us again. We will just have to be patient.'

Sal felt awash with tea by the time the driver finally appeared through one of the doors and walked past them without acknowledging them, heading for the drinks counter. He had clearly finished his shift some time ago as he was also in his own clothes.

There were very few spare seats, so it appeared perfectly natural when the other driver, Mohnid, brought his tray across to their table, which had a spare seat, and asked to join them.

As before, the man's dark, beady eyes were darting about incessantly as he sat down with his cup of tea. When he spoke his voice was so low that Sal had to bend forward to catch what he was saying, with all the noise going on around them.

'There may be a way I can help you,' Mohnid said. 'They are always looking for extra drivers where I work, it is very busy. Once you get a job there and I see that you can be trusted, I can talk about you to these people. You have a clean driving licence?'

'Yes, but not with me,' Sal said quickly, having prepared his cover story in advance, not wanting to give too much detail to this man. 'Khalid drove me here so I didn't bother to bring it.'

'Once you're in, I will see about some extra work being put your way. You will be asked to collect and deliver certain things. It could be anything. If you want this work, you need to do as you are asked without ever asking any questions. That is very important.'

Sal nodded. 'I can do that,' he said earnestly. 'I would be so grateful for any help to get these people off my back.'

'When you start to receive payment from these people, you will, of course, have to pay me an introduction fee. Help comes at a price,' Mohnid said with a smile like a sneer, revealing bad teeth. 'My share will be half.'

'Half?' Sal echoed in amazement, raising his voice in astonishment.

The man glared at him and made shushing noises and gestures. 'My risk is greater than yours. If I introduce you and you let them down, it will go very badly for me,' he said. 'If and when things start to settle down and all is well, I may be able to reduce my commission to one third. I will be in touch again with your cousin to see when you should come and ask for work. Then I will see to the rest of it. Now go, without saying anything. We are supposed to be strangers sharing a table.'

As they walked back to Khalid's car, Sal was still expressing amazement at the cut the other driver was proposing to take. 'If he's recruiting other drivers and taking half of everything they make, he must be doing very well,' he said. 'Now all I have to do is persuade my boss to let me go in under cover and see what I can find out from the inside. Persuading him won't be easy.'Not easy proved to be impossible. Ted was adamant it was too soon to put anyone in under cover when they currently had no intelligence on who they were dealing with.

'But, sir,' Sal argued, 'the only way we are going to get that intelligence is from the inside. I've got an in and I blend in perfectly. I could do this, if you'd just let me.'

'Even if I agreed with you, Sal, which I don't, at this stage, the Superintendent would never go for it,' Ted told him patiently. 'I've already discussed it with her and those are her instructions. We're not saying not ever, just not yet. You've done good work.'

'So what do I say if this other driver gets back to me about starting some driving work?' Sal asked, looking stubborn. 'If I turn him down now, I've blown it.'

'You're inventive, Sal, you can think on your feet,' Ted told him. 'He may not get in touch for some time, and by then we might be ready for you to go in. If he does make contact sooner, try telling him you're under so much pressure from the people you owe money to that you're too afraid to leave the house.'

He could tell that Sal wasn't happy about the decision but there was little more he could do at the moment. He was reluctant ever to put the lives of any his team at risk, especially when they had so little intelligence to go on.

It was the day for the self-defence club for kids and for Ted and Trev's judo session. Ted always tried to get away from work in good time if he could, and today more than most he was in need of the kind of release from tension he could find only through his martial arts. He wondered if Flip would be there tonight and if things would be awkward between him and the boy.

Living with Trev, Ted had come to like Queen rock music but sometimes in the car alone, he indulged in his guilty pleasure of listening to country music. Trev teased him mercilessly about his taste but always bought him the CDs.

It was only a short drive from the station to the house but long enough for Ted to enjoy singing along loudly to Willie Nelson. Ted had a good voice but lacked confidence to air it except on his own. Trev, on the other hand, frequently sang with great enthusiasm and always hopelessly out of tune.

Trev was in and watching the news on television as Ted walked in.

'Have you seen this?' Trev asked, pointing towards the screen, as Ted leaned over the back of the sofa to plant a kiss on his cheek. 'It's Rory the Raver, his house near Wilmslow is being raided for child porn.'

Ted looked at the screen, his heart suddenly pounding. Police were swarming round a big, impressive house while journalists, cameramen and even a helicopter were all over the scene.

'Who is he?' he asked.

'Modern rock, not anything you would listen to,' Trev told him. 'Plays in a band called Toof. Very alternative, but he models himself on the old classics. Likes smashing up hotel rooms, that sort of thing. Rumoured to like young groupies, very young, and not fussed as to the sex.'

'Toof?' Ted echoed blankly.

Trev smiled as he explained, 'Stands for Too Fucking Much.'

He was about to continue when they were interrupted by Ted's much more classical taste of Freddie Mercury singing Barcelona, his mobile phone ring tone. He knew who it would be without needing to look at the caller display.

'Inspector? I need you in my office, as soon as possible,' the Ice Queen said, sounding colder than usual.

'On my way, ma'am,' Ted replied and hung up. 'I'm really sorry, can you do club without me tonight? Ring Bernard to give you a hand. I have to go back in. The shit's about to hit the fan in a big way. Kevin and I were told about this upcoming raid a couple of days ago and it was firmly on the top secret list. There'll be all kinds of witch-hunts now to find out how it got leaked to the press. Heaven knows what time I'll be back. The Ice Queen is probably rolling out her rack and thumb-screws as we speak.'

'Good luck,' Trev said. 'No worries about club, I'll sort it, and I'll plate up some food you can heat up whatever time you get back.'

'I might not get back,' Ted warned as he headed to the door. 'She might send me to a Gulag if she can't find another scapegoat.'

Chapter Eleven

Kevin Turner had clearly not yet made his escape when the Ice Queen had issued her summons. He was lying in wait for Ted's arrival, lurking near the car park, as if he needed the moral support before facing the storm that was no doubt to come.

'You heard, then?' he asked Ted as they fell into step together and headed for the Superintendent's office. 'Heads are going to roll for this one, in a big way.'

'Trev had the news on when I got home,' Ted said. 'I didn't even know who he was. Modern rock's not my thing. Trev had to fill me in.'

As they got to the door of the Ice Queen's office, Kevin shoved Ted and said in a low voice, 'You go in first, you can do martial arts.'

'Sit down, gentlemen. We have a serious problem,' were her opening words. 'I take it you are both fully aware of the massive leak on this raid?'

The two nodded warily.

'The Cheshire top brass, from the Chief Constable down, are incandescent with rage,' she continued. 'So are the CPS. Unfortunately, we are right in their collective sights. They've been planning this operation for months in the utmost secrecy, with not a sniff of it leaked anywhere. Then they share it with Greater Manchester, this division to be precise, and suddenly the press are all over it like a rash.'

'Ma'am, surely no one seriously suspects either Inspector Turner or me of leaking this?' Ted asked. 'We have the murder of a little boy to wrap up and the possibility of intelligence which might help us in that. What possible motive would we have?'

The Ice Queen gave him a hard stare. 'Money, Inspector,' she replied coldly. 'Whoever has leaked this will have had a nice little hand-out for their efforts, no doubt.'

'But ma'am, without stating the obvious,' Ted continued, 'neither of us knew the name of the person being raided. You didn't give us that information.'

This time she studied him as if he were some strange laboratory specimen. 'Sometimes, Inspector, your naivety astounds me,' she said. 'You may not have heard of this character but the press have, of course. One simple phone call to say that a raid was going to take place on a rock star's house near Wilmslow would have been all that was required to set the circus in motion and cause this complete and utter fiasco.'

Ted rather wished he could kick himself in the seat of the pants. Somehow almost every time he opened his mouth in front of the Ice Queen he managed to make himself look like an incompetent idiot, and he knew he wasn't. He realised Kevin had exactly the right idea in keeping quiet and only speaking when spoken to.

'Let me outline for you both just how serious this leak is, then we'll talk about where it might have come from,' she continued. 'The target is Ruairi MacKenzie-Douglas, spelt the Gaelic way, although he keeps very quiet about that handle and is universally known as Rory the Raver. Lead singer with a group called Toof. Spoiled little upper-middle-class rich boy whose family are loaded. He's the black sheep but, because of his connections, he has very few convictions.

'He's known for heavy drinking, recreational drugs, and trashing hotel rooms. Rumours of under-age sex follow him everywhere he goes. He's said to like to take his pick from the youngest groupies. So far nothing has stuck. Some of the kids who follow him round seem to take it as some sort of badge of honour to be picked.'

Ted knew they were in for a long evening when the Ice Queen suddenly broke off and asked, 'Would you gentlemen like coffee? Please help yourself.' She indicated the coffee machine in a corner of her office. She already had a cup in front of her. Ted decided to do the honours for Kevin and himself. It gave him something else to think about, apart from what an imbecile he kept making himself appear. He hoped the fancy coffee machine was not as complicated as it looked or he would seem even more stupid if he fumbled with it.

She carried on speaking as he managed to sort the drinks. 'He's been under observation for some time now because of things he's been posting in various groups on the internet, some of it very graphic. It's believed that there is a lot more stuff, much worse, on his computer or computers inside the house, hence the need for the raid.

'But now, whatever they might find when they go in, it's going to be very hard to bring charges against him that can be made to stick. His lawyers are already ranting about pre-trial prejudice, and it certainly gives them grounds to challenge any attempt to bring this to court.

'Not only does that ruin the chances of getting this person, who is almost without doubt a piece of filth, behind bars where he belongs, it also means there is no chance of getting him to name names in exchange for a lighter sentence or protection on the inside. And we all know what fate awaits sex offenders like this once inside, unless they have negotiated in advance to be kept safe.'

Ted couldn't resist putting his head above the parapet once more. He knew he risked the Ice Queen writing him off as a lost cause but he had to have his say.

'Ma'am, is it just possible this leak has come from others involved as an attempt to discredit Rory as a witness, or even to stop him getting his chance to name names in court?' he asked.

'Go on, Inspector,' the Ice Queen said, watching him with a

new expression on her face.

'Well, ma'am, it's just an unformed idea at the moment and I'm not sure if it takes us anywhere,' Ted said. 'But now all of this is out in the open, the case might not only fail to make it to trial but it could also have ended his career, surely?

'His loyal fans will support him, but would venues want to book someone with this kind of rumour about him? And if he doesn't get his day in court, he can't name names to bargain with, and he can't trot them out in public in a courtroom to save himself. He's tainted now, surely? So even if he went to the papers with names, would anyone believe him?'

'A different way of throwing him to the wolves?' she asked, her tone reflective. 'A bit far-fetched, don't you think? Not to mention a colossal gamble to take. And it would still mean that the leak came from somewhere within the force, or the CPS.'

'To me, it makes as much sense as thinking either Inspector Turner or myself would break this news to the press,' Ted said firmly. 'And there are plenty of rumours about police officers and lawyers being involved in child abuse.'

'There will, of course, be an official investigation into where the leak came from,' she continued. 'In the meantime, we have to hope that the seizure of computers might just throw up something to help with our ongoing case.

'That will be all for now, gentlemen. Except, Inspector Darling, if I could just have a few more minutes of your time?'

Kevin threw Ted a sympathetic glance as he stood up and left him sitting there, wondering what else he had done wrong. When Kevin had left and closed the door behind him, the Ice Queen turned her attention back to Ted.

'You seem to have left rather early this evening, Inspector,' she said. 'I was surprised to hear that you had already gone when I was trying to contact you.'

Ted mentally gave himself another kick in the behind. He'd been running the self-defence club for so long, with the full knowledge and support of DCI Baker, that he had quite simply forgotten to mention his standing commitment to the Ice Queen. He hoped she wasn't going to raise objections to it. He never allowed it to interfere with his work and always stepped down and let Trev run it when necessary.

'Ma'am, yes, I apologise, I should have told you,' he said. 'I run a self-defence club for children at the local martial arts club I attend. We set it up to help combat bullying in schools and it's had a lot of success.'

Even the Ice Queen looked impressed. 'That sounds like a good initiative.'

'There's no charge to the children, the club covers the cost of the use of the dojo and Trevor and I run it as volunteers. The young boy Flip, Philip, who first told me about Aiden going missing, is a keen member. In fact he told me he used the techniques we taught him when he once went with Aiden on one of his trips,' Ted told her.

'You certainly have my support on this,' she said, to Ted's surprise, 'as long as it still leaves you the time to catch our killer or killers, as I feel confident you will. You have an excellent track record, Inspector. Don't let me down on this one.'

Ted checked his watch as he left the station. He hadn't been as long as he feared he might be. He would have missed much of the juniors' self-defence session by the time he got to the dojo, but he could still be in time for the adults' training session.

He could swing by the house to grab his kit and change quickly out of his suit. Then he would drive to the dojo rather than walk, as he and Trev usually preferred to do. After a day like today, he needed a fast and furious session of martial arts more than ever as a release for tension.

Chapter Twelve

Inspector Kevin Turner didn't often venture up into Ted's territory. He certainly seldom burst into his office uninvited as he did that morning.

'Bloody hell, Ted,' were his opening words. Then, as he sank into a chair, by way of emphasis, he added, 'Bloody hell! I'm not even going to offer to tell the Ice Queen this one. I'm going to hide behind you while you tell her then I'm going to run away very fast.'

Ted looked up from his paperwork. 'Care to stop talking in riddles and tell me what the problem is, Kev?'

'We've just had a call downstairs. A taxi driver's been found shot dead, in a quiet corner of the car park down by the viaduct,' Kevin told him. 'Apparently it looks like a very professional job. Two shots through the window, no robbery, nothing like that. Please tell me this is nothing to do with your line of enquiry and if it is, how the hell did word get out of who you've been talking to?'

'It must be a coincidence,' Ted said, with more optimism than he felt. 'I'll get down there straight away. Are your officers on the scene?'

'Everyone's on their way. I think I'll come with you on this one. I want to put as much distance as possible between me and the Ice Queen if she thinks there's another leak of information from this nick,' Kevin told him.

Ted smiled. 'Anyone would think you were afraid of her. I'm sure she's a pussy cat really. Your car or mine? I'll see you down in the car park. I'll put my head round the door of the witch's den and hope she doesn't throw me out of the window.'

As Kevin went off in search of a vehicle, Ted headed to the main office. Several of his team were out but Sal was at his desk, as was Steve, working away on the computer as usual.

'Just had a call about a shooting,' Ted told them. 'Taxi driver, shot dead at the wheel, near the viaduct. I'm on my way down there now with Inspector Turner. I'll call in when I know who I want working on this.'

Sal jumped to his feet, his face anguished. 'I'll go.'

'No Sal, I don't want you anywhere near this,' Ted told him.

'But sir, my cousin Khalid ...' Sal said pleadingly.

'Precisely. That's why I don't want you there. I'll let you know as soon as I get down there if we have any ID on the victim,' Ted said. 'It may be totally unrelated to what you've been working on but I don't want you showing your face anywhere near the scene if it is. It could put you at risk.' Then he added, 'I will call you Sal, I promise, as soon as I know anything.'

Ted headed to the superintendent's office, tapped at the door and waited for the Ice Queen's command to enter. Once inside, he lurked as close to the door as possible, hoping to make a quick getaway.

'Ma'am, we've just had a call. A taxi driver's been shot dead. No further information at the moment, no indication if this is in any way connected to our enquiries. It looks like a hit job rather than a robbery,' he told her. 'Inspector Turner and I are both on our way down there in case there's a link. We'll keep you informed.'

She looked up sharply at the news. 'See that you do, Inspector. If this is in any way linked, I want to know immediately. Any hint of a possible leak or another bungled operation will reflect very badly on this station.'

Kevin was waiting for him just outside the entrance, the engine of the area car running. He put the blue light on as they set off, giving him a clear run through traffic on the short drive.

The car park was close to Stockport's famous brick viaduct. As they arrived, they could see that a quiet corner was already taped off and there were signs of activity everywhere. Kevin drove across and stopped just short of the tape. Beyond it they could see a taxi parked.

Professor Nelson was already on the scene. She looked up as Ted and Kevin approached her.

'Morning, Inspector,' she said. 'My goodness, senior officers from both uniform and CID? I'm assuming there is more to this than just a random shooting?'

'Good morning, Professor,' Ted also opted for being formal in public, following her lead. 'Have you met Inspector Turner? There is a possible link with our other ongoing murder. What can you tell us so far?'

'Your sneezing chappie was here earlier to certify death. So far I've just had a cursory look. Two bullet wounds to the head from short range, very accurately done. The first officers on the scene tell me the takings appear to be untouched,' she told them. 'I'm just about to arrange for his removal. Quite excited about this one, ballistics is a bit of a thing of mine.'

Ted smiled to himself. It just confirmed his mental image of Bizzie Nelson as one of the huntin', shootin' and fishin' crowd. He wondered if she owned a Purdey, like her predecessor.

'Time of death?' he asked optimistically.

'No idea with any certainty,' she said briskly. 'Best I can do for you with what I have seen so far is probably some time late last night. I'll let you know more accurately as soon as I can. At least you shouldn't have any trouble with ID,' she told them as she prepared to leave. 'If the dead man is the driver of this taxi, his photo ID is hanging up inside.'

Both Ted and Kevin had gloved up as soon as they arrived on the scene. Kevin opened the passenger door of the taxi and reached in to take down the driver's ID badge hanging there, which he showed to Ted.

'I see your earlier "bloody hell" and raise you an "oh shit",' Ted said. 'Mohnid Ahmadi, the driver Sal has been talking to. The driver who claimed to know about getting paid to pick up kids and deliver them to the paedos. The Ice Queen will really love this. And it's your turn to tell her.'

'Rock-paper-scissors?' Kevin asked hopefully, before both men went into professional mode and started arranging the enquiry. As promised, Ted's first priority was to get straight on his phone to Sal.

'It's not your cousin,' was the first thing he said, and heard Sal's immediate sigh of relief. 'But it is your driver, Mohnid Ahmadi. Shot in the head, and his takings are still there so almost certainly not a simple robbery. Who's in the office to send out?'

'Me and Steve are still here, Sgt Hallam and Virgil have just come back in,' Sal told him.

'Send them down here, can you. There are uniform officers on site but I want some of the team as well, asking around. There may be witnesses and I want them finding as soon as. I'll be heading back in shortly with Inspector Turner. We both need to bring the Superintendent up to speed on this as soon as possible,' he said, with a pointed look at Kevin as he said it.

Kevin grinned at him and made the rock-paper-scissors hand signals in rapid succession as Ted rang off.

In the car on the way back, Ted said, 'Seriously, I'll brief her about this. If anything has gone wrong, it's gone wrong from my end so it's only fair. But you owe me one.'

The Ice Queen was anticipating his return. Ted went in and sat down, then laid out what he knew so far, as succinctly as possible.

'And you're confident that DC Ahmed took all precautions not to be identified as an officer?' she asked.

'He's a good and experienced member of the team,

ma'am,' Ted told her. 'He went to great lengths not to be seen leaving the station before meeting up with his cousin. I can't at the moment see, if this has occurred as a result of a leak of information, where any such breach could have come from.'

'So what are your initial thoughts?' she asked.

'One of two possibilities. The first, and most obvious, is that someone somehow knew he had been talking to the police and wanted to silence him. The second, from a completely different angle, he was not targeted because of that but because his actions had lead to the death of the boy Aiden.'

The Ice Queen nodded agreement. 'That has occurred to me, too. An execution, a retribution. But that also requires the killer to have knowledge of his involvement and from what you describe of his behaviour, he has been very cautious in sharing information with anyone.

'The boy had no family at all, from what you have told me. So who would be likely to take such action on his behalf? And again, how would they know of this driver's involvement?'

'Someone higher up in the ring? Housekeeping, because things went wrong? Maybe this is the first time there's been a fatality and people are starting to panic, cover their tracks,' Ted suggested. 'That's all I can offer for now, ma'am. I need to get back to the team now and see what else we can come up with.'

Chapter Thirteen

Mike Hallam and Dennis 'Virgil' Tibbs arrived on the scene shortly after Ted had left. They took time to liaise with the uniformed officers on the scene before going looking for witnesses. Virgil knew the area well, Mike Hallam was relatively new and still finding his way round.

'Do you want to try the shops and offices over there, Sarge, just on the off chance? I'll go and take a look over by the arches,' Virgil told him. 'There are often homeless people dossing there, it's just a possibility one of them may have seen something.'

Hallam nodded and strolled across the car park. They'd been told the body had probably been there since the night before so he wasn't optimistic, but they had to start somewhere. Virgil headed over to the furthest corner of the car park towards the arches of the viaduct.

There were a few sleeping forms, wrapped up in an assortment of old clothes and cardboard. One man was sitting up, watching him. The morning was chilly and damp and he was huddled inside a sleeping bag but still looked cold.

'I'm DC Tibbs, making enquiries into an incident which happened over there last night, on the car park,' Virgil told him, showing his warrant card. 'How long have you been here?'

The man looked at him. His eyes were bright, but the face was streaked with ingrained dirt, and his hands and fingernails, in his fingerless gloves, needed a good scrub. His hands were clasped tightly round a can of extra strong lager.

'What year is it?' the man asked.

'No, I meant have you been here since last night?' Virgil said.

'I have,' the man replied. He was younger than Virgil had at first thought and his voice was well-spoken. 'There was mix-up with my booking last night at the Palace Hotel, so here I am.'

Virgil squatted down to his level, intrigued by the man. 'Did you see anything last night, over there?' he jerked his head over to where tape marked out the crime scene, where the taxi was parked.

'I might have done,' the man said warily.

Virgil sighed and reached in his back pocket for his wallet. 'If I give you a tenner, will you spend it on drink and drugs?'

'If you give me money, without me asking you to, does it not then become my money, to do with as I choose?' the man parried.

'Would a tenner help you?' Virgil asked. 'I'm a bit light on cash.'

'I take credit cards,' the man said ironically. 'When you have nothing, ten pence helps. Are you paying me for what I know or giving me money to spend as I choose?'

'Did you actually see anything?' Fascinated as he was by the man, Virgil knew he needed to be getting on and finding witnesses, rather than just talking to a loquacious derelict.

'I did,' came the reply. 'Because I am a responsible citizen, I'll tell you anyway, but your ten pounds would be very welcome for a cup of hot coffee and a bite of breakfast. And perhaps another can of lager for later on.'

Virgil handed over the note and the man palmed it deftly, in a movement which spoke of practice.

'I saw a taxi drive into the car park and pull up over there, as if it was waiting to pick up a fare. The lights were on and the engine was running. Then I saw a motorbike come out of the shadows at the other side of the car park, come up behind the taxi and stop alongside the driver's door.

'There were two people on the bike. The one at the back produced a hand-gun, silenced, I imagine, as I didn't hear much of a noise, just enough to make out there were two shots. Then the bike went off at speed, leaving the taxi there.

'The engine stayed running for quite some time. I imagine it eventually ran out of fuel, and at some time in the night the lights went out, so the battery had probably gone flat by then.'

'Did you not think to report the incident?' Virgil asked.

'Well, of course, officer, as I told you, I'm a fine upstanding citizen. Unfortunately, I had forgotten to charge my smartphone so I was unable to,' the man said, with biting sarcasm.

'Sorry, stupid of me,' Virgil said and grinned. 'Can you tell me anything about the bike or the people on it?'

'It was dark, of course, although the street-lights were on. I could see that the bike was red and that both people were wearing dark helmets and dark leathers, but no more than that.'

'Any idea of the make of bike?' Virgil asked hopefully.

The man shook his head. 'I was never a biker. Believe it or not, back in the day, I drove a Porsche.'

'And around what time was this?'

'I stupidly forgot to look at my Rolex,' came the reply.

'Would you make a statement about what you've just told me, down at the station?'

'When you live like I do, you try not to get involved in anything that happens on the streets,' the man told him. 'This patch here might not look all that inviting to you but it suits me well enough for now.'

'Is there nowhere you can go, a hostel or something?' Virgil asked with evident concern.

The man laughed harshly. 'I don't suppose you've ever spent a night in one or you wouldn't ask. Believe me, this is the Ritz in comparison.'

Virgil straightened up. 'Would you tell me your name?'

'Haven't used it in a long time,' the man said.

'What do they call you, then?'

Again the short laugh. 'My wife called me Dickhead, several times, before she threw me out and changed the locks. My employers had much harsher names for me. I was a trader, and not on a market stall. My ambitious dealings cost them rather a lot of money. Mostly I'm known as Nat.'

'It's been nice talking to you Nat, and thanks for your help,' Virgil handed him his card. 'If I can ever help you, or if you remember anything else which might be useful to me, here's my mobile number. DC Tibbs. They call me Virgil.'

This time the man's laugh was full of humour. 'Shouldn't that be "they call me Mr Tibbs"?' he asked as Virgil walked away.

It was not only the best lead they got, it was the only one. Mike Hallam had drawn a blank. When Virgil filled him in on what little information he did have, the DS echoed what the homeless man had said. Anyone out on the street witnessing a shooting was unlikely to want to get involved.

When they got back to the station, DS Hallam headed for Ted's office and found him at his desk. He briefly outlined what Virgil had come up with.

'Boss, do you think this was a killing to silence someone who was on the point of talking to someone, possibly to the police?' the DS asked him. 'Or could it be someone who knew he was involved in delivering these kids up to the paedos, especially after young Aiden got killed like he did?'

'At this stage it could be either, Mike,' Ted told him. 'We have to keep an open mind until we get a bit more of a lead and know which direction we're going in.'

'Right, just so we do this thoroughly and by the book, can I take a witness statement from you, sir, as to what you were doing last night?'

Seeing Ted's look of astonishment, the DS went on, 'I've

told you before, boss, you helped me a lot when I first came here so I watch your back. We came back with a witness account of two riders on a red motorcycle involved in the killing of someone who probably delivered a young boy to his death. I've seen you and Trev riding into action together on a red bike, and I know you're a former firearms officer. I just want to cover all bases, especially as I know we're coming under investigation because of the leak to the press you told us about.'

'Good thinking, Mike, I appreciate it,' Ted told him sincerely. 'It wasn't me, tempting though it would be. Luckily I have an alibi for last night. I missed the kids' self-defence club as I was in with the Super but I went to the dojo in time for most of the adult session. Plenty of people saw me there. Unusually, afterwards, Trev and I went out for a drink and a meal with some of the lads from the club and we all went back to our coach, Bernard's, house for coffee afterwards. We were there till gone midnight.

'I can give you names and addresses so you can check it out and log it. And thanks, Mike, good to know you're covering my back, as ever.'

Chapter Fourteen

The water closed over Ted's head. It was filling his nostrils, the chlorine burning the back of his throat, making him gag. As he opened his mouth to retch, more water poured in, seeking its way to his lungs to choke and suffocate him.

He fought as hard as he could to regain the surface but he couldn't make any headway against the weight pressing him down. Lights were flashing in front of his eyes, coming from inside his head, not from anything he was looking at. By now his lungs were exploding with the pressure of the water. He was dying.

Suddenly the restraining grip on him was released and he was hauled back to the surface, shipping more water, starting to cough and heave in a desperate attempt to grab some vitally needed oxygen into his water-logged airways.

His ears were full of water so he couldn't hear much. All he could hear was derisory laughter, echoing all around him, and a man's voice, but he couldn't tell what it was saying. His eyes were streaming, as much with tears as with the stinging chlorine.

He was vomiting up water now, his stomach feeling as if it was being turned inside out. Then he was grabbed, dragged into even deeper water and pushed down under the surface again. Down, down and further down. This time he was sure he was going to die.

Ted shot upright in bed, gasping, choking, coughing. His whole body was wet with sweat and he shook all over as if gripped with a fever.

Beside him Trevor stirred awake and put a reassuring arm around his shoulders.

'Hey,' he said gently as he reached out the other hand to switch on the bedside light. 'It's all right. I'm here.'

He folded both arms carefully around his partner, attempting to stop the trembling, which was now violent.

'The same nightmare again?' he asked softly.

Ted couldn't speak. He couldn't even nod his head in agreement. He struggled to calm his breathing and regain control over the tremors. Trev just held him, murmuring soothingly, until, slowly, the shaking diminished to a slight shiver.

'You're freezing,' Trev said. 'Do you want me to make you a cup of tea?'

This time Ted managed to shake his head, glancing at the clock on the table at his side of the bed. 'It's time I was up,' he said, finally regaining enough control to speak.

'You look awful,' Trev told him. You can't go in yet, looking like that. Go and have a nice hot shower, while I make you some breakfast.'

'I can't eat anything,' Ted said, more sharply than he intended, then was immediately contrite. 'Sorry, I didn't mean to snap. It's just, you know.'

'Yes, I do know,' Trev told him. 'Are you sure you should be working on this case? It's so long since you had that nightmare.'

'I can't pick and choose the cases I work on. And I'm certainly not talking to the Ice Queen about why this one is so difficult for me,' Ted said firmly. 'I'll be all right, I just need to thaw out a bit.'

'Don't bite my head off but here's a suggestion,' Trev said warily. 'Have a shower, get dressed, phone Mike, tell him you'll be in a little bit later.' He held a hand up as Ted started to protest. 'I'll make you something really light, like a smoothie. Sit down and have some breakfast with me, then go in. You honestly do look absolutely awful. If the Ice Queen sees you like that she'll take you off the case anyway. Deal?'

Ted smiled at him. 'It does sound tempting,' he admitted. 'You have a deal.'

DS Mike Hallam had proved himself an invaluable right-hand man to Ted. He had got off to a shaky start but had quickly learned that his new boss was fair and respectful with all his team members, which in turn earned him their respect. He had the team sorted and working when Ted arrived, later than usual.

'Are you all right, boss?' he asked, looking and sounding concerned. 'You look a bit rough.'

Ted made light of it. 'Just a bit of a bug, I think,' he said dismissively. 'Where are we up to with the list of registered sex offenders on our patch?'

Steve was just printing out documents from his computer and handed one to Ted. 'Here's a copy, sir. I've marked the ones who are inside.'

'I've had Rob and Sal out checking whereabouts, and we've got a short-list of those without alibis,' the DS said. 'Maurice has done the ring-round to double check who's out and who's safely in custody. This is the list of those we're going to start hauling in for questioning.'

Ted glanced at the list. It was a depressingly long one. As his eyes scanned the names, the trembling began again and he started to struggle for breath. Hauling the hated tie down and loosening his collar didn't help. He was soon coughing and gasping, sweat springing out again on his forehead, starting to trickle into his eyes and sting them, the same sting as the chlorine, the smell of it filling his nostrils.

The DS hauled a chair closer. 'Shit, sir, you look shocking, are you all right?' he asked anxiously. 'Steve, get the boss a glass of water.'

Ted half fell into the chair, struggling for air, desperately trying to stop the shaking. He waved away Mike's concern with a trembling hand as he fought to regain control.

The TDC looked even more worried as he held out a glass of water to the boss. Water was the last thing Ted wanted but he took it anyway, hoping he could manage to drink at least some without spilling it everywhere.

'Thanks, both of you,' he said, once he could manage to speak. 'Honestly, it's nothing, just a bit of a virus perhaps, a touch of asthma or something. Sorry to have worried you.'

Neither of them looked convinced but they said no more on the subject.

'Do you want me to start interviewing the known offenders as we bring them in, boss, until you're feeling better?' the DS asked. 'By the way, the Super was asking for you first thing. I told her you weren't well and would be in later. Are you really sure you should be here? You really do look ill.'

'Mike, you'll quickly find the best way to get on the wrong side of me is to make a fuss, about anything,' Ted said, but he was smiling to take the sting out of it. 'I'm fine, really. I'm off down to see the Super. You've done a good job so far, keep at it.'

The Ice Queen looked searchingly at Ted when he went into her office.

'Good gracious, Inspector, you don't look well at all,' she told him, indicating the chair. 'Are you sure you should be here?'

'It's nothing, ma'am, just a bug,' he said. 'I have a murder to solve.'

'Well, please don't play the martyr,' she told him. 'You're no use to anyone if you're ill, even worse if you infect the rest of your team with a virus of some sort. For goodness' sake take some time off if you need to. Is this case causing you particular difficulty? Is there anything I should be aware of?'

Ted held her gaze unwaveringly. 'No ma'am,' he replied levelly. 'Like I said, just a bug, which I will soon shake off. I wanted to bring you up to speed with a possible eye-witness to the shooting.'

He briefly outlined what Virgil had found out from the homeless man, Nat.

'Two people on a red bike, you say?' she asked. 'Doesn't your partner ride a red bike?'

'Ahead of you there, ma'am,' Ted said. 'DS Hallam also spotted that coincidence. He has already taken my witness statement and is checking out my alibi.'

'Strange choice of getaway vehicle for what otherwise looks like quite a professional job, from what you've told me,' the Ice Queen mused. 'A red bike is easy to spot, so why not a black one? Why draw attention to themselves like that, even at night?'

'I was going to ask if we could release that information to the local press, even the national media, ma'am, ask for the public's help? Ask if anyone saw two riders on a red bike in that area, around the time of the shooting?'

'Good idea, do it. I hope you and your partner aren't out and about often on his, or we are going to have to do a lot of checking up on you.' It was the nearest thing to a light-hearted remark Ted had heard her make since her arrival. 'And seriously, Inspector, take some time off if you need to. As I've told you before, I'm not your enemy.'

Chapter Fifteen

There was an air of anticipation about the team. After a lot of leg-work, finally some tentative leads were starting to appear. There had been some response to televised requests for information on the red bike and its riders, although so far nothing definite. But at least the public were trying to help.

Jancis Reynolds had been doing well talking to children who had known Aiden. She told the team that the boy liked to boast of the places he went to and the people he met. Although some of it was no doubt exaggerated, a lot of it was consistent and had been helpful in tracking down a possible location for the hotel they were looking for.

Rob O'Connell had found the Hotel Sorrento, small, private and less than a mile from where Aiden's body had been found. It had a modestly-sized but impressive function room, complete with oak parquet dance floor and crystal chandeliers, which could perfectly fit Aiden's grandiose description of a ballroom.

Jancis began the feedback on their progress. 'Aiden also liked to boast of being in bedrooms which he said had poles and curtains round the bed, by which I'm assuming a four-poster bed and, Rob...?' she looked across at Rob to continue.

'Several of the rooms in the Sorrento have four-posters, complete with heavy brocade curtains,' he said. 'To a young kid with not much money, living in a home, it would look like quite a posh place. He may well have been impressed by it. And a possible clincher – cards for the right taxi firm on the desk in reception and in the bar.'

Ted was watching DC O'Connell closely as he spoke. Something was not right. Rob was one of his best officers, keen, enthusiastic. Now he delivered his input in a flat voice, where Ted would have expected him to be excited at the prospect of a real lead at last. He made a note to make time to talk to Rob on his own, to see if he could find out what the problem was.

It was Ted's turn for some input. 'The post-mortem hasn't shown up anything we weren't expecting,' he told the team. 'Two shots to the head from close range, very accurate. We've had the ballistics report and the gun was a Glock 17. Nothing unusual, in fact it's standard issue for a lot of police forces, for instance.'

The Ice Queen had been quick to point that out when Ted briefed her on the weapons report. Both she and Ted were former firearms officers who had trained with the same weapon and were proficient in its use. It was an easy enough weapon to get hold of on the street and often cropped up in gun-related crime on their patch.

'Right, Rob, I think it's time you and I paid an official visit to this Hotel Sorrento to ask them some searching questions about the day young Aiden died. I have things to do this morning so we'll make it straight after lunch. Mike, in the meantime, can we get everyone available out with pictures of young Aiden in the area around the hotel, any shops nearby, ask any kids hanging about, anything we can find that might place him in that area.

'But I want all of you to keep clear of the taxi ranks, and that goes double for you, Sal,' Ted told the team. 'That's dangerous territory for now, strictly off limits until we get a clearer idea of who we're up against. Let's not take any risks.'

Ted headed back towards his own office, asking DS Hallam to join him as he went.

'Is everything all right with Rob, do you know, Mike?' Ted asked as he switched on his kettle. 'Can I offer you a green tea?' he asked, although he knew most of his team disliked his favourite brew, even when laced with honey.

'He is quiet at the moment, boss, I had noticed that,' the DS said, shaking his head to the offer of tea as he sat down. 'I don't know of any reason, except I think most of us are finding this case a bit tough, because it involves kids.'

'It doesn't get much harder,' Ted said in agreement. 'Don't forget, there's no shame in anybody asking for other duties if they find they're struggling. I wanted to talk to you about interviewing the sex offenders, who's doing what on that.'

His tea was ready so he sat down with his steaming mug and picked up the list on his desk. He noticed his hand was again shaking slightly, so he put the sheet of paper back on his desk to look at.

'I think you and I should talk to the majority of these,' he told the DS. 'I daren't trust Maurice, he might thump someone. There's just one name on this list I can't get involved with, as it's someone I know, so it wouldn't be correct for me to question him.'

Ted found his throat was starting to constrict so he hastily took a gulp of his tea, which was too hot. At least it gave him an excuse for his sudden coughing bout and struggle to get his breath.

'Are you all right, boss?' Mike Hallam asked anxiously. 'I know you said not to fuss but you do still sound a bit rough.'

'Tea went down the wrong way, that's all,' Ted waved away his concern. 'This David Evans,' he said, forcing himself to say the name out loud without his voice betraying any emotion. 'He's the one I know, the one I can't interview, so that's down to you. Have Sal in with you on that one, and be ready for him. He's very devious, extremely plausible.'

Mike reached across to look at the list on the boss's desk, to remind himself of the offences for which Evans had served time.

'Ten years for serious sexual assaults on young boys,' he

said aloud. 'Nice.'

'There's a strong possibility that when you bring him in, he'll ask to speak to me, by name,' Ted told him. 'I am not available, at all, no matter how much he asks. In fact, don't even confirm my presence in this station. You don't tell him anything at all about me.'

'That goes without saying, boss,' Hallam said, with a hint of reproach in his tone.

'Yes, of course, sorry, Mike, teaching you to suck eggs, and all that,' Ted apologised. 'I just wanted to forewarn you that he will in all likelihood ask for me and the answer is no.'

Ted waited until Mike had left his office before he attempted to drink his tea. There was still a noticeable tremor to his hands and his throat felt constricted so it fought against swallowing the hot, sweet liquid.

He took the morning to clear the paperwork backlog from his desk, then collected Rob and they headed in his car to the hotel.

'Is everything all right, Rob?' he asked. 'You don't seem quite your usual self.'

'I could ask you the same thing, boss,' Rob parried. 'I heard you gave Steve and the sarge a bit of a fright the other day.'

'A slight virus,' Ted said quickly, 'and we were talking about you. If there's a problem, you know you can come and talk to me, don't you?'

'Yes sir, but it's fine,' Rob assured him, 'just not the nicest of cases to work on, for any of us.'

The Hotel Sorrento was set back from quite a busy main road by the parking area in front of the building. It was a large brick structure in Victorian style, with Virginia creeper covering part of the façade. It looked as if in some previous life it could have been a large vicarage or something similar.

Ted and Rob walked up the three steps to the entrance door

and went into a lobby with a reception desk where a young woman was on duty. Her badge announced her name as Maggie. She had what looked like naturally red hair and a sprinkling of freckles.

'Good afternoon, gentlemen, welcome to the Hotel Sorrento. How may I help you?' she trotted out what was clearly her standard script for phone or personal greetings.

Both men pulled out their warrant cards and held them up for her inspection. 'I'm Detective Inspector Darling, this is Detective Constable O'Connell,' Ted told her to save her the trouble of reading the cards. 'We'd like to speak to the manager.'

'Mr Rossi is busy at the moment, if you could just tell me what it's about …'

'I'm busy too,' Ted told her politely, 'but I have made time to come here to talk to Mr Rossi to save him the inconvenience of being summoned to come and talk to me at the station.'

The young woman hesitated for a moment before picking up the phone and calling the manager. He came bustling in after only a few minutes.

'*Scusi signori*, how can I help you?' he said, his Italian accent thick, almost theatrically so, Ted thought.

Ted introduced the two of them and said, 'Mr Rossi, we are making enquiries into a serious incident which took place a few days ago quite near to this hotel. I would be interested to know if you had any special functions at this hotel on the night in question. I would also like to see your guest register for that date.'

The man looked stricken. 'But is confidential,' he said. 'I cannot just show you this, without you bring a warrant.' He appeared to notice Rob for the first time and said, 'You already come here. You ask me about hotel for wedding.'

'That's still a possibility,' Rob told him dryly.

'I can, of course, go away and come back with a warrant, Mr Rossi,' Ted told him, 'but it would be so much easier for everyone if you just gave me the information I ask for. While you're making up your mind about what to do, perhaps you could show me your main function room? The one which has the dance floor?'

The man looked taken aback but led the way along a carpeted corridor to a solid light oak door, which he opened then stood aside to allow Ted and Rob to go in first. It was a large, bright room with French windows all along one side, opening out on to a small but pleasant garden to the rear of the building.

The floor was waxed honeyed oak, in herringbone blocks, buffed to a shine by hundreds of feet waltzing over its surface through the years. A grand piano stood at the side of the dance floor. Ted could easily see how impressive even this modest room might be to a young boy who had never known anything like it. He thought it very likely they had found Aiden's ballroom.

'So, Mr Rossi, can you tell me if this function room was booked on the twenty-eighth of last month and by whom?'

The man looked uncomfortable. 'Is not my hotel,' he said, spreading his hands apologetically. 'I have to ask my boss, the owner, before I do something like that. He is away, in Sicilia, at the moment.'

'I presume he has a mobile phone, Mr Rossi. Perhaps you'd be kind enough to telephone and ask him,' Ted said. 'That would be so much quicker than me having to apply for a warrant to search your records, which I will happily do if you prefer. In the meantime, I take it you have a restaurant? Serving authentic Italian food? My partner loves Italian food, I'll book us in and come back this evening, if that would be convenient?'

Chapter Sixteen

When Ted phoned Trev to say he was taking him out for a meal that evening, Trev's reaction was to laugh and ask, 'What have you done?'

Ted feigned offence. 'I do take you out sometimes,' he protested. 'But you're right, there's no such thing as a free lunch or a free dinner, when you live with a copper. I just want you to speak Italian to someone, to tell me if they're as phony as they sound.'

'Shouldn't be too difficult,' Trev said. Italian was one of many languages he spoke fluently and he was always pleased to have an opportunity to practise any of them. 'I'll see you later. Are you driving, so I can have a drink?'

'It's near enough to walk,' Ted said and heard Trev's laughing remark of 'Cheapskate!' as he rang off.

They both enjoyed walking. It was a time to relax and talk, sometimes the only time Trev could get Ted to unload whatever was troubling him. Ted seldom talked about his work at home, but as they walked he mentioned that the hotel had a possible link to the murder of the young boy.

'There's something about the manager, this Rossi bloke, which makes me suspicious. Maybe he just puts the whole Italian thing on a bit strongly as he thinks it goes with the image. It all sounds a bit B-movie to me so I need you to check him out,' he told Trev. 'Once I know someone is not being straight about one thing, it makes me suspicious about anything else they tell me.'

Trev laughed and threw an arm round Ted's shoulders to

hug him. 'Sometimes you are such a policeman.'

A group of youths was walking towards them. Seeing the gesture, one of them called out, 'Get a room, you fucking pair of bum bandits!'

Trevor stopped in his tracks and drew himself upright. He was six feet tall, all of it well-defined muscle. Grinning to himself, knowing what was in store, Ted stepped aside to leave him room to move.

Trev was making a strange incantation to himself in what may have been proper Japanese, another of his languages, but was probably just mumbo-jumbo. He began posturing and high kicking in an elaborate show of Shotokan karate. The youths looked shocked and backed up as Trevor advanced.

'He's a fucking nutjob,' the one who had shouted earlier said.

'He may well be,' Ted said evenly, 'but he has black belts in judo and karate and he doesn't take kindly to being called names.' Then to Trev he said, 'Come on you, behave yourself or I'll have to arrest you.'

The youths were feeling cocky again, now they'd moved away and felt safer. Ted was almost eight inches shorter than his partner, slightly built, though well muscled. Another of the boys jeered, 'You can't arrest him, you're no copper, they don't let short-arses in.'

Ted sighed and pulled out his warrant card. 'Not only am I a copper but I have more black belts than he does,' he said. 'So why not just jog on quietly, lads. I'm off duty.'

Still muttering and jeering, the boys crossed the street and disappeared hastily up a side road. Ted and Trev carried on towards the hotel, still laughing.

'They were right about one thing,' Ted smiled affectionately. 'You are a nutjob.'

There was no sign of the manager when they reached the hotel, and there was a different young woman on the reception desk. Her badge gave her name as Chiara. Her hair was black as jet, eyes rich chocolate brown. She trotted out the same stock greeting as the other had earlier on.

Trev launched into his flawless Italian, which seemed to delight her as she beamed and replied with the rapidity of machine-gun fire. The two were soon chatting away nineteen to the dozen. Ted stood by, admiring the effortless way Trev had of talking to almost anyone in one of many languages.

They seemed to reach a lull in their conversation and with a '*grazie mille*', Trev led the way along a carpeted corridor, in the opposite direction to the function room, following a sign that pointed them to the dining room.

'I asked to see the hotel records earlier on,' Ted said as they walked. 'Rossi was very evasive, said he'd have to ask the owner, he's just the manager. He said the owner is away in Sicily.'

'Whoa!' Trev exclaimed. 'Is he warning you off, hinting that you're messing with the Cosa Nostra? Anyway, I can tell you that the lovely Chiara is the real deal, impeccable Italian, born and bred there.'

The dining room was a modest size, intimate and attractively laid out. They were shown to a table by someone who was presumably the restaurant manager and left to browse the menu, which Trev announced looked promising. Their waiter, when he came, was a small, dark man who looked permanently anxious. Ted let himself be guided in his choice of dishes by his partner who was much more knowledgeable about Italian food than he was.

The waiter was back in good time, carrying two steaming bowls of spinach and ricotta tortellini. Ted noticed that the man had a disabled right hand. His fingers didn't seem fully functional, three of them folded over into a partial fist. As he went to set down the bowl in front of Trev, he lost his grip with that hand and the dish fell, overturning onto the table. Most of it spilled across the tablecloth, but some of the hot food fell into Trev's lap and he leapt to his feet with a yelp.

The restaurant manager appeared like a shot, apologising profusely to Trev, interspersed with berating the hapless waiter. He was dabbing ineffectually at Trev's trousers, looking miserable enough to burst into tears. In no time, the manager had arranged for the entire table to be cleared and reset, summoning other waiters as reinforcements.

The original waiter was despatched to fetch a fresh starter for each of them. This time he was only allowed to carry one at a time, so he successfully managed to serve both men. As he put Trev's plate in front of him, Trev said, '*Mulțumesc.*' The man positively beamed at him as he scuttled off back to the kitchens.

'What language was that?' Ted asked.

'Romanian,' Trev told him. 'That's his nationality and he doesn't seem to speak much Italian, other than enough to take our order. I just thanked him as I felt sorry for him.'

'I didn't know you spoke Romanian,' Ted said, surprised.

Trev laughed. 'I don't, I just recognise what it sounds like. And one rainy day when you were at work and I was at a loose end I decided to try to learn "thank you" in as many languages as I could.'

Ted smiled. It was so typical of his partner.

The starter was delicious. Once their plates were cleared away and they were waiting for their main course, Ted caught the eye of the restaurant manager and beckoned him over.

'Two things,' he said pleasantly. 'The first is we both accept that what happened with the waiter was an unfortunate accident. We'd hate to see him get into any sort of trouble. Secondly, would you please let Mr Rossi know I'm here and anxious to see him. Detective Inspector Darling, he should be expecting me. I need to arrange a time with him to come in and have a look at his records tomorrow. All of the records, including the employment ones,' he added, watching the sudden anxious look which crossed the other man's face.

When the manager had gone, Trev grinned across the table

at Ted. 'Naughty,' he said. 'But I like that you stood up for the waiter.'

Rossi, the hotel manager, came bustling into the dining room soon afterwards and headed for their table.

'*Scusi, inspettore,*' he blustered. 'I was busy elsewhere, I only just got the message that you were here. I hope the meal is good?'

'Very good, thank you. I hope you have contacted the owner and made the arrangements I requested?'

'Ah, *inspettore*,' he spread his hands wide in an extravagant gesture. 'The owner is very busy man, I have not yet been able to contact him. But I will arrange it all for you.'

'I will be here tomorrow afternoon, Mr Rossi, to see all of your records, with or without the consent of the owner,' Ted told him icily. 'By the way, this is my partner, Trevor, who is very fond of Italian food and wanted to pass his compliments to the chef through your good self.'

Trev launched into very rapid Italian. Ted watched the body language of the manager as he responded. He had no knowledge of the language himself, but even he could see that Rossi looked a little uncomfortable at times, as if fishing for a word.

Once the manager had gone and their still apologetic waiter had returned with their main course, fish for Trev, thin slices of chicken in a lemon and cream sauce for Ted, Trev said, 'Well your Mr Rossi is not a fluent Italian speaker, that's for sure. Possibly second or third generation. His accent is more Stockport than Sorrento or anywhere else, and he gets stuck on some pretty basic words. He called you *inspettore* instead of *ispettore,* and hoped I would enjoy my peach instead of my fish. I don't know if that helps?'

'Nor do I really,' Ted confessed, 'but at least it shows my hunch about him was right. Now I just need to find out what else about him is not on the level.'

When Ted asked for the bill, the restaurant manager came

over in person. 'Compliments of the management, *signori*,' he said, 'there will be no charge for your meal this evening, because of the unfortunate incident earlier.'

'I am a police officer,' Ted told him. 'I will pay for my meal, anything else would not be appropriate. But I will send the hotel the dry cleaning bill for my partner's clothes. And please remind Mr Rossi that I will be here tomorrow afternoon to inspect all the records.'

Chapter Seventeen

Ted took Rob with him again for his return to the hotel Sorrento. The DC was still unusually quiet but kept insisting he was fine.

The hotel manager, Rossi, was in the reception area, the red-haired young woman called Maggie on duty behind the desk. He had clearly been waiting in anticipation of their visit.

'*Inspettore*,' he greeted Ted, as if he were a valued client. Now Trev had pointed it out to him, Ted heard that he again made the same error with his Italian.

'Mr Rossi, I hope you have all your bookings records available for our inspection, as I requested?' Ted began.

'Please, *inspettore*, call me Tonino,' Rossi invited.

'Mr Rossi,' Ted said formally, 'may I begin by asking you for some form of identification? Do you have a driving licence, a passport, something with your name on?'

The man looked taken aback. With seeming reluctance, he pulled out a British driving licence and handed it to Ted, who scrutinised it.

'Mr Anthony Ross, town of birth, Stockport,' Ted read aloud, then looked at the man. 'Can we please drop the pretence now, Mr Ross? My partner spotted last night that your Italian was far from fluent.'

The manager looked apologetic. When he spoke again, it was with a broad Stockport accent with no trace of an Italian inflection. 'Sorry, Inspector,' he said, 'it's just that the punters like to think this is an authentic place. My dad's Italian, I learned the language from him but not brilliantly. It's just for show, for the job.'

At that moment, the waiter from the previous night came through the reception area, his coat on, clearly heading home at the end of his lunchtime shift. When he saw Ted standing talking to the manager, he looked stricken, his expression something between embarrassment and fear.

Ted excused himself and took a few steps towards the man.

'*S-a întâmplat ceva?*' he asked. Ted was no linguist but Trev had spent some time when they got home patiently researching how to ask 'are you OK' in Romanian then coaching Ted in how to pronounce it and what likely answers it might elicit.

The man looked astonished and replied, '*Sunt bine, mulțumesc.*'

Ted knew he was saying he was OK and thanking him. He didn't believe a word of it. The man had looked really afraid when he had dropped the food last night. Ted took out one of his cards and handed it to the man, making the universal telephone gesture with his hand and saying in English, 'If you need help, call me.'

The man took the card, thanked him effusively then said something else that Ted's crash-course had not equipped him to understand before bolting out of the door.

Ted turned back to the manager and said, 'As I said last night, Mr Ross, I wouldn't like to think of that man getting into any kind of trouble because of the unfortunate incident last night. Now, what about those records?'

The manager spread his hands expansively. He had kept the Italian gestures while reverting to his native accent. 'You're really not going to believe this, Inspector, but we've had a major computer crash and lost a lot of stuff.'

'That's very unfortunate,' Ted replied. 'However, luckily, I have a young officer back at the station who is an absolute genius with a computer. He can retrieve things which appear to have been lost forever. I'll arrange for him to come and look through your system for you. He can probably also help you to restore everything and get it working again. It won't cost you anything and it'll save you having to get an expensive IT expert in.'

Rob chipped in at this point and asked, 'Do you perhaps keep a written back up of your main bookings, Mr Ross? Something for just jotting down bookings which might come in over the phone when you're not in front of the computer? Or perhaps someone might remember? The twenty-eighth is not all that long ago.'

'That's a very good point,' Ted said. 'Surely, Mr Ross, if you had a function on that night, your chef will remember? Perhaps we could all go and talk to him?'

Ross looked as if he knew he was backed into a corner and was trying to find a way out of his dilemma. It was clear the two officers were not going to leave without some answers.

'It was a block booking,' he said finally. 'I remember now. The bedrooms, the restaurant, the function room, all booked for a private party.'

'And who made the booking, Mr Ross?' Ted asked, trying to keep his rising irritation out of his voice.

'A firm called Parish's Pies,' Ross told them, clearly reluctantly. 'I can't give you their contact details off the top of my head, but once the system is up and running again I will have them. It's a small, family firm. It was their works do, like a dinner-dance, and most of them stayed over.'

'Are they a local firm?' Ted asked.

'Not very local,' Ross said evasively, 'I think there were some people there from their head office, in London.'

'And there was no one else here apart from this firm? No other bookings?' Ted asked, making a mental note of his reference to a London head office for a supposedly small, family firm.

'No, just them. They had the meal, the function room, the bedrooms, and they all left after breakfast, those who stayed over. Some of them left after the dance in the evening.'

Ted reached in his inside pocket for the picture of Aiden they were using to try to find any sightings of him in the area. It was a school photo and he was scowling at the camera, looking every bit the rebellious young boy. Ted kept the photo in his hand, turned away from the manager, while he continued to question him.

'Were there any children at the function?'

'It's a family firm, some of them brought their children with them, yes,' Ross replied. 'There were a few at the dinner, and some stayed up for the dancing, although I think some of the younger ones went to bed when it got late.'

Ted turned the photograph round and held it up for the man to see. 'And did you see this boy there that night, or have you seen him at any other time in or near this hotel?'

Ted's keen sense of observation meant that he could see the slight muscle twitch around Ross's eyes. He was sure that Ross had seen the boy at some time.

'No, I don't think so, Inspector,' Ross said glibly. 'I didn't really pay much attention to the children, I was busy making sure that everything ran smoothly for the adults and that they had everything they needed.'

Ted looked at him levelly for a long moment. He could see that it made the man uncomfortable. Finally, he said, 'That will be all for today, Mr Ross. I will be back tomorrow with someone who can hopefully help to find the missing information on your computer.'

Rob and Ted headed back to the car.

'Thoughts?' Ted asked.

'Lying bastard, boss,' Rob said promptly. 'He definitely reacted when you showed him the photo. Aiden's been in that hotel at some time, I'd put money on it. What's the next move?'

'We need to check out this pie company, find out if they are genuine. I highly doubt it. Why would a small, family firm need a London head office? That's one for Steve or Sal to investigate online,' Ted replied. 'I also want to get him in there to have a look at that computer. This loss of data for the night in question is all a bit convenient. I'd like to find out if it's genuine or not.

'If we get anything a bit more positive to go on, I'll talk to the Super about perhaps getting a warrant to go in and search, see if there is any trace of Aiden's DNA anywhere. At the moment, I don't see us having enough to do that, we need a bit more of a lead to go on.

'Fancy a quick coffee on the way back to the station? Be good to kick around some ideas, away from the nick.'

Rob's hesitant acceptance sounded almost suspicious. He was usually much more at ease in the DI's company than he appeared to be today. Ted was keen to try and find out why, in an informal setting. He took the welfare of his officers seriously. It concerned him that Rob was not his usual self and seemed reluctant to talk about the reasons.

They sat together over coffees in a small café Ted knew, not far from the station. Ted tried to make small talk, but he was not good at it at the best of times and felt that Rob had the shutters firmly down, which didn't help.

'So how are the team bearing up on this one?' he asked eventually. 'I don't imagine it's easy for anyone. I suppose Sgt Reynolds has the most experience with this sort of case of any of us. Are you up for sitting in with either me or DS Hallam on interviewing some of those on the Offenders' Register who've not yet come up with an alibi?'

'Are you asking me if I might thump someone, boss, like Maurice threatened to? I might feel like it, but I don't think I will,' Rob told him.

'Okay, Rob, here's the thing, I'm no use at being subtle,' Ted smiled ruefully. 'I'm worried about you. You don't seem yourself and I want to know if it's the case that's getting to you or if it's something in your private life, something you'd prefer to stay private.'

'About as subtle as Maurice on a bad day, boss,' Rob returned his smile, much more like his normal self with his joking reply. 'It's fine. I'm fine. Like all of us, I'll just be glad when this case is over.'

Chapter Eighteen

'Today will be quite a difficult day for most of us, I imagine,' Ted said, beginning the morning briefing. 'We're going to be starting to interview those people on the Sex Offenders' Register who live on our patch. Those who have not so far provided an alibi, or at least not a convincing one, for the twenty-eighth, the night that Aiden was killed.

'I just want to make it clear at the outset that, no matter what any of us feel about those who commit sex crimes, especially on children, these are people who have been convicted and served their time. We are professional police officers. No matter how hard it is for any of us, we put aside our personal feelings and do our job.'

He looked round at his team, letting his glance linger a moment longer on Maurice Brown, to make his point. They all looked solemn today. There was none of the usual relaxed air and ready banter.

'Rob, I want you and Steve to go back to the Hotel Sorrento so that Steve can have a look at their computer system. Tell me if this so-called crash is genuine or if the records are still there somewhere. Steve, I also want you to find out anything you can about this Parish's Pies, the firm which is supposed to have made the block booking.

'Maurice, you and Sal are in charge of ferrying these people in for Sgt Hallam and me to interview. And Maurice, I'm counting on you not to do or say the slightest thing which could compromise this enquiry. I know I can trust you.'

'I can't promise it will be easy, boss, but I won't let you

down,' Maurice assured him.

'Right, that leaves Virgil and Jan to sit in with me and Sgt Hallam. Are you both comfortable with that? Please say if not.'

The two nodded in silent agreement. Ted looked across to his sergeant. 'Mike, have you a rough running order of who's coming in when?'

'Yes, sir,' Mike told him. 'We've warned all those on the list that we'll be bringing them in for questioning. I preferred to do it that way to make as sure as we can that we get them and they don't just disappear. For ease, I've arranged it that I'll take the morning ones, you take over at the start of the afternoon, then I'll mop up any that are left at the end of the day.'

He looked significantly at Ted, who realised that he was actually telling him the man David Evans he had mentioned as knowing, would be one of those coming in early on. Almost unconsciously, Ted's hand went up to loosen his tie and top button as he immediately started to feel the familiar shortness of breath.

'We won't get through them all in a day,' Mike Hallam continued. 'The list is worryingly long, and of course, there will be those who just disappear. But we're hoping we can make a good start at least and possibly start eliminating some of them.'

'Meanwhile, of course, forensics are cross-matching DNA samples on all those on the list against traces of anything found on Aiden's body,' Ted told the team, trying to keep his voice as steady as possible. 'In the meantime, we mustn't overlook this taxi driver shooting. There's a link there somewhere and we need to find it. Virgil, if you work with Sgt Hallam this morning, can you get back out there afterwards, see if you can find any more witnesses? Maybe talk to your homeless person again, see if he remembers anything else? Straws are all we have to clutch at, so let's not neglect any of them.'

Mike Hallam followed Ted as he went back to his own

office and headed straight for the kettle. 'I just thought you'd like to know that David Evans is supposedly up first, at ten o'clock, if he comes quietly when Maurice and Sal go to fetch him. Sir, can I ask you how you know this man?'

'You can ask,' Ted said guardedly. His meaning was clear. He wouldn't necessarily answer.

'Were you involved in his arrest?' Mike asked.

Ted shook his head. 'I was in firearms then. Can we leave it at that for now, Mike? It's handy that he's in first. Inspector Turner and I have been summoned to see the Super at that time. Have you worked on sexual offence cases before?'

'Luckily not, boss, this is my first experience.'

'Just something you need to be aware of, when you're speaking to some of these people. Often in their eyes they've done nothing wrong,' Ted told him. 'Don't forget it's not all that long ago that there was an attempt to remove the age of consent altogether, to make sex with children legal. I'm just flagging it up for you because it can come as a nasty shock if you've not come across it before. Right, good luck, let me know when you want me to take over.'

Ted went to find Kevin Turner in plenty of time before their meeting with the Ice Queen. He was particularly anxious to avoid any possibility of crossing paths with David Evans when he went downstairs. They went to her office together and Ted knocked on her door on the stroke of ten o'clock. They waited for her invitation to go in.

'Come in and sit down, gentlemen,' she greeted them. 'We may be some time, so help yourself to coffee if you need to. I wanted to update you on what has been happening with the raid on Rory the Raver's house, and the leak to the press. There have been significant developments.

'To start with, the enquiry into the leak has taken rather a back seat since it's become almost academic. In short, a large quantity of child porn was found in the raid, some of it of the worst possible kind. It should have been an open and shut case with a strong likelihood of a conviction.

'However, as soon as the story leaked, Rory simply hopped on the next plane and left the country. It's clear he has no intention of coming back. His career would have been over anyway, after something like this, and it's not as if he's short of money. Rumour has it he's gone to the Philippines, which should suit his particular proclivities ideally.

'It would be tempting to call that a result in itself, one fewer sexual predator in our area. However, it's highly likely that he could and would have named names, given the opportunity for a deal.'

Kevin Turner shook his head in bewilderment. 'I still don't see what anyone gained, apart from money, in leaking this and giving him the chance to slip away.'

'I'm coming round more and more to Inspector Darling's theory that the leak was precisely to achieve what it has done, to get him out of the way before he could start incriminate other people,' she said. 'There is now so much against him that he could never safely come back to Britain. But if he did, who would believe anything he said if he tried to implicate others?

'Physically removing him, an assassination, for example, would have been risky. This way he is rendered harmless. But that, of course, means that the leak came either from inside the force or from the CPS. It would not be the first time, though, that corrupt police officers or lawyers have been behind something like this on a paedophile case.

'Which brings me to the main reason for this meeting today.'

As she spoke, the Ice Queen got up and served coffee for them all. Ted was surprised. It was the first time she had shown any signs of such a loosening of formality. He expected that it didn't bode well for what was to come.

'Some of the material recovered is of Rory himself, with young boys. Cheshire think there is a good chance that it may be possible to identify locations, or at least get a clue, from the material they have found.

'I realise it is asking an enormous amount from you gentlemen, but would you be willing to view it, bearing in mind that it could give us the breakthrough we need? They have already sent over a number of stills which, whilst still shocking, are probably not quite as bad as the videos, which I would ask you to view only if all else fails.'

Ted desperately needed a drink of his coffee. He could feel his throat constricting and his pulse starting to race. He was afraid that if he reached out a hand and attempted to lift his cup, the other two would see how much his hands were shaking.

'If you do not feel up to it, please say so at the outset. No one will think any the worse of you, certainly not I. There is counselling available for you should you need it,' she stressed. 'Above all, I don't want you thinking you have to be macho…'

As soon as the words were out of her mouth, she realised her mistake and looked flustered, for the first time since Ted had known her. She was even going red.

Kevin couldn't retain a guffaw of laughter, giving Ted a sharp nudge with his elbow. Even Ted smiled, relieved to have something to break the tension threatening to consume him and provoke another panic attack.

'I'm so sorry, that's not what I meant at all, it was a completely inappropriate thing for me to say …'

'It's absolutely fine,' Ted assured her. 'I know it wasn't meant to give offence, and absolutely none was taken. I'll certainly take a look at the photos, and later at the videos, if it becomes essential.'

Kevin was nodding in agreement.

'It is something I would undertake myself, in the interests of the case, but I do not yet have the sort of local knowledge you two have, which is what is needed,' she said.

'It's fine, ma'am, really,' Ted almost felt sorry for his new boss at that moment. 'Kevin's a local boy, born and bred here. I've lived in the area since I was six, Lancashire lad by birth. It's not something either of us will relish, I'm sure, but as you say, if it moves the case forward, it has to be done.'

Chapter Nineteen

This time the water was even deeper. So deep that each time Ted sank like a stone, he feared he would never reach the bottom. It was only when he did, that he was hauled back to the surface, sometimes by the hair.

He'd lost count of the number of times already that he had been pushed under then pulled back up. Sometimes he was not even sure if he was conscious all of the time. He wished he could just die and get it over with. But whenever he felt himself slipping away to where he was safe and could no longer be terrorised, he was dragged back up and his reflexes forced air back into his lungs to keep him alive.

This time as he shot back up to the top, he felt strong hands grabbing his swimming trunks and pulling them down. By the time he broke the surface, he knew he was completely naked. The hands holding him shoved him contemptuously against the wall of the pool, with such force that the skin on his knuckles split and his hands began to bleed, colouring the water.

He made a wild grab for the rail, and hauled himself towards the steps which were tantalisingly close. As his hands felt the welcome touch of the rough metal, he was convinced he would suddenly be snatched back for more torture but it seemed his tormentor had grown bored. He just idly trod water nearby as Ted scrambled frantically up the steps and out of the pool.

They were at the deep end, which meant a long sprint back to the changing cubicle where his clothes were. Ted used his hands to cover his nakedness and ran as fast as he could, skinny legs pumping like pistons. As he ran, he heard the jeers and catcalls of other boys in the pool ringing in his ears. He also felt the warm flood of urine on his hands as the terror robbed him of all control.

The cubicle was the last place on earth he wanted to be. A place where he felt more in danger than in the pool. But his clothes were there. He desperately needed to cover his body and get out of there, as far away from his attacker as he could.

Trembling all over, and not just from cold, he didn't even bother trying to dry himself. He just pulled on his clothes over his wet body then ran out of the swimming baths, clutching his towel and his kit bag, and just kept on running.

Down the road he ran, blindly dodging traffic as he crossed over. Past shops and offices, on down the pavement, over a bridge. The marketplace was full of people, the metal and glass market hall heaving at the seams.

Ted was gasping for breath more than ever, totally disorientated, with no idea of where he was heading, just that he wanted to keep on running. He ran round the side of the market hall, seeking somewhere less crowded, and bumped straight into two patrolling police officers.

It was Ted's first ever ride in a police car as the two kindly constables took him back to his school and handed him over to the school secretary. There had been a bit of a panic on when he had not been on the bus returning the pupils to school after swimming, and he was nowhere to be found.

His form teacher was summoned, as was his swimming teacher.

'He had a bit of a fright when he slipped in the deep end and went under the water,' the swimming teacher said. 'Didn't you, Darling? You had us all worried for a moment there.'

He laughed and looked reassuringly from the secretary to the form teacher. 'Don't worry, next week I'll personally spend time with Darling in deeper water, showing him there is nothing to be afraid of.'

'That's very kind of you, Mr Evans,' the form teacher replied. 'I'm sure Darling is very sorry for all the trouble he has caused, and is grateful for your kindness, aren't you, boy?'

Ted shot upright in bed and realised in panic that he was on the point of pissing himself with fear. He leapt out of bed and ran for the bathroom, shaking like a leaf and soaked with sweat. He emptied his bladder, shuddering in self-loathing, then doubled up and retched and choked over the toilet bowl.

When he had straightened up and washed his face in the basin, he turned to see Trev standing quietly in the doorway, lines of concern etched on his face. He held out a fleece blanket, which Ted meekly allowed him to wrap round his shoulders. Then he led him back to the bed, sat him on the edge and gently hugged and soothed him, until the shaking stopped.

'You can't go on like this,' Trev told him. 'This is worse than it's ever been before. You need to see someone. I can't help you through this, it's too dark.'

Ted patted his arm with a hand that was still shaking. 'You can help, you do help. You're what gets me through the darkness,' he said. 'I'm sorry I worry you. I will be fine, I promise.'

'Ted, you're not fine,' Trev said gently. 'You need proper professional help with this. You need to talk to someone who can help you, who can end these terrors for good.'

Ted paused for a moment to make sure his voice was back under control. 'I'll talk to you more, I promise,' he said. 'Look, it's nearly the weekend. Let's make plans. Sunday, you, me, the bike, a picnic, the Peak District. Miles from anyone. That's all I need, honestly.'

'You know I'll help you if I can,' Trev told him. 'It's just that this is getting too serious. If it's the case you're working on, you need to talk to someone at work about getting some help.'

Ted snorted. 'If I tell the Ice Queen I'm cracking up, she'll pull me off the case altogether. I don't want to be packed off to shrinks or therapists or whatever. I just need you to listen while I talk but outside. Out in the open. On top of Kinder Downfall.'

It was a cheap shot and Ted knew it. Kinder Downfall was their special place, where they had shared their life histories and a first brief kiss. He knew Trev could never resist the chance to go back there. It was also one of the few places where Ted felt comfortable talking about himself and the demons from his past. Trev knew most of it already, though not why it was coming back to haunt him so violently with his current case.

'If you can't talk to the Ice Queen, could you talk to Jim?' Trev asked. 'You used to get on so well with him when he was your boss, and you've listened to enough of his problems over the years.'

Ted shook his head. 'That would be compromising him professionally. It's too much to ask of an old and valued friend. He would feel obliged to tell the Ice Queen everything I told him, even if I asked him to keep it confidential. He's a copper first and my friend afterwards.'

'You need to talk to someone,' Trev repeated doggedly. 'Kinder Downfall isn't the answer to everything in life. We'll go there on Sunday, we'll sit and talk, but you have to agree that you will talk to someone else, and Jim is your best bet.'

Ted still looked reluctant, so Trev pushed for a compromise. 'All right, if you have no more nightmares after Sunday, I'll let it drop. But if you do, you have to promise me that you will do something about it. Deal?'

Ted nodded, yawning, suddenly incredibly tired. He slid back under the duvet, not making any fuss as Trev tucked the fleece blanket around him, and was asleep again almost before Trev had gone round to his side of the bed and got in beside him.

Chapter Twenty

Ted was in early as usual the following morning and was surprised to find young Steve there ahead of him.

'Morning, sir,' the TDC greeted him. 'I was hoping to catch you before the others got in. I just wanted to tell you about my findings in private first, as I threw up something very odd in looking into the computer systems at the Sorrento.'

Ted was really pleased with the progress the young officer had made since joining the team. To begin with he had been painfully shy and clearly uncomfortable in speaking up in front of his DI. With Ted's encouragement he had really come out of his shell. Now, especially when talking about his area of expertise, he was quite happy to voice an opinion.

'Go ahead,' Ted said, intrigued.

'Well, sir, before I forget, I can't yet find any trace of this Parish's Pies anywhere on the Internet, which is strange in itself. I've tried all the spelling variations I can think of, and even words that sound similar, in case it was misheard, but nothing so far.'

There was never any hesitation when Steve was talking about computers or Internet research. He knew what he was talking about.

'Now, on to the computer system,' he continued. 'We're not talking about a crash or any kind of accidental loss of data. The system has been thoroughly and very professionally wiped. It's not something that can be done quickly, either. A job as thorough as this one would need several hours, by someone who really knew what they were doing.'

'So the data's gone for good? No one could recover it?' Ted asked. He knew as much about computer matters as he did about brain surgery, which was next to nothing.

'Cheltenham could, with the resources they have, and with a lot of time,' Steve replied.

'Cheltenham?' Ted echoed blankly, wondering if he appeared as stupid as he felt.

'GCHQ, sir,' Steve told him patiently. 'Government Communications Headquarters.'

Ted looked even more puzzled. 'Why on earth would someone go to that amount of trouble to wipe the records of a small private hotel?' he asked.

'Perhaps we're getting closer to the truth?' Steve suggested. 'There could have been something in the records which might lead to people very high up in the establishment who were involved.

'There is more, too, sir, but I need to show you stuff on my computer and I know the rest of the team will be in shortly. Maybe we could do that at the end of the day? I wanted you to decide how much of this you share with the others at the moment, sir, as it brings in some pretty sinister possibilities, I'd say.'

'Brilliant work, Steve, thanks,' Ted said.

The rest of the team members were arriving, but there was no sign of Rob O'Connell by the time Ted was ready for the morning briefing.

'Anyone know what's happened to Rob?' he asked. There were blank stares and head shakes.

'So, Mike, since we all had so much fun yesterday with the sex offenders, I take it you have more of the same on the agenda for today?' Ted asked ironically.

'Yes, boss, we've still got quite a few to sift through, then we need to check their stories,' the DS said. 'Hard to know really where to begin when some of them have the form they have. Of the ones I spoke to I could pretty much imagine any of them being involved. What about yours, sir?'

'Like you say, most of them have the form, although it has to be said that some of them only seem interested in girls. The DNA cross-matching should hopefully help narrow it down a bit for us.

'If Rob doesn't appear before the suspects start arriving, do you want me and Sgt Reynolds to take the morning shift?' Ted asked. 'Then if he turns up, you and Rob do this afternoon. If he doesn't appear for some reason, Virgil can you take over from him, please. How are you getting on looking for your homeless man?'

'No sign at all of him at the moment, boss,' Virgil replied. 'Nobody's seen him for a few days. He seems to have gone underground somewhere. I'm just hoping he's all right, and no one realised he was a witness to the shooting.'

'Keep looking, keep asking around,' Ted told him. 'Right, let's crack on. We need to make some progress.'

Ted's first interviewee of the day was tall and distinguished-looking, silver haired and in his early seventies. Ted knew from his record that he was a former house parent at an expensive boarding school. He had served time for having sex with under-age girls in his care. He seemed not the slightest bit perturbed to be summoned to the station. His whole attitude oozed arrogant self-confidence.

Ted started with the formalities then began, 'Mr Armitage, we have asked you to come in today to account for your whereabouts on the evening of the twenty-eighth of last month. I understand you were not able to do so when my officers called on you. At this stage it is purely routine. We are asking the same question of all people on the Sex Offenders' Register living in this area.'

'Let me save you some time, Inspector,' the man replied, with the hint of a sneer. 'As I read the newspapers and watch the local news, I believe this is in connection with the sexual assault and killing of a young boy. I have absolutely no interest whatsoever in boys, I find that a complete perversion.'

'But Mr Armitage, you must understand that we need to speak to anyone with a record of having sex with children.'

'Children!' the man almost spat. 'I slept with girls of fourteen and fifteen. Have you any notion of how adult they can appear? If you saw them out for the evening, you would take them for nineteen, twenty, easily.'

Ted could feel the revulsion rising in him. He struggled to keep control. 'As a house parent at their school, though, you would have been perfectly aware of their ages, surely?'

Quietly, Jancis Reynolds laid a hand on Ted's arm and said, 'Sorry to interrupt, sir, but as time is a bit short, can I just ask Mr Armitage if he can account for his movements on the evening in question?'

'Since the court case and subsequent prison sentence, I have very little social life,' the man told them. 'My wife left me. I can no longer work. I am hounded wherever I go, so I tend to stay in my flat rather a lot of the time. In the evenings I often play Scrabble online. I imagine it is possible for you to check that? That's about all I can offer you for now.'

Ted concluded the interview with almost indecent haste. As soon as the man had left the room, he turned to Jan. 'Sorry about that, Jan, I nearly lost it for a moment there,' he said apologetically. 'I just find it very hard the way these people try to justify their actions by blaming the children.'

'No worries, boss, at least you didn't karate kick him all round the room,' she laughed. 'The team hasn't told me how to control you if you do.'

Ted smiled in turn. The touch of humour was a big help for a difficult morning. There was plenty more of the same, but they were no nearer finding a possible suspect. When they had finished the morning interviews and headed back upstairs, Rob O'Connell was at his desk, head down, working on something.

He looked dreadful. He was unshaven, looked as if he had slept the night in his clothes and even from across the office,

Ted could smell the alcohol oozing from his pores. He was shocked; it was so unlike him.

'Rob, have you got a minute, please?' he asked, heading for his office. The DC followed him, not looking at any of his colleagues.

Ted headed straight for his kettle. He was in need of green tea after the distasteful morning he had just experienced. He kept coffee in his office for visitors who didn't share his taste. He made a strong one for Rob, put it in front of him, then sat down opposite him.

'So, Rob,' he said, 'what's wrong?'

'I went out and got absolutely hammered last night, sir,' he began. 'The girlfriend wouldn't let me back in the flat. I had to sleep in the car.'

'I guessed that much. Do you want to tell me why?' Ted asked.

Rob took a long gulp of the hot coffee. 'You were right, it is this case. It was sitting there yesterday listening to those bastards talking about what they did, without any sense of guilt or remorse.'

Ted sensed there was more to come and waited patiently in silence, sipping his tea.

'I was in care for a time, when I was a kid,' the DC continued. 'My mum was very ill, in and out of hospital for a long time. She was a single parent, no family. I was lucky, in a sense. I was placed with a foster family, not in a home, and they were wonderful. My foster mum's brother, though, my "uncle Derek", was a different story altogether.'

Both men paused to drink. Ted noticed that his own hands had started to shake so he gripped his mug tightly between both of them to try to steady them.

'He … he kept touching me. Intimately. At every chance he got. And there were a lot of chances. They left him to babysit me and their own children, two girls, quite often, as he was "so good with children".'

Ted stayed quiet, letting Rob talk. He sensed it was what he needed most, the opportunity to unburden himself.

'I never told them. I was terrified they wouldn't believe me. I was afraid they'd say I'd encouraged him, or made it up or something and I'd be put in a home. I just shut it away in my memory and thought I'd forgotten all about it. Until this case.'

'Thank you for being honest, Rob. There is help available, if you want it, but that's up to you. I don't want to push you into anything, but if you need me to arrange something, just say the word,' Ted told him.

'For now, I want you to go home, have some food, have a shower and get some proper sleep. Come back in the morning and I'll assign you to something else. Nobody will know the reason.'

Rob shot him a look of gratitude as he drained his coffee then headed for the door.

'Oh, and Rob,' Ted said before he left. 'Maybe get a bunch of flowers for the girlfriend on your way home, eh?'

Chapter Twenty-one

The day had been long and hard. Ted, unusually, was clock-watching until he could get away. It was his night for both the self-defence club and his own judo session, and he could hardly wait. He needed to feel the healing power of a hard physical workout, to help him regain some inner balance.

He had attended Aiden's funeral, out of respect. It had been a depressing affair, with so few people there. There was just a token presence from the children's home; Flip, with both his foster parents and, to his surprise, Professor Nelson had put in an appearance. She immediately went up even further in his estimation.

He had also been affected by listening to Rob O'Connell's account, although he had suspected something of the sort. However, it hadn't helped with the emotional scars of his own troubled past, which he was trying his best to keep buried until he could wrap up the case.

Although he had suggested arranging counselling for Rob, it was not a route he would personally contemplate going down, unless pushed into it. Ted was a good listener, but found it incredibly hard to talk about his own feelings. Only with Trev could he do so, out walking in the hills. And even with Trev he could only manage to vocalise his emotions if he were looking somewhere else, up at the sky, off to the far horizon. The prospect of sitting in a room talking to a stranger was the stuff of his worst nightmares.

Although he was keen to get away, he was also intrigued to hear what else Steve had to tell him, from his computer work.

The implications of his disclosures that morning had rather rattled Ted, but he had not yet had the time to discuss them with either the Ice Queen or Kevin Turner.

He was feeling a little out of his depth at what Steve had told him so far and badly needed to kick some ideas around with someone who knew more about the subject than he did himself. He suspected that would include pretty much everyone else in the station, since he was a total techno-phobe. He knew enough to do his job, but no more.

As soon as the others had left, Ted pulled up a chair and sat down next to the TDC's desk, where Steve was at the computer waiting for him. In a couple of clicks, Steve opened the page he had bookmarked earlier.

Ted stared at it for a moment in evident incomprehension. Seeing his expression, Steve said, 'It's like a blog, sir. Things someone has posted, and where people can comment. But look at the title.'

Ted read the name of the page: PIEdpiper. He couldn't work out what it meant or why it was written in that format.

'I'm an idiot with this stuff, Steve,' he confessed, 'you'll have to spell it out for me in words of half a syllable.'

'Right you are, sir,' Steve was clearly in his element to be helping his boss with stuff he couldn't grasp. 'Well, the Pied Piper, perhaps you know, was a rat-catcher in Hamelin, but it's quite a sinister story. On a fairy tale level, the children followed him because of the sound of his pipes. But some legends have it that up to a hundred and thirty children followed him out of the town and were never seen again.

'Now PIE, written like that, also stands for Paedophile Information Exchange which, you probably know, was a pro-paedophile activist group set up in 1974, which ran for ten years. Initially it was above board and official. The stated aim was the abolition of the age of consent, so that sex between adults and children could become legal.'

Ted nodded. 'I've heard about it. Mind-boggling.'

'I've been researching it, in connection with this website. There were top diplomats involved, all sorts of respectable establishment figures, even a senior intelligence operative. The group also received grants from the Home Office. Eventually a lot of the major players were arrested and convicted, some not all that long ago.'

'So what I don't understand, is this a page that's promoting paedophilia?' Ted asked.

Steve shook his head. 'Far from it. It's set up to expose people who are allegedly involved in child sex abuse.' He clicked to open a new page. 'Someone like this face you may well recognise.'

Rory the Raver's face stared out at Ted from the computer screen. Underneath the photo were several paragraphs of text outlining allegations against him in connection with his activities with under-age fans.

'How do they get away with publishing this stuff without getting sued?' Ted asked.

'Everything that's written here is littered with "alleged" and similar words,' Steve told him. 'Plus people running sites of this type are proficient and clever. They make it as difficult as possible to track them down. Not impossible, of course, to anyone with the right knowledge. It can be done but it needs to go higher up than we are.'

Ted caught sight of the clock at the bottom corner of Steve's computer and exclaimed, 'Shit, is that the time? Sorry, Steve, I must just make a quick phone call. Hang on.'

Trev had carefully stored his number in Ted's phone and showed him how to speed-dial it, which he did now. When Trev answered, he said, as ever, 'Hi, it's me.' He always forgot that Trev could see his name on the screen and had set the ringtone for his calls to Ted's own favourite song, Barcelona. 'I'm running late. Sorry. Can you start things off and I'll get down there as soon as I can? I'll just nip home to change. I'm not letting Bernard and the lads see me in a suit. See you as soon as possible.'

He turned back to Steve. 'Sorry about that, it's the self-defence club tonight, the one we run for kids. I like to think it's because of what Flip learned with us that he didn't finish up like Aiden. So go on, what else.'

'You better brace yourself for this one,' Steve said with a grin. Ted noticed he was so relaxed he'd dropped all formality and wasn't calling him 'sir' every other sentence.

He clicked another link which brought up a different photo, one which Ted recognised instantly.

'Holy shit!' Ted couldn't help but exclaim. It was of a senior police officer from a neighbouring force. He rapidly scanned the text underneath in disbelief. Most of it centred on allegations that the officer was particularly fond of administering spankings to young, naked boys. 'I know there have been rumours, but this stuff is beyond anything I imagined.'

'Ready for another?' Steve asked, and clicked on another tab. This time Ted gaped at the screen as a photograph of a former Crown Court Recorder he had known appeared on the page. He knew that this man was now dead, which perhaps explained why some of the allegations against him were more graphic and left little to the imagination.

Ted leaned back in his chair, amazed. 'I get that these are just rumours, but if there is any truth in any of them it's no wonder there's not much progress in catching and bringing these people to justice.'

'I've saved the best to the last,' Steve told him, with the air of an illusionist about to produce the best trick of the evening to a packed audience. 'Ready?' he asked teasingly, then said, 'Ta-da!' as he clicked the link.

This time Ted said, 'Bloody hell!' staring at the picture on the screen of a minor royal. He was no royalist so he could not begin to guess how far down the line of succession the man who appeared in front of them was. But not so far down that

Ted didn't recognise him immediately.

'How high does this go?'

'I dread to think,' Steve replied. 'Bear in mind, as you said, this is all just rumour and speculation. But lately a lot of what started out as rumour has proved to be true. Jimmy Savile, for instance.'

'But I thought this one was married, with a child? And why do they call him the Knave of Clubs?' Ted asked.

'The Knave or Jack is the lowest court card in a pack, so that's a reference to his lowly status amongst the royals,' Steve explained. 'Yes, married, with a child, but then that's not all that unusual for paedophiles, from what I've read. And the Clubs bit is a reference to his public image of a bit of a Jack-the-lad, night-life lover, party animal.'

'Steve, you have absolutely excelled yourself this time, fantastic piece of work, well done,' Ted told him. 'Let's just sit on this for now, until I can get my head around it. It's very big, if it's true, and is going to need some extremely careful handling. Thanks for all your hard work. Now I'd better go and equip some more kids with the means to defend themselves against this sort of stuff.'

Ted left Steve grinning from ear to ear, clearly pleased with himself. If he really got his skates on, he could still arrive at the sports centre in time for part of the junior club, then do the much-needed full judo session with the seniors.

When he got to the dojo, he was surprised to see Flip's foster mother, Mrs Atkinson, sitting on one of the benches watching the session. Trev was working the kids well. Ted went over to the mat and bowed before stepping onto it.

Flip saw him, stopped what he was doing and immediately rushed across, beaming. 'Ted! I was worried when you didn't come last week. I thought I'd done summat wrong and got you into trouble.'

Quietly, Ted reminded him of correct etiquette, not

breaking off to talk during a training session, but added in a low voice, 'It's fine, Flip, nothing you did, I just had to work.'

Now Ted had joined him, Trev was able to up the pace a bit, using his partner to help him demonstrate more techniques. With encouragement from the juniors, they finished up with a little high-speed workout between them, Ted showing some of his lightning fast Krav Maga self-defence moves, which he knew the kids loved to see.

Once the session was over, while Ted and Trev were still out of breath from their display, Flip's foster mother came over to speak to them.

'Inspector, that was incredible to see,' she said. 'I think I misjudged you on our recent meeting. What you've done for those children is just amazing. Flip thinks the world of you, and I can now see why. Thank you. My husband and I want to get him a judo outfit to encourage his interest, so we'd be really pleased if you could help and advise us.'

Chapter Twenty-two

Rob O'Connell looked much more like his old self when he arrived, ahead of time, the following morning. He was cleanly shaven, correctly turned out and clearly raring to go. Ted had decided to send Rob and Virgil to check out the records of the taxi firm where the murdered driver had worked. He wanted them to see if there was any discernible pattern in their visits to the Sorrento, especially on the night Aiden died.

Since the shooting of the taxi driver, Ted had been wary of pushing any harder to find out information from that direction. He and Kevin Turner had now agreed between them, their decision having been sanctioned by the Ice Queen, to put a high-profile uniformed presence near the taxi ranks in their area. If they couldn't yet find Aiden's killers, at least they could perhaps prevent other children falling victim to the same abuse.

Ted and Mike Hallam were still wading through the interviews, waiting for all the DNA test results to come in so they could at least eliminate some of the suspects on the Offenders' list. Once they had spoken to everyone on the list, they would get together to discuss which of them to question further.

The phone on Ted's desk rang. When he picked it up, a cheery voice greeted him.

'Hello, Ted, me old mucker. It's Brian Donohue, at Manchester City. How's life under the reign of the Ice Queen?'

Ted groaned. 'About how you'd imagine,' he said. 'She has me wearing a suit and tie, can you believe? What can I do for you?'

'Well, for starters, you can stop littering my patch with your stray bodies. We're busy enough without, thank you very much.'

'Meaning?' Ted asked.

'You know the old railway station near here? A body's been found there, shot in the head. Would normally be one for us except this body is clutching your card in his hand, so he clearly knows you,' Donohue told him. 'Have you time to come over and see if you know him, or can shed any light on the matter?'

Ted was not due to start interviews until the afternoon, leaving him time to go and visit the crime scene near Central Manchester's Piccadilly. 'Setting off now, Brian, I'll be there as soon as traffic allows. See you at the scene?'

Traffic was not too dense so he was there in good time. He parked near several police vehicles, showing his warrant card to a young uniformed constable who tried to move him on, and asked where to find Inspector Donohue.

Brian Donohue and Ted knew one another of old. They had been on various courses together and had always kept in touch intermittently. When Brian saw him walking down the old deserted platform towards him, resplendent in light grey suit, striped shirt and tie, he let out a whistle of admiration.

'Wow, Ted, loving the new image,' he laughed.

'Which martial art would you like me to use to inflict extreme pain on you, Brian?' Ted asked pleasantly in reply. 'This is the Ice Queen's doing, not mine. Now, where's this body that you say is one for me?'

Still laughing, Donohue nodded further up the platform. 'Just along there, where the action is, down in the rails. Mind you don't crease your nice new suit.'

He tossed Ted gloves and shoe covers and they both headed in that direction. The two men jumped down carefully on to the old track-way.

Ted could see the body of a man lying there, face down. One arm was thrown out to the side and Ted saw immediately that the body had a disabled hand.

'I know him,' he said. 'At least, I don't know his name, but I know who he is. He's Romanian, a waiter, from a hotel we're investigating as part of a child sex abuse enquiry we're running. It's called the Hotel Sorrento, on my patch.'

'Trev and I ate there the other night. This man served us and dropped Trev's starter in his lap. He seemed much more afraid than I would expect him to be just for something like that. I wondered if he was an illegal, or if he knew anything about the goings-on at the hotel we're looking into. What else can you tell me for now?'

'I would say an execution rather than just a straight-forward shooting,' Donohue told him. 'Single gunshot to the back of the head, very precise. He'd also been thoroughly frisked and all personal possessions and any ID removed. They only missed your card because it was inside the closed hand, not easily visible. The pathologist just spotted it by chance.'

'You've probably heard,' said Ted. 'We've got a little lad who was raped and strangled on our patch, we think maybe at this hotel, but we've got nothing to tie him to it at the moment. We're assuming we're looking at a paedophile ring, sex parties with kids, that sort of thing. Can we get DNA from this body cross-checked against our boy? It's looking as if this chap may have been killed in connection with our case, either because he was involved or he knew too much about who was.

'We've also had a taxi driver shot on our patch, a possible suspect in our case. Weapon was a Glock 17. I'd put money on this one being shot by the same weapon. We need to work together on this if we possibly can.'

'Always a pleasure to work with you, Ted,' Donohue said, and sounded as if he meant it. 'Have you got time for a coffee before you head back? Strictly business, of course. We need to get our heads together on this one from the start.'

They walked the short distance to the nearby mainline railway station for a drink at a coffee bar there. It was good to catch up but Ted still felt as if he was playing truant from school, even though they talked shop a lot of the time. He wouldn't have given it a second thought had DCI Jim Baker still been his boss.

'So, what's the Ice Queen like to work for?' Donohue wanted to know. 'Must come as a real shock to the system after Jim Baker and his relaxed ways.'

'Very efficient, even colder than I imagined, extremely intelligent,' Ted summed up. 'I turn into a complete idiot every time I open my mouth in her presence.'

'She's seen your record, though, she knows you're a good cop,' Donohue told him, then asked, 'So where do you see this stiff fitting in with your enquiry? Is he one of your paedos, do you think?'

'I don't think so, based on nothing more than the wages he'd be likely to be getting as a hotel waiter, possibly an illegal immigrant to boot. I don't see how he could afford to be moving in those circles, on that money,' Ted replied. 'I also doubt if he could have identified anyone, or would have. I don't know how long he worked there but he didn't seem to speak any English and hardly any Italian, and it's an Italian hotel. I'm guessing that perhaps, for some reason, if this young boy was killed at the hotel, this waiter may have been given the job of dumping the body.

'Whoever did dump it wasn't very bright. They left it in a skip not all that far from the hotel, where it was easily discovered. So, if someone higher up was not best pleased about that, this might be another housekeeping job. The same as taking out the taxi driver who may have delivered the boy and who could have been on the point of talking about it.'

When Ted was back at his own station, he briefly informed the Ice Queen of the latest body and its possible connection to their own case. Then he steeled himself for another afternoon of the distasteful task of talking to known paedophiles.

He called the team together quickly at the end of the day, so they were all kept in the loop about the body and the new line of enquiry it would involve.

'I got a call from Manchester City this morning about a gunshot victim. It turned out to be the waiter from the Hotel Sorrento. He dropped Trev's hot starter in his lap when we ate there. He was shot once in the back of the head, execution style.'

'Bloody hell, boss,' Maurice blurted out. 'Remind me not to drop hot food on your Trevor. Are you sure you don't still have your service weapon?'

Ted tried to look stern and disapproving but failed and had to chuckle along with the rest of the team. 'It wasn't me, Maurice,' he smiled. 'But it begs the question why he was killed, and why in this way.

'Rob, tomorrow, you and I will go back to the hotel, get a full ID on this man and start finding out a bit more about his background. I want to know if he had a car and if so, where it is. My current thinking is that he may have been the one to dispose of Aiden's body. So if we find a vehicle, we need to get forensics on to it, looking for any trace at all of Aiden's presence in it.

'We're working with City on this one because of the strong possibility of a tie-in. I think we're getting nearer. We just need to keep working away until we crack it.'

Chapter Twenty-three

After the briefing at the start of the day, Ted told Rob O'Connell they would go to the Sorrento some time later that morning. He had something to do first, something he had been putting off and dreaded tackling.

Back in his own office, he took off his jacket and hung it on the back of his chair. He pulled off the hated tie and stuck it in the jacket pocket, opening the top two buttons of his shirt, crisply ironed for him by Trev. He made a mug of green tea, stronger than usual, and doubled the amount of organic honey he normally added. Then he fished an old box of tissues out of a drawer. He wanted to be prepared.

Only then did he unlock the top drawer of his desk. He took out a large envelope containing the still photos taken from the videos seized in the raid on Rory the Raver's house. Ted tried to prepare himself mentally for what he would see, but just the sight of the first photo alone nearly caused him to lose his breakfast.

It was of Rory the Raver, in close-up, with a young boy, barely into his teens by the look of it. The shot left nothing at all to the imagination. Ted didn't recognise either the boy or the surroundings. He steeled himself to continue.

A lot of the stills were in close-up; not much of the background was visible in many of them. Where it was, Ted separated out the photographs, desperately trying to concentrate on the surroundings rather than what was happening in the centre of the shot.

Ted was not one for therapy or counselling. He had been

offered it on occasion when cases had been tougher than usual, especially in Firearms when he had shot people. He'd been obliged to go at times but only paid it lip service. He instinctively felt it was not for him, but he knew the principles. Find a safe place in his mind and go there when things got too hard to manage.

He leaned back in his chair and turned his face up to an imaginary sky, eyes closed against the sunlight. He could feel the soft, springy heather under his back, hear the sound of water in Kinder Downfall, splashing over rocks. Larks were singing, buzzards, wheeling high above, gave their pitiful mewing cries.

There was nobody for miles around. Only a hesitant sheep nibbled experimentally at the laces of his boots. Yet he knew that Trev was lying in the heather close to him, their hands not far apart. All he had to do was to reach out his fingers and he could make contact.

It would take him many virtual visits to Kinder to get through the pile of photos. He had just about sorted them all, collecting together those that showed any sort of background which might help him identify the location, when there was a hesitant knock and his door started to open.

'Wait!' Ted barked, his voice much sharper than his normal calm tone. He scooped up the worst of the pictures, slid them back into the envelope and locked it back in his drawer. He turned the remaining pile face down on his desk and only then said more quietly, 'Come in.'

Rob O'Connell came cautiously into the small office and looked shocked at the sight of his dishevelled boss. Ted's shirt was wet through with sweat which trickled down his back and left damp rings around his armpits. His hands were visibly shaking, although he tried to disguise the fact. Seeing Rob's look, Ted grabbed some tissues and mopped his face.

'Are you all right, sir?' Rob asked in evident concern. 'Is it still the virus thing? You look shocking.'

119

Ted shook his head dismissively. 'Just had to do something rather distasteful, Rob. I've been looking at some of the stills from the child porn videos seized in the raid on Rory the Raver's place. Some of them show background of the rooms they were shot in, which might be identifiable. There are some shots of what could be part of a four-poster bed.

'I don't want you to look at the content of these photos. It's not necessary and it's asking too much. Just wait outside a couple of minutes, will you, and I'll mask out the worst of the shot with blank paper, see if any of the backgrounds look familiar to you.'

'Boss, I'll look at it all if it will help catch these bastards …' Rob began.

Ted shook his head. 'No, Rob, you won't. Just please do as I say.'

When Ted called him back in, he reminded him not to move the paper, just to focus on what he could see of the backgrounds of the shots he had laid out on his desk.

'I can't be one hundred per cent certain but it is possible that some of these are in one of the rooms at the Sorrento that I looked at,' Rob said hesitantly.

'Right, wait for me in the main office, I'll collect these shots up and we'll head off down there now. Oh, and Rob, I might just show our phony Mr Rossi one of the full photos, just to see his reaction, so make sure you don't look at it when I do.'

Ted used a few more tissues to try to dry off the worst of the sweat on his face. He put on his jacket but left the tie stuffed in the pocket, hoping he wouldn't cross the Ice Queen's path, looking as bad as he did.

Steve was at his desk in the main office when he went out. 'Steve, Parish's Pies. I think we both know now what that actually stands for. Find them, please, whatever it takes.'

'Ahead of you. Already on it,' the TDC said, without raising his head from his computer. He was too involved even to add a 'sir', his fingers flashing over the keys like the flying feet of Irish dancers.

As they drove to the hotel, Ted outlined to Rob how he wanted the visit to go. First he needed an ID on the waiter, but he also wanted to get a look at some of the bedrooms, to see if they could identify any from the photos he had with him.

'We also need to find out if the waiter had a car, and where it might be. If he did have anything to do with Aiden's death, perhaps in disposing of his body, we'll need to get it thoroughly tested for traces. I've already asked Professor Nelson to cross-reference his DNA when she gets it from City against traces found on Aiden's body and clothing.' Ted told him. 'We're getting close to a breakthrough, Rob, I'm sure we are.'

Ross, the manager of the Sorrento, didn't look pleased to see the two police officers walk through his doors again, but he went into smiling professional mode. Ted noticed that he no longer bothered with the phony accent.

'Gentlemen,' Ross beamed, 'what can I do for you?'

'Your Romanian waiter,' Ted said, 'the one who dropped the starter all over my partner. Is he working today?'

Ross spread his hands. He still kept the flamboyant gestures. 'We haven't seen him for a couple of days. Sometimes these immigrants are not very reliable'

'What's his name?' Ted asked.

Ross shrugged. 'I'm not sure, Josef, Iosif, something like that. I don't remember and as I already explained, and your young officer verified, all our computer records have been lost in a crash.'

'Is he legally employed here? With the correct papers?'

'Well, sometimes we don't ask too many questions,' Ross said evasively. 'If we can help someone out with a bit of work, we try to.'

'Very public spirited of you,' Ted said dryly. 'Does he

have a car?And do you have an address for him?'

Ross was starting to look uncomfortable. 'I think he drives an old Ford. I'm not sure where he lives. What's this about, Inspector?'

'I have to tell you, Mr Ross, that the body of a man has been found, a man who appears to resemble your waiter. No formal identification has yet been made. If we are unable to trace any next of kin, I may have to ask you to identify the body,' Ted told him.

Ross was looking increasingly shaken. Ted pressed on relentlessly. 'Next, Mr Ross, I want to take a look at some of your bedrooms, in particular any rooms which have four-poster beds. I have reason to believe that your hotel may have been used to host so-called sex parties, those involving serious sexual abuse of under-age children.'

Now Ross looked pale and seriously worried. He started to bluster but Ted cut him short. 'I'd like you to accompany me and Detective Constable O'Connell now, and show us some of the rooms.'

Again the manager tried to prevaricate. 'Some of the rooms are currently occupied, I can't show them to you … '

'We can either do this now, informally, without a warrant, or I'll go and get one and come back with a lot of officers in uniform so all of your guests can see what's going on,' Ted told him pleasantly. 'The choice is yours.'

Reluctantly, Ross got his pass key and led the way up the stairs to the first of the bedrooms. Ted told him he was at this stage only interested in those with four-poster beds, of which the hotel had several. When they entered the third such room, Ted walked across to the bed and looked at the posts, the brocade curtain and a picture hanging on the wall behind them.

'Mr Ross, I would like to show you photographic evidence to support my belief that your hotel has been used for child abuse,' Ted took one photo of several he had brought with him out of the envelope. He gave Rob a meaningful glance warning him not to look at it, then turned the photo over so Ross could see.

'In light of this evidence, Mr Ross, I am going to have to ask you to come to the station with me now to answer a number of questions in connection with serious offences.'

The manager only just made it into the en suite bathroom in time, where they could hear him heaving up his stomach contents.

Chapter Twenty-four

As Ted and Rob escorted Ross through his own reception area to the front door, he called across to the young woman at the desk to contact his boss as a matter of urgency, to let him know what was happening. All the way to the car and for most of the short journey to the station, he kept demanding to call his solicitor. Ted assured him he would be able to do so as soon as they arrived there.

When they got to the station, Ted asked Rob to book the manager in and see that he got his phone call, while he went off in search of the Ice Queen. He wanted to ask her to put the wheels in motion to obtain a warrant for a thorough search of the Sorrento Hotel.

He quickly brought her up to speed on his preliminary identification of a room at the hotel from the photos, and of his decision to bring in the manager for questioning. He also mentioned the deliberate wiping of the hotel's computer system, at which her eyebrows went up visibly but she didn't comment.

'You can leave the search warrant for me to organise while you get on with questioning him,' she told him. 'It sounds to me as if we need to keep him here for as long as possible, until we can get that place thoroughly searched. Do you have a holding charge in mind, if needs be?'

'I'll think of something, ma'am, even if it has to be speaking Italian badly,' he told her dryly.

To his surprise, she smiled at his humour and said, 'That sounds fair enough to me. Good luck, and keep me posted. I'll let you know as soon as I have your warrant, and I'll bring Inspector Turner up to speed as well.'

Ted headed for the interview room. Rob O'Connell was sitting there with Ross, waiting for him. There was a uniformed officer standing just inside the door. Ted asked the officer to wait outside when he arrived, in case he was needed for anything. He then took the seat opposite the hotel manager.

'I've called my solicitor, but it will take him a while to arrive,' Ross told him. 'I'm not saying anything at all until he gets here.'

'That's absolutely fine, Mr Ross,' Ted told him pleasantly. 'That is your right and I'm quite happy to wait for as long as it takes.'

'You're going to regret this,' Ross told him with a sneer. 'You have absolutely no idea of the type of people you are messing with.'

'Are you trying to threaten me, Mr Ross?' Ted asked.

The man gave a hollow laugh. 'You'll see,' he said. 'You have nothing at all on me and even if you did, it wouldn't go any further.'

'I think, perhaps, Mr Ross, that it would be wise for you to follow your stated intent of saying nothing further, until you have legal representation,' Ted told him. 'In fact, I'll get someone to find you a quiet cell and a cup of tea, or coffee, whichever you prefer, so you can wait for him.'

'You can't put me in a cell, I'm not under arrest,' Ross told him.

'It's merely for your own protection, so that you don't inadvertently incriminate yourself,' Ted assured him. 'If necessary, I could find a charge on which to hold you, if that would make you happier?'

He had Ross taken away, protesting, and he and Rob went back upstairs.

'What d'you make of that?' Ted asked Rob on the way.

'Is he hinting this mystery boss of his has a long arm that

can protect him, even from Sicily or wherever he's meant to be?' Rob speculated.

'He certainly thinks someone, somewhere, is going to protect him,' Ted said, as they reached the main office. 'Let's give him a nasty surprise and show him he's wrong on that score.'

Most of the team were out. Steve was still working away at his computer and Mike Hallam had just come back in.

'Mike, stand by for a search on the Sorrento,' Ted told him. 'The Super is organising a warrant right now. I'll want SOCO all over those bedrooms like a rash. We've got the hotel manager downstairs and we're just waiting for his brief to arrive.

'We found a match on at least one of the rooms there, from photos seized in the raid at Rory's place. Some of the activity almost certainly took place there. I need as many of the team as you can rustle up to get down there and start finding out about this dead waiter. Where he lived, where his car might be. We desperately need to start pulling all these links together.

'We also need someone looking into their employment records. It's possible Ross was taking on illegal immigrants knowingly. At the moment I'm looking for something, anything, that I could charge him with to hold him longer if I need to.

'Rob, can you nip to that sandwich place on the corner and grab something for me, and for yourself, so that we can hopefully eat quickly now, before Ross's lawyer arrives. I've a feeling we may be in for a long session.'

He pulled a note out of his wallet and handed it to Rob, who disappeared out of the door. He was happy to keep Rob on this interview. He didn't at this stage suspect Ross of any abuse himself. He thought he was probably paid to keep quiet and say nothing.

They managed to munch their way through most of their baguettes before they got the call that Ross's solicitor had appeared and they could go back down to interview him.

Ted was surprised when he saw the solicitor whom he knew by sight. He was from a real street-fighting outfit that certainly didn't come cheap. He wondered who was picking up Ross's legal bill and whether it was an indication that the manager had wealthy friends in high places.

Ted knew he was going to have to play everything by the book, but he didn't have a problem with that. He was a old-fashioned, orthodox type who generally stayed within the rules. He set the tapes running and began by identifying those present. Before he had time to say anything else, the solicitor announced, 'I have advised my client to say nothing at all at this stage, Inspector.'

'That is, of course, his right, Mr Richards,' Ted said calmly. 'I have to tell you that we have applied for search warrants for the Hotel Sorrento and Mr Ross's home. I am making enquiries into the rape and murder of a young boy. Mr Ross, I think it may be possible that you can help me with those enquiries.'

Ross opened his mouth to speak but the solicitor immediately put a restraining hand on his arm and said again, 'I have advised my client to make no comment on anything at this stage.'

'Mr Ross, are you aware that rooms booked in your hotel may have been used for sexual activities with under-age children?'

Ross glanced at his solicitor, who shook his head.

Ross replied, 'No comment.'

'Are you aware that video footage showing this abuse and appearing to identify your hotel as the location is circulating on the Internet?'

'No comment.'

'We believe that a young boy, a child, might have been killed in your hotel as a result of this activity. What do you have to say to that?'

'No comment.'

'Have you any explanation as to why one of your hotel waiters appears to have been killed by a single gunshot wound to the head?'

'No comment.'

They continued relentlessly, like an endless tennis volley with no advantage to either player. After some time, there was a knock on the door and Mike Hallam came in. Ted introduced him for the tape.

The DS came up close behind Ted and bent down to speak to him quietly, so no one else could hear. Ted listened to what he had to say then thanked him and announced his departure for the record.

'Mr Ross, I have just had confirmation that the warrant has been issued,' Ted told him, full of silent admiration for the speed with which the Ice Queen had arranged it. She clearly knew which strings to pull to move an enquiry along. 'We will shortly be carrying out a complete and thorough search of your hotel and your home. This will require anyone staying at the hotel to move out until the search is finished. Obviously, we apologise for any inconvenience caused.'

Ross half leapt to his feet. 'You can't do that!' he shouted. 'I need to be there, I need to sort this out. This is very damaging to the hotel's business. The owner is going to be very angry.'

His solicitor was doing his best to get him to sit down and stay quiet, but Ross was starting to look very agitated.

'Mr Ross, if we find absolutely nothing untoward, I will personally apologise to any of your guests who have been inconvenienced in any way,' Ted said. 'However, we are investigating very serious offences here, so I am sure you will understand that we must do everything possible to try to find out what has gone on in the hotel, which you manage and for which you are therefore presumably responsible.

'As I've already outlined to you, photographic evidence

appears to show at least one child being abused in one of your rooms. We are hoping that our search and the forensic testing can confirm or disprove that premise. In addition, there is the question of your former waiter who appears to have been murdered, and the fact that you tell us all your hotel records were lost in a computer crash.

'I have to tell you, Mr Ross, that our initial enquiries lead us to believe that those records were not lost but systematically deleted, very professionally. I'm sure that, in these circumstances, both you and your solicitor can see why we are keen to question you at length.'

Ross was starting to look panic-stricken. Ted noticed the tight set of the solicitor's jawline as he once again shook his head at his client.

Ross's voice was much less steady this time as he replied, 'No comment.'

'In addition, Mr Ross, I also require you to provide me with a DNA sample and your fingerprints. Your solicitor will explain to you that I am within my rights and will no doubt advise you to co-operate. As I told you, I am also applying for a warrant to search your house and, in particular, to seize and search any computers that you have there.'

This time Ross couldn't find his voice to reply at all.

Chapter Twenty-five

'Good morning, Edwin,' a brisk voice said when Ted answered his office phone the next morning. Ted smiled to himself. There was only one person other than Trev who knew what his full name was.

'Morning Bizzie, how are you?' he asked. He was already growing rather fond of the decidedly eccentric new senior pathologist.

'I'm very well, thank you, and I hope I may be the bearer of some good news, at least,' she replied. 'I've been shamelessly slave-driving underlings to try to rush some results through for you. Your colleagues at City sent me the DNA of their body, which I gather might be connected to your case. I can confirm that traces of his touch DNA appear on the clothing worn by your little boy in the skip, and on parts of his body. So he definitely came into contact with him, though in what capacity, I'm not able to tell you yet.'

'That's brilliant, Bizzie, thank you, I really appreciate your speed on this one,' Ted told her. 'We're pulling out all the stops to find the dead man's car to see if it might have been him who dumped the body, which is my hunch. We've also started searching the hotel where we think young Aiden may have been killed. Hopefully we'll get a DNA match that will definitely put him in the hotel. It's progress of sorts, but still very slow.'

'Slow and steady wins the race, Edwin,' she told him breezily. 'The tortoise and the hare. You'll get there in the end. I have every confidence in you.'

Somehow her words cheered him and he started the day feeling positive.

Despite the solicitor's protestations, Ted had kept Ross in overnight, telling him he was being held on suspicion of involvement in the murder of young Aiden. It was flimsy, but he was anxious not to let him go anywhere he could start warning others off, people higher up in the operation.

The solicitor was on the offensive from the start this time. 'You have no right to hold my client, you have nothing on him at all and you know it, Inspector.'

'I beg to differ, Mr Richards,' Ted said politely. 'I have photographic evidence of a graphic nature. It appears to show serious sexual abuse of a child in the hotel which Mr Ross manages. I would be willing to show you the photographs if you wish?'

The solicitor grimaced in distaste. 'I don't think there is any need for such shock tactics. I think you were considerably out of order showing them to my client.'

'Mr Ross, I apologise if I caused you any distress. I felt you had a right to see the photograph. It appears to show quite clearly an act of sexual abuse taking place in one of your hotel rooms,' Ted told him. 'Do you accept that the photograph showed the room you and I were in at the time of our conversation?'

'No comment,' Ross said again.

Ted had a feeling they were not going to get any more out of him for the moment, so he called for a break. The solicitor was even less pleased at this.

'I've come in to advise my client, now you are breaking off again already? It's time you showed your hand, Inspector. You clearly have nothing with which to charge Mr Ross, so you must let him go.'

'Oh, I think we both know we're not even up to the first twenty-four hours yet, Mr Richards,' Ted said smoothly. 'And an application has already been made to hold Mr Ross for longer, as this is a murder investigation.'

The solicitor was clearly furious. He went off, muttering darkly, in search of coffee. Ted dreaded to think what his firm's bill would be for so much waiting time. He would put money on the fact that Ross was not picking up the tab himself. He was just making a mental note to ask Mike Hallam to find out who the registered owner of the hotel was, when his mobile phone rang and it was the DS himself.

'Great minds, Mike,' Ted said as he picked up the call. 'I was just about to call you.'

'You first, boss, then I have some news for you.'

'Just to say to make sure you find out who the mystery hotel owner is, though I'm sure you'd already thought of that. Now what have you got?' Ted asked him.

'Hidden cameras in some, but not all, of the bedrooms. Certainly in all those with the four-poster beds, which seems to be where the main action has taken place,' the DS told him. 'That's clearly how the videos of Rory the Raver were taken, and he presumably knew about them since he had copies. I'm just wondering, though, if some of it may be covert, for blackmail purposes?'

'Quite likely. Now make my day and tell me you've found some film,' Ted told him.

'No can do boss, sorry,' Mike said apologetically. 'At a guess, whoever wiped the computers also cleared out all photographic evidence. I reckon Steve's your best bet there, sir. I understand that there are places on the Internet where this filth is posted, like Rory was doing. That means that there may be more out there.

'In the meantime, we've got forensics crawling all over everywhere for the slightest trace of anything. Oh, and we have a possible address for the waiter, so Virgil and Maurice have gone round there, to see what they can find out and check out if the car is there.

'The staff are tighter than clams, they're saying as little as possible. They're clearly very scared, and obviously under orders from higher up not to talk.'

'Nice work, Mike, thanks. I'm still not having much luck with Ross and his heavyweight brief,' Ted said. 'Keep me posted of any new developments, no matter how small. And can you remind SOCO, with my compliments, that I need the results yesterday, if not the day before.'

Ted had made it back to his office before Mike's call came through. Now he went back into the main office and said to Rob, 'We're back on with Ross, I've got new intel from the hotel search. Can you rustle up his brief again and let's get back to it.'

As soon as they were all sitting in the interview room once more, Ted said, 'Mr Ross, the officers searching the Sorrento Hotel have discovered a number of hidden cameras in the bedrooms. What do you have to say about that?'

Ted caught a sudden change of expression on the solicitor's face but couldn't easily interpret what it meant. Shock? Anger? It was gone in a flash. Ross was easier to read. He looked absolutely petrified. His mouth opened but he was unable even to articulate his usual 'No comment.'

'Were you aware of the presence of those cameras, Mr Ross?' Ted asked.

The solicitor looked furious now. 'Inspector, I request a break in order to take further instruction from my client,' he said icily.

'Really, Mr Richards?' Ted asked smoothly. 'We're only just back from a break, one to which you objected, if I remember correctly?'

'In light of your further allegations, I insist that I speak further with my client in private,' Richards replied.

'Then of course you must,' Ted said pleasantly. 'DC O'Connell and I will be just outside the door, out of earshot I assure you. Please let us know when you are ready to continue.'

He and Rob went outside and, true to his word, Ted led the way a short distance down the corridor before stopping and saying, 'DS Hallam wondered if the delightful Mr Ross was doing a little bit of work on his own initiative. Was he perhaps filming the goings on either to sell them, as it looks like someone did with the Rory tapes, or even to do a spot of blackmail. At the moment the search hasn't found any more film, but they're still looking.'

'Did you see the way his brief looked, sir?' Rob asked him. 'The hidden cameras were clearly news to him. If Ross does have people higher up protecting him to save their own skins, I don't give much for his chances if they find out what he's been getting up to. He'd probably feel safer going down for a stretch rather than being back out, if they get wind of that.'

'If Ross has been moonlighting to line his own pockets, there's at least a chance that there is evidence out there to find. Wouldn't be the first time we got lucky when someone posted something they shouldn't on the Internet,' Ted replied. 'People complain that they're being watched by Big Brother, but in a case like this I hope they are. And I hope it will throw up something we need. I'll talk to the Super, see what we can come up with. She knows how to go about it.'

At that moment, the interview room door opened and Richards, the solicitor, put his head out looking for them. 'You are welcome to resume your interview now, Inspector,' he said, 'but I should warn you that my instruction to my client remains precisely the same – to say nothing at all at this stage in the enquiry.'

Chapter Twenty-six

Richards was right. They got nothing more than several 'no comments' from Ross for the rest of the day. It was frustrating but to be expected. A solicitor of the calibre of Richards was not going to let his client say anything until he knew exactly how much evidence there was against him.

Ted's one consolation was that they had been granted another twenty-four hours to question him, because of the possibility of serious charges arising out of the interview. He hoped another night in police custody would loosen Ross's tongue somewhat, although there was no sign of it at the moment.

He couldn't put his finger on what exactly, but there had been a definite change in atmosphere between the solicitor and his client since the revelation about the hidden cameras. It was almost as if Ross was now even more afraid of his solicitor than of the prospect of being charged with murder.

Ted was pinning his hopes on getting good news from Mike Hallam and the team, and especially that forensics were going to turn up something for them. Mike had phoned him to say that they had found where the waiter had been living, in cramped, shared accommodation with several other illegal immigrants, as it now seemed certain that he had been as well. They had also found his car at the address and it had been taken away for testing.

Once again, Ted passed the word that he wanted miracles working and he wanted them in record time. Everyone from the station knew they were up against the clock on this one, desperate to find something to give Ted enough to charge Ross with, before he was obliged to let him go.

With luck, and the prospect of enough to make a serious charge stick, he could get an extension to hold him for up to ninety-six hours. If he didn't have enough to charge him with anything after that, he would have to release him, which was the last thing he wanted to do.

Mike and the rest of the team came back to the office at the end of the afternoon, looking tired and frustrated by the lack of further progress.

'It's like talking to a brick wall, interviewing the staff, boss,' the DS told him. 'They're clearly scared stiff and no one is willing to talk, which makes me think they do know something. I can't even get anyone to tell me who the owner is.'

'I've got that, Sarge,' Steve piped up from in front of his computer. 'I did a Companies House search just now. I've done you a print-out.'

'Great, Steve, thanks,' the DS said, then continued, 'Forensics found lots of samples, human hair and the like. They've gone off with them all and have promised to pull out all of the stops for an early result. There were hair and blood samples in the boot of the waiter's car. Iosif Petrescu, his name was, we managed to find that much out, at least, but not much more.

'No one would talk to us about him, not at the hotel or his home. The problem at the house where he was living was we couldn't find anyone who seemed to speak much English. They were clearly scared when the police came calling,' the DS told them.

'Right, we've made a start. We've perhaps not made as much progress as most of us would have liked to, but at least we've got a bit more time to hold Ross. Time to wrap it up for today and we'll all hopefully start back fresh tomorrow,' Ted told the team.

As everyone was getting ready to go, Steve followed Ted into his office and said, 'Boss, can I show you something online before you leave?'

Ted smiled to himself at the informality, the first time he could ever recall Steve calling him boss rather than sir. At the same time he hoped it was not going to be anything requiring a lot of time. He'd promised Trev he'd try to be home in time to get to their karate club. As well as the training, there was going to be a get-together over a meal afterwards. Ted was trying hard to make sure that he and Trev got out together a bit more. A social life was never easy for a police officer, but it became nearly impossible at times with an ongoing serious crime case.

Ted followed Steve back to his workstation and pulled up a chair alongside his. Steve was already opening pages on his computer.

'We know that Rory the Raver was at the hotel, at least once from what you've told us about the photos,' he began. 'But from what you said, those photos date from before Aiden was killed. It made me wonder who else from the PIEdpiper site might have been in our area on the day of the murder. Nothing much locally going on at all, so I widened the search, and look what I found.'

He pulled up a saved page with a newspaper article from a town in the Midlands. The headline was about a royal visitor opening a new community centre.

'The Knave of Clubs?' Ted asked, looking at the photo.

'The very same. Just an hour or so's drive down the motorway from where young Aiden was murdered, later the same evening,' Steve told him. 'The photo's not brilliant, worse when I enlarge it, but do you recognise any other faces there?'

Ted looked a little more closely. He had good eyesight, never having needed glasses for either distance or close work. At the front of the picture was the minor royal, accompanied by his wife. There was a collection of dignitaries slightly behind and to either side of them. He spotted a police uniform, and saw the same senior police officer that Steve had pointed out to him on the PIEdpiper website.

'So, two people fingered by this blogger as being possibly implicated in child sex abuse, close to our patch, the night Aiden died,' Ted said.

'More than two, boss,' Steve told him, pointing to another figure in the group. 'This character is the local Member of Parliament for the town in the article. Now look.' He toggled between screens and pulled up a another page from the PIEdpiper website.

Ted quickly scanned down the page, with talk of various allegations against the MP never getting far. There were vague hints of processes being blocked by an unspecified high-ranking police officer.

'It's all just rumour, though,' Ted said, partly to reassure himself.

'Rumour, yes, until a decent, honest copper starts investigating,' Steve replied. He was now looking at Ted with expectation on his face. It was the kind of hero-worshipping look a boy might bestow on a father whom he believed could do anything, including walk on water.

'So tell me more about this Knave of Clubs,' Ted said, partially to change the subject. 'I don't know much about him at all, except I know he's a marginal royal. Do you know how far down the line of succession he is?' Ted asked.

'I've just started looking a bit more into him. Pretty much off the scale, I think,' Steve told him. 'Most references only list the first dozen or so, some of them up to fifty, although I gather in theory there are four thousand or more people with a claim. He's not listed by any source I've found so far, so he's too far down to count.'

'Does he work, or is he in the forces or anything?

'Certainly not forces; they wouldn't even let him in,

according to rumour,' Steve said quickly. 'This site says it's because of doubts about a certain sadistic streak he's said to have. As for work, I don't know yet, perhaps some consultancies somewhere. I'll check.'

'Thanks, Steve, but not tonight,' Ted told him. 'You've done incredible work again, thank you, it's time you were going. And if I don't turn up in time to take Trev to karate club tonight, you are likely to have to investigate my untimely death tomorrow.'

'Just before you go, boss,' Steve said. 'Parish's Pies. I've found a closed and very secretive group on social media which appears to relate to it. There's a newsletter, but I didn't want to sign up for it using a computer inside the station, in case it later compromises the enquiry.'

'Don't go doing it from your home computer either, Steve,' Ted told him firmly. 'I need to give this some thought, and talk to someone who knows more about this type of enquiry than I do. It's clearly your field of expertise, but it's a long way from mine. I need to be absolutely sure what the protocol is. As you say, there's no point in us working hard on this and getting within sight of an arrest, only to find we've blown it and our actions are deemed to be those of an *agent provocateur*.'

'Now I'm going to pass a pleasant hour or so kicking people, which is my way of unwinding at the end of a hard day. What's yours, Steve?'

'Playing on the computer, sir,' the TDC smiled, switching back to formal mode.

Ted laughed. 'Well, absolutely no going near any sites which might get you into trouble Not until I've found out how to cover your back when I unleash you as our secret weapon on this enquiry. And you can take that as a direct order.'

Chapter Twenty-seven

After the usual morning briefing, Ted called both sergeants, Mike and Jancis, into his office for a more in-depth discussion. He wanted to leave Ross cooling his heels a little longer. He was hoping he might just get some test results in soon, to help him to persuade the hotel manager to talk.

'Looking at the photos from Rory's computer was not a pleasant task. But it has at least given us a link to the Sorrento,' he told them. 'But the shot of him there is with a different little boy, not Aiden. This is where I have to ask a lot of you, Jan. Somebody needs to go through the stills we have, concentrating on the kids, to see if any of them are from our area, from one of the homes, or posted missing from there.'

'No problem at all, boss,' Jan said promptly. 'I'm trained for this sort of stuff. It's only right that I'm the one to do it. And I've seen a lot of these kids while I've been asking about Aiden, so there's a good chance I might recognise a face or two.'

'Thank you,' Ted said sincerely. 'Mike, we need to pin down which of the registered offenders we've spoken to is a possible suspect. I'm not convinced about any of those I've spoken to, even without alibis. Their form is not right for this sort of thing. I want to talk to the Super about getting warrants to search the homes and computers of anyone we think may be involved.

'My money is firmly on David Evans, boss,' the DS told him. 'He has no alibi, and he has form with little boys. But he doesn't seem bothered, almost as if he doesn't see that what he's done, what he's been convicted of in the past, is anything wrong. I personally would like to see what sort of things might pop up on his computer.'

Ted's hand subconsciously went up to loosen his collar and tie as the DS spoke. 'I'll see about getting a warrant then. Do you want to haul him in again, question him further? Or go round to his place to talk to him, see if he even has a computer?'

'Boss, what about showing Flip some photos, including this man Evans, see if he recognises anyone from the time he went with Aiden?' Jancis suggested. 'Worth a try?'

'Anything's worth a try on this, Jan,' Ted replied. 'Now this next bit I'm not sharing with all the team just yet because I need to go and talk to the Super about it before I do. We've got information that some very high profile suspected paedophiles might have been in our area the night that Aiden was killed. I'm talking the highest level, including one senior police officer, from outside our area.

'We have absolutely nothing concrete to back this up at the moment. I believe there is a way to access the content of someone's computer, and certainly to see what they are distributing, without their knowledge, but all of this is way over my head. I need to talk to the Super to ask if it can be done. However, she may just dismiss the whole thing out of hand so we can't move any further forward on it. And she may just think I have totally lost the plot and send me to see a shrink.'

He grinned at the others, although he was not really feeling the humour. He knew he was way out on a limb and rather wished it was Jim Baker he was going to talk to, not the Ice Queen. He always felt like a complete moron in her presence, although he knew he wasn't.

Just as he was getting ready to wrap up the discussion and head down to see her, his desk phone rang and he took the call. He listened in silence, then turned to the other two.

'Getting closer,' he said. 'That was forensics. A definite tie-in on Aiden's DNA in one of the hotel bedrooms and in the boot of the car driven by the waiter. I'll let Ross sweat just a little longer, then I'll ask him how he explains those facts and see what else he has to say for himself.'

He headed down to the Ice Queen's office with a lighter step. He'd got Steve to print out for him the addresses for the websites that they had been looking at. He knew there was only a slim chance she would take any of it seriously, certainly not enough to look into ways of covertly accessing email accounts, but he felt he had to give it a try.

Like any honest copper, he was tired of reading in the papers about alleged cover-ups and corruption within police forces. By the very people who should have been protecting the children, not those who might have been abusing them.

He started out with the news of the DNA match, as it was something positive and concrete. He also mentioned the possibility of Evans being involved and asked about getting a warrant to seize and search his computers.

'DS Hallam is on his way over there now to question him further, ma'am. He has no alibi for the night in question. We don't even know if Evans has a computer but at least if the DS talks to him in his home he might be able to find that out,' Ted told her.

'You're not interviewing this suspect yourself?' she asked curiously.

'I have enough on for now with Ross,' he told her. 'I also wanted to talk to you about something else, ma'am. It's highly speculative at this stage and I don't know how to take it forward, if indeed we can, but I thought you would know.'

Ted gave her the list of websites and carefully talked her through what he and Steve had been looking at. He half expected her to dismiss the mere suggestion but she remained impassive as she clicked from page to page, carefully reading what she saw there.

'This is all total speculation, of course, most of it actionable,' she said. 'What makes you think there is any grain of truth in it?'

'That most unscientific thing of all, a good old-fashioned hunch,' he said honestly. 'We have DNA to put Aiden in the Sorrento at some point. We have video evidence that a known paedophile, Rory the Raver, used the hotel, though nothing to put him there on that day. At the same time we have some alleged paedophiles just down the road from there on the right date. Is it just coincidence?'

Her phone rang at that moment and when she answered it, she handed it across to Ted. 'For you.'

Ted listened briefly then hung up. He tried hard to suppress a grin as he asked, 'Permission to punch the air and shout 'yes', ma'am?'

'As long as you never, in my presence, propose a high five,' she replied dryly.

Ted smiled. It was the nearest to a relaxed and friendly exchange they had ever shared.

'That call was to let me know that Ross's DNA is also on the sweatshirt Aiden was wearing when he was found. Just a trace, on his arm, but enough to show that Ross came into contact with the boy. Got 'im.'

'Let's not get carried away, especially with the calibre of brief he has,' she warned. 'You could perhaps go for an accessory charge on that but I agree, it's an encouraging start.

'Now, as to the other matter, are you seriously asking me if we should tap into the emails of all the people on this list? Even if I knew how to go about it, can you imagine the can of worms it would be opening up?'

'So we just look the other way when children are being sexually abused?' Ted asked defiantly.

'No, of course not,' the Ice Queen said sharply. 'But what we have here is nothing but rumour and speculation, nothing

143

on which I could legitimately base any such request and, I repeat, that's even if I knew how to.'

'Ma'am, there have been constant stories circulating about bent police officers involved in cases like this,' Ted said, keeping his tone as moderate as he could. 'Should we not perhaps at least look a little more closely into this particular senior officer? How are we ever going to get justice for these kids unless one day decent police officers like you and me stand up and do something?'

The Ice Queen regarded him closely, so much so that it started to make him feel uncomfortable. 'You do know you can talk to me, in confidence, about anything, don't you?' she asked. When he didn't reply, she continued, 'Very well. I will see what can be done. I expect shutters to come down all around, but there's no reason why I can't at least find someone to peep through the cracks for us.

'Meanwhile, let's not have any procedural mistakes anywhere on any of this. Nothing which would mean that suspects would slip through our grasp at the eleventh hour. You may only have a sprat in custody at the moment, but if we start with the sprats, it hopefully won't be long before we start to reel in the mackerel.

'I'm very impressed with the work of the TDC. But working on cases like this is always difficult and harrowing. I hope you are making sure he's not getting in too deep with his online activities and putting himself at risk?'

'Trying my best, ma'am, but he's like a hound on the trail.'

The Ice Queen looked serious as she continued, 'It's alarming how many people have had personal experience of sexual abuse as children. A case like this can bring up long-buried and distressing memories for anyone on the team who has, sometimes the unlikeliest of people. Don't forget there is counselling available for anyone who needs it.

'Above all, as well as being supportive of our team

members, we need to be making sure that the case is not compromised in any way, by anyone in this category.

'Now go catch your sprat. Good luck, and keep me posted of all developments.'

Chapter Twenty-eight

Suddenly Ted was on a roll. The good news kept coming. Another phone call told him that Ross's fingerprints were all over the hidden cameras, and the search of his home had revealed a large quantity of pornographic material on his computer. Some of it was the footage with Rory the Raver that they already had. There was none date-stamped for the night Aiden died but there was plenty of it from other dates before that.

Kevin Turner had agreed to go through it, to see if he could recognise anyone else in any of the shots. Ted didn't envy him the task. The team working on it were also going to pull off more stills in the hopes that they may be able to track down some of the adults in them.

Ted had asked the custody sergeant to get Ross's solicitor in for later that morning. He wanted to get as many results as possible to throw at them before he spoke to Ross again. He didn't expect Ross to say anything more, not with his solicitor keeping him on a tight leash, but with what he had so far, he was happy there was enough to charge him in connection with Aiden's murder, at least, and CPS were in agreement.

He wasn't sure about the dead waiter. Unless they found a gun or a red motorbike in the search of Ross's premises, he couldn't see anything there to pin that murder on him. But for now, he would be happy with anything which would keep Ross in custody and stop him contacting those higher up the chain. He strongly suspected, though, that the solicitor was already talking to anyone connected.

All of the team members, except for young Steve, were out, so Ted decided to prise him away from his computer to sit in with him on the interview. The young officer had shown in the past that not only was he adept at IT, he was also quick to pick up on minor details in interviews that could have an important bearing on a case.

The solicitor was prompt. Ted noticed he was wearing a different suit to the one that he had worn the previous day. Even Ted's untrained eye could tell that it had probably cost far more than all of his own modest new wardrobe put together.

'Mr Ross,' Ted began, 'in light of new information I have received, I think the time might have come to start talking to us.'

Ross looked anxiously at his solicitor, who shook his head firmly.

'First of all, Mr Ross, we have found your fingerprints on all of the hidden cameras in the hotel. Would you care to tell me how they came to be there?'

The tension between the man and his solicitor was palpable. Ross seemed as if he wanted to start talking but the looks Richards was giving him made it clear he was not at liberty to do so. This time he contented himself with a shake of the head.

'Next we come to what was found on your computer, Mr Ross,' Ted continued. 'We discovered a large quantity of indecent material of a serious nature, involving children. This material, which we have reason to believe that you may have made yourself with a view to distributing, is sufficient, should you be convicted of its possession, to get you a sentence of up to ten years in prison.'

Ross looked terrified, all the more so under the cold glare his solicitor threw at him. It seemed clear that all of this was news to the manager's legal adviser.

Ted put his arms on the table and leaned forward, making direct eye contact with Ross. 'Mr Ross, can I just say to you at this stage, whilst you are of course entitled to have your solicitor present at all times while you are being questioned, it does not necessarily mean that you are obliged to follow his advice.'

'You're out of order, Inspector, and out of your depth,' the solicitor told him, with barely concealed contempt. 'You're clearly on a fishing expedition, hoping to trap my client into giving you information when you obviously have very little. That is why I am continuing to advise him to say nothing.'

'Fair enough, Mr Richards,' Ted said pleasantly. 'Now, Mr Ross, we come to something much more serious. We have identified traces of your DNA on clothing worn by a young boy who was found raped and strangled not far from the Hotel Sorrento. This shows us that you, at some point, came into contact with this young boy.

'In addition, we found traces of the boy's DNA in a car belonging to Mr Iosif Petrescu, a waiter at your hotel, who was later found shot dead. Can you explain when and why you came into contact with this boy, Mr Ross?'

Ross opened his mouth and looked as if he was actually about to break the silence at last, but his solicitor rapidly cut across him.

'My client has nothing further to say at this stage, Inspector.'

'Then unfortunately, I have no alternative other than to arrest Mr Ross for possession of indecent images of children, and for involvement in the murder of Aiden Bradshaw. Mr Ross, you do not have to say anything. But it may harm your defence if you do not mention when questioned something which you later rely on in court. Anything you do say may be given in evidence.

'You will now be taken and formally charged. You will appear before a magistrates' court in the morning, where we will oppose any application for bail that your solicitor might make, on the grounds of the serious nature of the allegations against you.

'Do you understand everything I have said to you, Mr Ross?'

Ross was looking wildly about him, as if unsure what was happening. His solicitor was tight-lipped and saying nothing.

Ted and Steve saw Ross safely processed and charged, then went back upstairs to their respective desks. Ted finally felt as if he had achieved something. Maybe he might just get away at a reasonable time today and suggest to Trev that they go out for a meal somewhere.

'Have you found out anything else, Steve?' Ted asked him. 'I hope you haven't signed up to anything you shouldn't have?'

'No, sir, I don't want to do anything to jeopardise the enquiry so I've been waiting for the green light before I do anything,' Steve assured him. 'I've just been looking into that MP a bit more closely. It seems there have been several allegations made against him in the past but nothing has ever come of it. There is a lot of speculation that it's because he has friends in high places.'

'I've put feelers out, to see if there is any way at all we can find out if any of the people listed by the PIEdpiper are distributing material involving indecent images of children,' Ted told him. 'It's a bit like an elaborate game of dominoes at the moment. Once one of them falls, they quickly start bringing the others down all around them. At least that's what I'm hoping, and counting on.

'You've done some really good work lately, Steve, the Superintendent was most impressed. Why don't you get off home now and do something to relax? Something that doesn't involve computers, perhaps.'

Steve smiled. 'Not sure I would have any idea of relaxation which didn't involve them, sir, but thanks, yes, I'll do that. See you tomorrow.'

Ted headed back to his desk thinking he might well do the same, if he could just shift the pile of paperwork which was awaiting his attention. He had made quite a dent in it when his mobile phone rang. The caller display told him that it was Trev phoning him and he smiled, thinking perhaps he had had the same idea of going out that evening.

As soon as Trev began to speak, Ted could tell by the thickness of his voice that he was in tears. 'Ted? Can you come home? Please. It's John. He's been killed. Someone's hanged him, in the back garden.'

Ted was shocked rigid. John was one of their seven cats, like family to them, especially to Trev, who doted on them.

'I'm on my way. I'll be there as soon as I can.'

Chapter Twenty-nine

Ted pushed his elderly Renault to the speed limit all the way home. He left the car on the drive rather than putting it away and went straight into the house. Trev was sitting at the kitchen table, looking shell-shocked. The body of the little cat was lying on a work surface near the back door. There was a noose around its neck, and the end of the rope had been cut.

Trev got up as Ted came into the kitchen, threw his arms around him and buried his face against his partner's shoulder.

'God, Ted, it was awful. John wasn't in the house with the others when I got home so I looked out of the window and I saw him hanging from the cherry tree.'

Trev was still in tears. Ted had no idea what to do or say to make it better, so he just hugged him fiercely.

'I cut him down,' Trev said. 'I didn't know what to do. He was already dead. Who on earth would do something like that to a little cat like John?'

Ted had his own suspicions, but there was no way he was going to voice them, certainly not now. His trained eye was checking out every detail of the kitchen as he asked, 'Was everything else as normal when you got home? Was the alarm set?'

Trev lifted his head and looked at him, his face tear-stained. 'You think someone got in through the house? But the alarm was set, how could they, without setting it off?'

'I'm just trying to understand what happened,' Ted told him. 'Look, you take the others into the sitting room and put the telly on, help take your mind off it. I'll make you a cup of tea, then I'll go and lay poor little John to rest in the garden.'

'Don't put him near the tree,' Trev said quickly. 'I couldn't bear that.'

Trev scooped up an armful of cats, shepherding the rest along, and obediently left Ted to it. After he'd made Trev's tea, Ted got a spade and a cardboard box from the garage. He put on a pair of gloves before carefully putting John in the box, having taken off the tight noose from around the cat's neck. He didn't for a moment imagine that there would be fingerprints anywhere, but he was not taking chances. He carried box and spade into the garden but before he started to dig, he got out his mobile and called Kevin Turner.

'Kev, it's Ted. I'm at home, we've had a break-in. Can you send someone round for prints?'

'Sorry to hear that,' Kevin responded. 'Much taken?'

'It seems like nothing was taken, but they killed one of the cats,' Ted told him.

There was a pause then Kevin said, 'Ted, is this a wind-up? You know I don't have the manpower to investigate every break-in on the patch and you want me to send a team round for a dead cat? Look, I'm sorry about the moggy but come on, can you imagine what the Ice Queen would say if she got wind of that?'

'Kev, you know I wouldn't ask unless it was something serious,' Ted said. 'I think this is related to the case. It's too much of a coincidence that it happened on the day I charged Ross with involvement in Aiden's murder. I think it's a warning to me.'

'I still can't put that on the paperwork or the Ice Queen will think we've both lost the plot. Surely they must have taken something?' Kevin said, hinting heavily.

'You know what, you're right, I just noticed they took all my Bisley shooting trophies,' Ted told him.

'Right, I'll get a team over as soon as. In fact, I'll pop in myself shortly, I was just on the point of leaving,' Kevin told him. 'And seriously, Ted, I am sorry about the little moggy.'

Ted dug a hole at the end of the garden, well away from the cherry tree, and laid the box containing the little cat into it. He had a look all round the garden. He could see no signs of anyone having got in over the high mesh fencing that he and Trev had put up to keep the cats from straying onto nearby roads. He was certain whoever had done it had come in through the house, and that meant a professional, if they had disabled the alarm then reset it, and done it all in broad daylight. He didn't hold out much hope of them having left any evidence, but when Kevin's team arrived, he showed them around and left them to it.

Kevin wasn't far behind. When Ted let him in, Kevin went first into the living room and shook hands awkwardly with Trev, mumbling, 'Sorry for your loss, Trev,' as he wasn't sure what the correct form of condolence was for a dead cat.

Ted led him into the kitchen. 'Do you want a drink? There's some decent wine open, I think.'

'I'm not much of a wine drinker,' Kevin confessed. 'Wouldn't mind a cuppa though, as long as it's not that poison you drink.'

Ted made tea for everyone then showed Kevin out into the back garden so SOCO could get on with lifting prints. The two men sat down in the steamer chairs on the small patio.

'So, what makes you think this is connected to the case?' Kevin asked. 'Why couldn't it be your friendly local dog fighters, for instance? You got a couple of them put away not long ago and they must know where you live.'

Ted shook his head. 'This is a bit too subtle for scallies like that. If it had been them, I would have expected to see the mesh fence down somewhere around the garden where they climbed in. It looks as if whoever it was came in through the house, and knew how to deactivate and reactivate the alarm. They got in in broad daylight. That suggests professionals to me.'

Kevin was looking sceptical.

'Bit far-fetched though, isn't it? A paedophile ring thinks you're getting too close to unmasking big names so they send someone round to hang a cat? Good luck with convincing the Ice Queen of that.'

'Anyone who knows anything about me knows those cats are like family to me and Trev,' Ted told him. 'And it's the fact of coming into our house and doing that. That's a warning, more than revenge, which I would expect from the dog fighters.'

'So what with wiping computers and killing cats, what sort of people do you think we're up against?' Kevin asked.

'I've no idea,' Ted replied. 'But I know a man who might, and I think it's about time I went to see him.'

'Oh, by the way, I've been going through the stills from the hidden cameras at the hotel,' Kevin said, with an expression of distaste. 'Dreadful stuff. Not really identified anyone as yet but we may have a bit of luck. There's one delightful character who appears a few times, without ever managing to get his ugly mug into a clear shot, but he has a birthmark, and it shows up. Like a big port wine stain, at the top of his left thigh.'

Ted's hand twitched involuntarily and his mug flew out of his grip to smash into a dozen pieces on the paving slabs of the patio. Ted grimaced and made a show of shaking his arm.

'Damn cramp,' he said, 'I think my salt levels must be low. All that sweating I do at the dojo and in the Ice Queen's presence. I'll just clear that up.'

He came back with a dustpan and brush. Kevin was looking at him strangely.

'Are you all right, Ted?' he asked. 'I mean, I know the cat was a bit of a shock and an upset, but you seem very jumpy just lately in general.'

'Yes, I'm fine, it's just a combination of this case and having to dress in a monkey suit and kowtow to the Ice Queen,' Ted told him. 'I never thought I'd miss Jim Baker's ugly mug quite as much as I do.'

Kevin drained his tea and stood up. 'I'd best be getting off,' he said. 'Sorry again about your little cat, Ted. We'll see what, if anything, the fingerprints reveal. If you're right about them being professionals, I doubt we'll find anything. Don't forget about that birthmark though, it may just give us a lead.'

After Kevin and SOCO had left, Ted went back into the sitting room and sat down next to Trev, putting his arm around him and hugging him close.

'I'm so sorry,' he said. 'I've laid him to rest. I will do whatever I can to find who did it.'

'Is this something to do with work?' Trev asked him. 'With a case you're working on?'

Ted sighed. He wasn't about to lie to his partner.

'I don't know,' he said, 'but it is possible. We seem to be up against some very nasty types. I may need to go away for a couple of days, three at the most. Would you be all right if I did?'

'If you have to,' Trev replied. 'Just not yet though? I don't want to be on my own at the moment. Is that all right?'

Ted hugged him closer. 'I'm not going anywhere right now. I'm here for you.'

Chapter Thirty

From talking to Kevin Turner, Ted was starting to think that Ross's activities with the cameras in the Hotel Sorrento were a freelancing sideline of his own, without the knowledge of anyone higher up. Kevin told him there were two distinct types of shot in the stills he had seen. He had not yet braved looking at the videos.

One lot, such as the ones that were found in Rory the Raver's house, were good-quality shots, with the adult involved clearly visible and in focus. That suggested that whoever was behind the camera was in the room, and filming with consent. Ted suspected Ross was selling these, a suspicion partly confirmed by the search of his home, where bank statements showed he had been squirrelling away nice little lump sums of money.

The other shots were clearly covert, using the hidden cameras operated remotely, without the knowledge and consent of the participants. Ted strongly suspected those had been taken for blackmail purposes, which would explain the reaction of Ross's solicitor, and the obvious change in their relationship after the hidden cameras were mentioned.

These were not always successful. Often it was hard to see the faces of those involved because of the camera angle, but sometimes there were distinguishing features, like the birthmark. They would probably be enough to blackmail anyone involved, certainly sufficient to panic them into paying up.

Jancis Reynolds had recognised the face of one of the

young boys in some of the shots and had gone off to try to track him down. They wanted to make sure he was safe first and foremost, but he might be able to provide useful information.

Ted called Mike Hallam into his office after the morning briefing to talk to him about Evans.

'How did you get on with Evans?' he asked him. 'Does he have a computer?'

'Had a laptop in his flat,' the DS told him. 'He was very quick to close it when I came in. I didn't refer to it at all. Just said I wanted to ask him a few more questions, which I did.'

'How long has he been out now?'

'Just over a year, boss. He served the full ten years, no chance of remission because the charges were so serious and he showed no signs of remorse.'

'I'll sort out warrants to seize his computer and search the house. I want you to go back and bring him in for more questioning. Take Virgil with you, he can look solid and intimidating when needed, in case Evans has any ideas about trying to make a break for it,' Ted told him. 'Inspector Turner passed some new information on to me, from the films on Ross's computer. One of the suspects has a birthmark, on their left thigh, quite a noticeable one.

'When you bring Evans in, take his clothes away, tell him it's for forensic testing. Make sure someone is there while he undresses, look out for that birthmark and let me know. There was no mention of a birthmark on the waiter and I doubt it would be worth blackmailing him, he wouldn't have been earning enough.

'I'll chase up more forensic results from the hotel. It's possible Evans hasn't been there all that recently but with any luck, if their housekeeping is not flawless, he may have left a stray hair or a finger print behind somewhere. I think he's small fry, in a sense. There are much bigger fish out there to catch, but he'll do for starters, so let's see if we can nail him before the end of the day.'

'Sir, he did ask about you,' Mike began, picking his words carefully. 'Is there anything I need to be aware of about you and him?'

'Nothing at all,' Ted said brusquely.

'It's just that, some of the things he was saying …'

'Don't even go there,' Ted said warningly. 'Water long under the bridge, not remotely relevant to this case, and don't believe everything he says.

'Now, once we've got him safely into custody, I might need to disappear for a few days. I'll sort it with the Superintendent. I'm sure you can hold the fort while I'm away. It's very likely I'll be out of phone contact but you can always liaise with Inspector Turner in my absence, he's fully up to speed.

'There are aspects of this case which are way outside my experience. But there is someone I know who would probably have the knowledge I need. It just that he's a little, shall we say, unorthodox, so I can't say exactly how long I'll be away.'

Ted's next stop was to see the Ice Queen to talk about taking a few days off. With Evans on his way in, and the likelihood that they would be charging him, he felt it gave him a reasonable bargaining point.

She looked surprised when Ted mentioned time away. She arched an eyebrow and looked at him in that searching way she had which made him feel like squirming.

'Isn't it rather a strange moment to take time off, Inspector, in the middle of a case like this?'

'It's not a holiday, I assure you, ma'am,' Ted said hastily. 'There are some strange things going on that I don't entirely understand but I know a man who might. And don't worry, he does have full security clearance for me to discuss things with him.'

'How very mysterious,' the Ice Queen said. 'Apart from asking for covert surveillance of emails, what else is outside your experience?'

Ted hesitated. He wasn't keen on mentioning the break in and the death of the cat to the Ice Queen. He certainly needed to phrase it in such a way that there would be no come back on Kevin if he did.

'We had a break in yesterday, at my home,' he began. 'In and out through the house, in broad daylight. They killed one of our cats, hanged him in the garden. I think it was a warning, and I think it may be related to this case.'

To Ted's surprise, she didn't dismiss his theory out of hand. Instead she said in a measured tone, 'I see. I'm sorry to hear about your poor cat, very distressing. Certainly, take some time away if you need it and if you feel it will advance your enquiries. Your DS Hallam seems competent, I'm sure between him, Inspector Turner and myself we can manage in your absence.'

After leaving the Ice Queen's office, Ted went to see Kevin Turner to let him know he might be going away for a few days.

'How's Trev today?' Kevin asked.

'Gutted,' Ted told him. 'He's taken the day off work. I explained that I couldn't really manage to do the same. Luckily he understands about my job, especially after living with me for years.

'I wanted to let you know I may be going away for a few days, probably next week. There's someone I need to see who may be able to help me with some of this stuff. I just wondered if you could ask some of your lads to keep half an eye on the house, and on Trev, while I'm away?'

'With all the huge manpower resources at my fingertips, eh, Ted?' Kevin said ironically. 'You don't really think he's in any danger, do you? That someone might go after him?'

'I know it's a lot to ask, and I don't know whether I'm just being fanciful, but I really would appreciate it, Kev. It would be a big favour I owe you, one which you can call in at any time,' Ted said.

Kevin sighed resignedly. 'I'll have a quiet word with the lads, see if they can't swing by your place once a day at least. If the Ice Queen should ask I can say we think the dog fighters are starting up again. At least Trev is handy enough to look after himself against your average knuckle-dragging thugs.'

'Trouble is, Kev, I'm not sure that's all we're up against on this one, which is why I need to go away for a couple of days.'

There was more good news waiting for Ted when he went back up to his office. He had a message to say that a partial print matching those of David Evans had been found on a bedpost in a room at the Hotel Sorrento. Ted sent young Steve in search of DS Hallam, who was down in one of the interview rooms with Evans, to let him know.

With that and the evidence of the birthmark, if it showed up, they would have another good result today in charging Evans. They had nothing to link him to Aiden but if a search of his computer revealed what Ted expected it to, along with his previous conviction, they had enough to get him sent back down for a long time.

It was another sprat in the net but Ted wanted the mackerel as well and at the moment he didn't know where to begin to haul them in. He made a quick phone call which should both help him and also make sure he was up to the mark for any challenges that still lay ahead.

Mike and Virgil were jubilant when they came back up to the main office later. It was good to see his team members smiling.

'Bingo, sir, Evans has the birthmark,' Mike told him. 'He wasn't a happy bunny when I showed him the photo of him naked in the hotel bedroom with what is clearly an under-age child. I've had him locked up until we know what was found on his computer but I would say we have enough to charge him, whatever shows up.

'He didn't want a solicitor but he is getting more and more

insistent that he should speak to you,' Mike added.

'Forget about it, Mike, not going to happen,' Ted told him. 'He's personally known to me, I'm not going to compromise the enquiry by speaking to him. If he wants someone of a senior rank, I'm sure Inspector Turner would be happy to oblige. Good work, both of you. That's a nice result on which to end the day.'

Ted got away as soon as he could, anxious to get home to Trev. He found him sitting on the sofa, watching old films, with the remaining six cats squatting possessively on top of him.

'Sorry I had to leave you,' Ted said as he kissed him. 'Do you want me to cook you something?'

'Thai green curry?' Trev asked with a wan smile. Ted's culinary repertoire was a bit limited and that was about as imaginative as it got. 'I'd like that, if you're not too tired. How was your day?'

'Not bad, as it goes. We have David Evans in custody,' Ted told him.

Trev sat upright and looked at him. 'Wow,' he said. 'No more nightmares?'

Ted smiled back. 'No more nightmares – hopefully.'

Chapter Thirty-one

Ted found time to have a quiet word with Rob before the start of the day, to ask him how he was getting on with the counselling he was receiving. The DC certainly looked a lot happier, almost back to his old self, but Ted wanted to check that it was not just bravado on his part.

'It's going well, sir,' Rob told him, as the two of them sat in Ted's office. 'I never thought it would, I was very sceptical about it but I'm glad you sorted it for me. It really has helped. I thought it might be a bit touchy-feely, role-play sort of stuff, and I would have run a mile. But it's just talking, and I've never found the strength to talk about a lot of it before.'

'I'm pleased it's working. I needed to ask if you feel up to doing some of the paperwork on the case now? But please feel free to say no if it's too soon. I may have to go away for a few days next week, and I want to make sure the file on Evans is absolutely right for the CPS.'

'It's fine, boss, I can do that,' Rob assured him. 'It's amazing the difference it's made to me. I'm back on good terms with my mother for the first time in years. When I was a kid I blamed her for putting me into a situation where I got abused. Crazy, I know now. She was very ill, she had no choice.

'But she's much better now and we're in contact again. In fact, I have some good news for her,' Rob said with a smile. 'I haven't told anyone else yet, boss, but I'm going to propose to the girlfriend this weekend. I think now I've got rid of some of the stuff from the past, I may be ready to make a commitment.'

Ted smiled and shook his hand. 'Congratulations, Rob, I'm really pleased for you. Just don't push yourself too far, too soon, please, and remember you can back away from this case at any time you need to.'

Virgil's phone rang while he was working at his desk. He didn't recognise the caller ID on his screen so just said a non-committal 'Hello' as he answered.

'Do they still call you Mr Tibbs?' asked a voice.

Virgil realised at once who it was but searched in vain for the man's real name so instead joked, 'And do they still call you Dickhead?'

The man laughed.

'The word on the street is that you were looking for me. I have to tell you that you were not the only one.'

Virgil immediately became serious. 'Care to tell me more?' he asked.

'I would be happy to do so over a cup of coffee.'

He named a supermarket near the town centre and Virgil arranged to meet him there in quarter of an hour, rather surprised at the choice of venue.

Virgil put his head round the boss's door before leaving.

'Just had a call from that homeless man who saw the taxi driver shooting, boss. I left him my card to get in touch and he just did. I'm off to meet up with him in town, see what he has to say.'

Virgil was even more surprised when he arrived at the supermarket. He was looking round the foyer for the unkempt homeless man he remembered from before. Instead he was approached by a smart, cleanly-shaven man in the supermarket's uniform, wearing a badge which announced his name as Nat.

'Good morning, sir, my name is Nat and I am here to help you,' he said, with a broad grin, clearly his scripted speech for supermarket customers. 'This is my break time. Let's get that coffee and I will treat you, in recognition of your kindness to me on our last meeting. Of course, I get staff discount so the offer doesn't amount to much, but it's all I can do at the moment.'

They chose their drinks and took a seat in a quiet corner of the café.

'I have fifteen minutes, so we'd best make it quick,' Nat told him. 'After you spoke to me and left, I went to the nearest coffee place, armed with your kind donation, to thaw out a bit. There's one close by that doesn't refuse admission to the homeless, from where I could keep an eye on my pitch and my pathetic possessions.

'That's when I noticed the motor bike again. Of course, I can't be sure if it was the same bike but it was a big red bike, with two people on it, and it was cruising around the arches, near to the place where I and the others hang out. That's when I decided it was time to find another pitch.'

'Can you tell me anything else at all that might help us?' Virgil asked him. 'It was in daylight this time, I imagine, so could you tell the make of bike or any other distinguishing features?'

'Sadly, as I told you before, bikes were never my thing. Sports cars, yes, I could tell you the make, model and year of manufacture but bikes are a bit too boys' toys for my taste.

'I can tell you that there were two people on the bike. The rider was taller than the pillion passenger, on both occasions, and it was the pillion passenger who shot the man in the taxi. Other than that, I can't tell you any more than I did last time. Dark helmets, dark leathers, and in daylight I could see the visors were dark too.

'That's it, really, I just wanted to tell you that they had come back and were sniffing around after you'd gone. That's what led me to move on, which in turn led to an extraordinary set of circumstances, resulting in the startling metamorphosis you see before you.'

Nat told him that the return of the bike and its riders had

made him nervous enough to move to a pitch on the other side of town. On his way there, he had bumped into someone he had known from his previous life but had long since lost touch with. That old friend was shortly leaving to work abroad for a year and had been delighted to let Nat use his flat while he was away, in return for him keeping it in good order and looking after his tropical fish.

'With an address of my own once again, I could take a step back into the world of normality. First I could sign on, then I started job hunting and now I spend my days welcoming people into a supermarket, helping to pack their bags and sometimes carrying the bags back to their cars. So much responsibility!'

He laughed. 'A few years ago, I was handling millions of pounds, every day. Now I work for the minimum wage, I live in a flat I don't own, and won't be able to stay in forever, but strangely I feel happier than I have done in a long time.'

'Well, you certainly look very different from the last time we spoke,' Virgil told him. 'If there really is someone out there looking for you, they're not going to find you easy to recognise.'

'And now my tea break is over, I must get back to my meet and greet duties.' Nat shook Virgil's hand. 'Good luck with your case, Mr Tibbs, I hope you catch the villains.'

Virgil headed back to the office with the latest news for the boss. Ted didn't like the development.

'Do you think this Nat is safe now?' he asked Virgil.

'I didn't recognise him and I'd spoken to him before,' he replied. 'With luck, if it really was the same bike again, they were just cruising round to see if there had been any witnesses, and hopefully scare them off. No one could have known I had spoken to him.'

'Unless they were watching while you did. But surely they would have made a clean getaway while they could, rather than hanging around?'

Sal was at his desk in the outer office so Ted went to the door and called him in. There was only one spare chair in the small space so Sal perched on the edge of the boss's desk. There was never any need to stand on ceremony in Ted's presence.

'This is asking a lot, after what happened to the driver, Sal, but we need to try to find out if anyone else knows anything at all about what was going on. If anyone had any idea of what the driver … what was his name again?'

'Mohnid Ahmadi,' Sal told him.

'What Mr Ahmadi was up to, where his money was coming from, who his contacts were. Anything. Without putting either yourself or your cousin in danger, Sal, can you find out anything that might give us a lead?'

'I could go in, as a driver …' Sal began but Ted shook his head firmly.

'We've been over this before, Sal. Not yet, not until we know a lot more about who we're dealing with. The more I hear about these people, the more uneasy it makes me. Just find out what you can, without putting yourself or anyone else in danger.'

Chapter Thirty-two

There was only one other vehicle in the remote and windswept car park in the Brecon Beacons when Ted pulled up in his Renault, a battered-looking ex-army Land Rover. The man he had come to meet was leaning nonchalantly against it, arms folded.

His only form of greeting to Ted was, 'Leave your mobile in your car or I'll smash it,' closely followed by, 'there's your bergen, Gayboy. Let me know if you need any help picking it up.'

Then he set off in the familiar loose-kneed, rolling gait Ted knew to his cost that the man was capable of keeping up for long hours at a time. Ted lifted the backpack he had left for him, wincing at its weight. It contained far more than the two of them would need for the two to three day training hike Ted had asked for. He strongly suspected there were a couple of house bricks in there as well, to make up the weight, which was probably pushing up above the hundred pound mark.

Ted had first met the man, whose name he knew as Marty Green, when he was a Specialist Firearms Officer, training for a particularly difficult role. Green's job was to teach Ted and other SFOs the basics of survival techniques and also of Krav Maga. He was the highest-graded instructor of the martial art in Britain. He practised it far beyond its self-defence application to that of deadly unarmed combat. He was also a crack shot with a sniper rifle.

He was ex-SAS and had undertaken all kinds of undercover missions around the world, according to the legends that surrounded him He was always in high demand for special operations because he spoke fluent Russian and Hebrew. Ted, in reality, knew very little about him for sure, and suspected that Marty Green was not his real name.

In his training role he showed no respect for anyone of any rank. Ted knew that by comparison with other names he used, his own nickname of Gayboy was so mild as to be almost affectionate. Ted had seen him reduce senior officers of both police and armed forces to tears with his punishing regimes.

Inevitably, on the training courses he'd been on with him, Ted had always been the smallest there and the only gay. He went in with the advantage of already holding several martial arts black belts, including Krav Maga and he had once, but only once, had Green on the ground with a lucky tackle. He suspected both of these factors contributed to the tiny amount of respect that the man sometimes showed him.

Martial arts gave Ted the safety valve he needed when work became too hard to handle. It was usually Krav Maga he turned to in order to release the most tension. From time to time he needed to put his body under extreme physical stress, so that his brain could work to its maximum level of efficiency.

This was one of those times and that's what this short training session was all about. That, and the chance to pick the brain of the one person he knew who would probably have at least a good idea of what was going on, possibly even who was involved.

Conversation would be impossible until Green stopped for the night, if indeed he chose to. No matter how hard Ted pushed himself under the energy-sapping weight of the backpack, he seldom got within a few hundred yards of his trainer. He had no choice but to keep on going as he was starting to lose all sense of direction, which he knew was part of the plan.

Finally, just as he was convinced he could go no further and would have to drop to his knees in the damp heather and scattered sheep droppings, Ted crested a small hill and saw ahead of him his trainer-turned-torturer sitting on a large rock, waiting for him.

'What kept you, Gayboy?' was his only comment as Ted staggered up and sank on to a nearby rock, chest heaving He was ready to sob with relief as the rock took the weight of his backpack.

'You said you wanted some serious training,' Green said dryly. 'I took you at your word.'

Ted nodded, still too out of breath to speak.

'Come on, Gayboy, get the bergen off and the kettle on, then you can tell me what this trip is really all about and what you need to know.'

Freed from the weight of the rucksack, Ted felt all his muscles trembling with relief but got the pack open and broke out the high-speed gas cooker that was conveniently near the top. He'd taken the precaution of stuffing a fistful of his green teabags in his pocket, knowing he would need them.

Over tea, he told Green of his current case. He knew his security clearance was of the highest order so had no concerns about doing so. When he got to the part of describing the break-in at his house and the hanging of the cat, Green let out a snort of derision.

'Bloody theatrical. Something as flashy as that has Spooks written all over it.'

'Security Service?' Ted queried incredulously. 'You really think they're involved?'

'Wake up, Gayboy. You've got a distant royal as a suspect. Who did you think would be watching his back and clearing up behind him. The Brownies?'

'I imagined it was a warning to me to back off, but I wasn't sure who from. Do you think Trevor might be in danger?'

Again, a scornful noise from Green.

'You clearly don't as you've come out here playing soldiers with me and left him on his own. What do you think they might do to your boyfriend? Kill him? Then what hold would they have over you? Kidnap him? They would know it's not in your power to back off from a case like this. I'd say he's safe enough until you get back to hold his hand. Although looking at the soft state you've let yourself get into, we've got an awful lot of work to do before you're of any real use to him or to anyone else. I thought you kept up your training?'

'I try to but I spend too much time driving a desk these days,' Ted said ruefully.

'Right, we've not all that much light left, you break out the basha and get us sorted for the night, I'll fix something to eat. This spot should do us well enough.'

Ted rummaged in the rucksack and found the basic nylon sheet that would make a cover of sorts, strung between a couple of scrub thorn bushes, the only kind of tree around, and fixed down with bivouac pegs. He was pleased to see that there were two ultra-light sleeping bags, folded away to next to no volume in compression sacks. He had feared there might be nothing more luxurious than a space blanket apiece to keep them from hypothermia in the night.

Ted thought his reflexes were still pretty good. He tried to practise judo and karate once a week and fitted in his Krav Maga training whenever he could. He saw the blur of movement out of the corner of his eye as he crouched, hammering home tent pegs, whirling and attacking as fast as he could. He pulled out every blocking move he knew. He still finished up in short order on his back in the rough grass, Green straddling him, with the cold steel of a knife hard up against his throat.

Green wasn't even breathing hard. He clicked his tongue in disappointment. 'Sloppy, Gayboy, very sloppy. Be thankful it's friendly, cuddly me holding this knife and not some nasty Spook. I can see now why you asked for training.'

He held Ted down for just long enough to make him feel vulnerable and totally humiliated, then sprang easily to his feet and carried on preparing their supper. It was basic army ration packs, high in calories, low in imagination, but it would sustain them.

Ted sat warily down, not too close to Green, to eat the plateful he was offered. Green grinned at him and said, 'Don't worry, I'll declare a truce for mealtimes. I also need to eat.'

Green ate quickly and methodically, refuelling rather than savouring his food, always alert, ready for action. He was ten years older than Ted, yet his reactions were those of a man half his age. He couldn't help Ted solve the case but he could, hopefully, bring him to a mental and physical state where he would be more capable of doing so.

Darkness fell fast in the mountains at that time of year, where the only light pollution was away in the distance. Before they crawled into their sleeping bags under the basha, both men scrupulously examined their feet for injury and cleaned them with medicated wipes. Neither would be any use out on a training hike with infected blisters.

Ted remembered from his previous training with Green to put his boots back on and sleep in them, just loosening the laces. Tired feet risked swelling and he might otherwise find himself unable to put them back on in the morning.

'On your performance so far, Gayboy, I don't see how you think you can crack a case like this, when bigger fish than you have tried before and failed,' Green said as they crawled under the basha.

'Because I want to badly enough,' Ted said simply. 'You have just two more days to make it possible.'

Chapter Thirty-three

There was barely the faintest streak of light in the eastern sky when Ted was unceremoniously kicked awake by the toe of a boot in his ribs.

'Get up, Gayboy, where's my breakfast in bed?' Green demanded.

Ted opened eyes which he felt as if he had only just closed them, and managed to crawl out of his sleeping bag. Every muscle in his back seemed to be screaming at him at once. He groaned silently to himself at the thought of hoisting the bergen back on to his shoulders shortly, its weight lightened only to the extent of two meals.

Breakfast was high-energy muesli bars and a hot drink. Ablutions consisted of a quick face rinse in cold stream water, which Ted followed up with a brief scrub of his teeth with his folding toothbrush. Then he was left to break camp and reload the rucksack, working as fast as he could because Green was already disappearing over the skyline without a backward glance.

They didn't hike all that far during the day. Every time Ted caught up with Green he was ordered to take off the bergen, then confronted with another martial arts session. Although his hiking boots were light and flexible, they still hampered him. He was a long way from making any impression on Green, although he mostly managed to keep himself upright and out of knife range, at least.

By the end of the day, Ted was fighting a rearguard action, barely able to keep upright long enough to defend himself.

Green called a halt and ordered him to pitch the basha for the night.

'And you think you're ready to go back and face the world tomorrow?' Green asked him scornfully. 'You need three more days' training at least.

'I haven't got three days,' Ted panted. 'I need to be back tomorrow night.'

Green held out a hand. 'Give me your car keys,' he ordered.

Ted hesitated.

'Give me your cars keys,' Green repeated. 'Don't make me take them from you.'

Reluctantly, Ted fished the keys to the Renault out of his pocket and handed them over.

'When you can get these back from me, then you're ready to go back,' Green told him.

'Like that's going to happen,' Ted said despairingly.

'What happened to wanting something badly enough to make it happen?' Green sneered. 'PMA, Gayboy. Positive Mental Attitude. First you have to believe.'

That night seemed even shorter to Ted than the one before, partly because he made several unsuccessful attempts to take the keys from Green when he appeared to be sleeping. He was lucky he didn't get himself seriously injured on the first attempt, in the seconds before Green was fully awake enough to know who his attacker was.

The next day was one humiliation after another as Ted tried ever more desperately to get hold of his keys. He had promised Trev he would try to be back by the third night, which was tonight, the morning of the fourth day at the latest, but it was looking increasingly impossible.

He woke up on the fourth morning with a mounting feeling of frustration, bordering on desperation. As they hiked, he dug deeper into his reserves to try to find the elusive PMA. He was feeling even less capable of tackling Green successfully than he was of breaking the paedophile ring.

Unusually, Green called a halt mid afternoon and told him to make tea. Then he sat down opposite him, looking relaxed, with no hint of imminent attack in his posture.

'What's stopping you, Ted?' he asked, in a quieter tone than usual, softened by dropping the nickname. 'You're capable of doing it, you've had me down before. What's stopping you believing you can? I'm not just talking about getting your keys back. I'm talking about your case. Where's your self-belief?'

The thing that Ted found hardest to handle. To look deep inside himself for answers and then share them with someone else. He would rather have fought toe-to-toe until he collapsed from exhaustion, but he was cornered, with no way out. He looked desperately off towards the horizon, searching for something on which to focus.

'The case has brought a few skeletons out of the closet,' he said finally. 'Stuff I've not worked through yet.'

'Then sort it, man,' Green said impatiently. 'It's blocking your energy. You're no use to man nor beast if you let shit from the past into your brain. Find something to replace it with. Hate, if necessary, but deal with it, or you'll never solve the case. Or get your keys back.

'On the subject of your case, no matter how high up it goes, in my experience I find these things have a way of getting sorted out, one way or another. It may not be exactly the result you're looking for, but I think you'll find there will be a result.'

Ted was at a low ebb by the time they stopped for the night. He was desperate to get back to Trev, aware he would now be getting worried by his unexplained, extended absence. Part of him knew Green was right. He had to start dealing with his demons but he felt he still lacked the moral courage to do so.

But Green had been right about using hatred if he could

find nothing else. As Ted saw the man calmly going about preparing their supper, something deep within him finally snapped. When he leapt at him from behind, it was with a speed and ferocity that took even Green by surprise. Ted had the huge satisfaction of seeing him go down, albeit briefly. But he was dealing with a master of martial art, so Green's time on his back was fleeting, just enough to give Ted a flash of hope and satisfaction. The next minute the tables were turned and Ted was on his back, completely immobilised.

To his surprise, Green was laughing. 'Nice try, Gayboy, your best so far. So because of that, tomorrow morning, you can have your car keys back and trot off home to your toy boy.'

Thinking of that prospect, Ted fell into his deepest sleep of the hike so far, finally feeling that he had crossed some mental barrier. He only woke when the first tentative rays of sunlight fell on his face. At that moment, he snapped awake and sat bolt upright.

The sun's rays were hitting his face because the basha had gone. Green had gone, so had everything else, including the bergen. The only things he could see, sitting on a flat stone nearby, were a couple of high energy bars, a bottle of water and his car keys.

Ted looked around, disorientated, desperately trying to get his bearings and work out in which direction his car was parked. It took him the best part of the day, using all the survival skills Green had ever taught him, to find his way back to the car park where his Renault was waiting. Green and the Land Rover were long gone.

Ted threw the lightweight sleeping bag, squashed down in its compression sack, the only other thing Green had left him, into the back seat, and grabbed his mobile phone from the glove compartment, praying for a signal. There was a weak one, enough to show him a long list of missed calls from Trev, ending with a text message which simply said, 'Where are you? Worried sick. Call me!'

Ted hastily sent off a text reply. 'So sorry, no phone. Leaving now. Back in under 4 hours', then floored the accelerator and headed back north, keeping up the speed as much as he dared, only just missing a police radar trap near Wrexham.

It was early evening when he wearily turned the Renault into the driveway of their modest house. Trev's red Triumph motorbike was already in the garage as Ted put his car away and headed into the house.

He found Trevor in the kitchen, surrounded by cats.

'I'm so sorry,' he said as soon as he got through the door. 'I've had no phone all week so I couldn't contact you. I didn't mean to worry you. I honestly meant to be back by yesterday morning at the latest but it just wasn't possible.'

He moved closer to Trev, arms out to hug him. Trev sidestepped and held up a hand to repel him.

Ted laughed. 'Yes, sorry, I probably smell like a badger's arse. I've not washed or changed any clothes all week. Let me go and have a shower then I'll explain everything and make it up to you.'

Trev's blue eyes were colder than Ted had ever seen them.

'Five days, Ted,' he said. 'Five days. You said three. I've been out of my mind. I didn't know where you were or what had happened to you. Nor did any of the team. I phoned Sal to ask. Have you any idea how that made me feel?'

'I really am sorry, I didn't mean to worry you.'

Then Ted noticed Trev's holdall sitting on a kitchen chair, and looked at him questioningly.

'I need some time away now, Ted,' Trev told him, his voice tight. 'You're in too dark a place, I can't go there with you and I can't make it right for you.'

Ted looked at him, astonished, seeing a raw emotion on his partner's face which he couldn't identify. 'Are you leaving me?' he asked, with a catch in his voice.

Trev reached out and gently touched Ted's face, his thumb stroking the stubble on his cheeks.

'I don't yet know the answer to that.'

Chapter Thirty-four

After Trev had gone, Ted knew he needed a hot shower, a change of clothes and something to eat. He couldn't find the motivation for any of them. He felt totally numb.

He and Trev had hardly spent any time apart in the eleven years they had been living together. He was just back from five days away, now Trev was gone and he had no idea for how long, or even if he was coming back.

He drank several glasses of water as his mouth was suddenly dry, then curled up on the sofa, at last able to take off his boots. He pulled a throw over himself and decided to try and sleep. The cats climbed cautiously on top of him. Although they knew and liked Ted, it was Trev they all worshipped unreservedly.

He fell into an exhausted but fitful sleep, punctuated by the usual nightmare, repeated over and again. Deep water, the feel of lungs exploding, nakedness, scornful laughter. Every time Ted was catapulted awake, one or other of the cats would hiss reproachfully at being disturbed.

Somehow he got through the night. The first thing he did when he woke up was to check his mobile phone, although he had left it on all night and not heard any alerts. There were no calls and no texts.

He took a long, hot shower, put on clean clothes and put those that he had been wearing all week into the washing machine. He felt as if he was running on autopilot, going through the motions of everyday tasks, feeding the cats, tidying the house, cleaning the litter trays.

About mid-morning, he phoned Mike Hallam, apologising for disturbing his Saturday, and asked to be filled in with what had been going on during the week. There was nothing much more to report. Evans had been further remanded in custody and bail had been refused once again.

Ted left it until after lunch before he tried phoning Trev, thinking it might be best to give him some space. His call went straight to voicemail and he had no idea what he could say to make things right. He left a stumbling, clumsy message of apology and hung up.

When he had heard nothing by the evening, he tried calling Willow. He and Trev had known her for a comparatively short time but they had become close friends, Trev especially, with both her and her fiancé Rupert. He thought Trev might possibly have gone there. He had no family, or none that he was on speaking terms with.

Her voice was guarded when she answered, knowing from the caller display that it was Ted. 'Hang on a minute,' she told him when he began to speak, and he heard the sound of a door opening and closing, realising she had moved to a different room.

'Yes, Ted, he's here, with me and Rupert,' she told him. 'Just at the moment, I think you'd perhaps better leave it, give him time. He was so worried about you, so scared of what might have happened. He just needs a bit of time away to calm down.'

'Can you at least tell him how sorry I am?' Ted pleaded. 'How can I make it right?'

'Be patient,' she said. 'He's not punishing you, he's just hurting. I know you're having a hard time with this current case but perhaps you've lost sight of how much it's affecting Trev as well.'

'What has he told you?' Ted asked.

'Do you really know him as little as that?' Willow replied. 'Nothing, of course, only to say that it's been hard. We're pampering him and making a fuss of him. He will come back, Ted, just give him time.'

After another night on his own, Ted faced the prospect of a long and lonely Sunday. He realised that he had long since lost track of what single people did with themselves at the weekend. He ironed a couple of shirts ready for starting back to work the next day, then decided he might as well go in to work to catch up. He had nothing else to do. At least he could go in wearing his favourite casual clothes. If he happened by chance to bump into the Ice Queen he wasn't officially on duty, so even she couldn't insist he should be in suit and tie.

It was quiet and orderly in the main office. The rota showed him that Sal and Virgil were on duty over the weekend, both out working somewhere. The white board they had started for Aiden's murder showed nothing more recent. It didn't take long for Ted to clear the paperwork on his desk and catch up with internal emails. Not nearly long enough to occupy his time.

He had a computer with Internet access on his desk, though he was not all that adept with it. But he decided that, as he had nothing else to do, he would see if he could find out more information from the sites Steve had been showing him. He was particularly interested in taking a closer look at the senior police officer.

After a couple of false starts, he successfully navigated to the PIEdpiper page. He searched around until he found the link he wanted. No real names were used, except where someone had been convicted. Ted knew the officer, a Chief Superintendent, was called Simon Danielson. He was not surprised to find him under the nickname of Simon the PIEman.

Everything was vague speculation and allegation, but there was a common theme in his case. There were recurrent suggestions that he particularly enjoyed inflicting corporal punishment on young boys, with a sexual connection.

Ted read on with mounting revulsion and incomprehension. There were links to follow to other sites, all making the same sorts of claim. But they were often so subtly made that their meaning defeated Ted, and increased his sense of frustration. He knew Steve could have made sense of it in seconds. It was likely to take him hours, but then he had nothing else constructive to do with his time, and at least it was distracting him from thinking about Trev.

What he was looking for was something to link Danielson to their patch and, in particular, to the Hotel Sorrento. It was like trying to decipher cryptic crossword clues. If someone told him what the clue meant, Ted could often come up with the correct answer, as his general knowledge was not bad. But some of those clues, and some of the subtle hints in what he was reading, may as well have been written in secret code.

He decided to make a day of it, so slipped out at one point for a smoked salmon bagel from a nearby delicatessen. He kept himself topped up on green tea as he worked. As well as toggling between sites claiming to expose known paedophiles, he also took time to check Danielson's police record, which looked exemplary. His rise through the ranks had been swift and seemingly unstoppable. Friends in high places for sure, Ted thought to himself. He wondered just how high.

There were plenty of photos of the man, showing a tall, somewhat gaunt figure, with slightly rounded shoulders and a hooked nose, which gave him the look of some sort of bird of prey. As well as his own senior position in a Midlands force, he seemed to travel around the country delivering lectures on various police matters. Ted noted that he had been in Stockport on a few occasions. He could find no specific mention that he had been there on the night that Aiden Bradshaw died, however, although he had been not far away, as had the Knave of Clubs. But that was based on his own limited search skills. He made a mental note to ask Steve to dig deeper.

Ted was intrigued by something on the PIEdpiper's page. It was a reference to the man liking to watch 'a child at play' whilst listening to his favourite Tina Arena song. It meant nothing at all to Ted. He was just about to take out his phone and ask Trev how he could find out what it meant. Then he remembered. For the time being at least, he was on his own.

He knew he would have difficulty sleeping alone again that night, but guessed it would be much worse if he didn't at least try to work the puzzle out for himself. He smiled as he thought of Trev telling him over and over, 'Remember, Google is your friend.'

Tentatively, he entered 'child at play' into the search engine. He got plenty of results, but nothing like what he was looking for. He tried adding the name Tina Arena to the phrase. In less than a second, results appeared and this time, the fourth result to display took him to a lyrics page for a song called 'Sorrento Moon (I Remember)'.

'Got you, you slimy bastard,' Ted shouted triumphantly at the screen. It was pure hint and conjecture again, but it was something, at last, which linked Danielson's name with a Sorrento reference. It couldn't be coincidence, surely.

Guiltily, Ted caught sight of the time at the bottom right of his computer screen. It was much later than he had realised. The cats would be hungry, waiting to be fed. He thought optimistically that there was even an outside possibility he would find that Trev had returned.

He was surprisingly hungry, despite the earlier bagel, so he called at an Indian restaurant on the way back and got a takeaway. There was plenty for two, just in case. But there was no red bike in the garage, and no one to greet him when he went into the house, just six disgruntled cats prowling round in search of fresh food.

He fed the hungry felines then got out his phone, hesitating over whether or not to try Trev's number again, despite

Willow's words of caution. In the end he opted for a short text.

'Hope you ok. All well here, cats fine.' He reflected a minute before adding, 'We miss you,' hoping it didn't sound as pathetic as he felt.

Chapter Thirty-five

Ted wanted to talk to the Ice Queen before he briefed his team on his first day back from his time away with Green. He had returned burning with determination to bring in some of the bigger fish. He wanted her agreement on what their next moves and priorities should be.

Like Ted, the Ice Queen was always in early, so he was able to catch up with her before his team members were all at work. She scrutinised him as he entered her office and sat down as instructed, then said candidly, 'I hope your time away was successful. I must say you look marginally worse than when you went away.'

'There was some hard training involved, ma'am I think you may know Mr Green so you can well imagine. But I did come away with some possible answers,' he told her. 'Green, who is of course well versed in such matters, confirmed my suspicions that we might have Spooks involved, due to the possible involvement of even a minor royal, and the security implications that entails.

'I don't even know how we would begin to go after someone at that level. That's one for you, I think. What I'd like to do now, if you agree, is go after some of those near to the top but at a slightly lower level. Like Chief Superintendent Simon Danielson.'

He outlined for her what he had found out from his internet searches the day before, pointing out that it was all pure conjecture, then added, 'I'd like to start bringing in more of the hotel staff, particularly the receptionists, to see if we can loosen a few tongues that way. We could perhaps suggest that they could face conspiracy to murder charges.

'I'm hoping, too, that Sgt Reynolds will have found the boy from the video. I would like him and the hotel staff to look at some photos. Those of David Evans, of course, and Danielson, to see if we get any sign of recognition from any of them.'

Her tone, as ever, was measured when she replied.

'I think that would be acceptable at this stage. I have nothing concrete for you immediately, but I have reason to believe that we may shortly be in possession of something very interesting, as far as the Chief Superintendent is concerned. I'm sure I have no need to remind you that we must proceed with extreme caution with a potential suspect of his rank. You must ensure that every action you take is beyond reproach.'

The team sensed a new resolve in Ted from the moment he opened the briefing. They quickly brought him up to speed, each adding detail of what they had done individually.

'Right, where is the owner of the Sorrento?' he asked them. 'We've effectively shut his business down. I'd have expected him to be kicking and screaming, but there seems to be nothing except a deafening silence. Why is that?'

'Staff are all still tight as anything, boss,' Mike Hallam said. 'The only thing any of them will say is that he's still in Sicily and can't be contacted.'

'So what happened to the info Steve found on the Internet? Has anyone been round to the address lodged with Companies House?' Ted asked.

There was a sheepish exchange of looks, then Mike Hallam spoke up. 'Sorry, sir, my fault, I should have checked up on that straight away. Maurice, can you get round there this morning and find out what's what?'

'Next, I want as many hotel staff as possible, and in particular the receptionists, brought in individually and questioned. If they're too frightened to speak, I want them to understand that they could potentially extremely serious charges including conspiracy to murder, see if that produces any results.

'I want them shown some photos, which I will sort out, to see if we get any flicker of recognition at all from any of them. We'll include shots of David Evans, of course, plus any other known offenders on our patch. I also have another potential suspect. I don't want to name him at the moment, but I do want to see if anyone recognises him. We'll call him Suspect A for now.

'Sal, you did such good work on that last fraud case, I want you and Steve to find out everything you can about the Sorrento's owner. The hotel is a limited company, so who are the shareholders? You know the sort of thing.

'Jan, any luck yet with the boy you thought you recognised from the photos?'

Jancis Reynolds explained that she had tracked him down to a different home to the one where Aiden had lived, although the two had been to the same school. He was a frequent absconder from the home and had not been in residence when she had visited. The staff there had agreed to call her as soon as he reappeared.

'The Sorrento is the link for us here, that's the lead we have to nail down. The more we can tie suspects into it, the more chance we have of getting convictions. I can't yet tell you who the new suspect is, but I can say that it's someone satisfyingly high up. Right, get to it,' Ted said in conclusion.

The phone on Ted's desk was ringing as he returned to his office. A voice he didn't know announced, 'I'm the governor of the prison which is currently holding your man Anthony Ross on remand. He's been to see me and is asking to see you, in person.

'He says he has information for you but he wants to do a deal. Of course, as you know, every single man in here is innocent, they've all been framed, or so they say. I get requests like this all the time. But I'm the father of five small boys and I particularly dislike paedophiles, although I know I shouldn't let personal feelings get in the way.

'I'd just never forgive myself if I dismissed what he's saying out of hand and didn't get in touch with you. If you want to talk to him, I can get him shipped over to you later today.'

Ted thanked him profusely, grateful the man had shown some initiative and co-operation, and agreed a time for Ross to be brought to the station. Then he went back down to see the Ice Queen to bring her news of a potential breakthrough.

'I hope he realises we can't offer him a deal on the spot,' she said. 'It will have to go higher up for clearance. But if there is the potential to bring down those further up the chain, there's a chance something could be worked out.'

'I wondered if you would care to preside over this meeting, ma'am?' Ted asked her. 'It might show him we are taking him seriously to see someone senior willing to listen to him. And certainly you can tell him more than I could about his chances of getting any sort of a deal.'

'We will have to proceed with extreme caution from the outset with this. I take it he is coming without his solicitor present?'

When Ted nodded, she continued, 'Even if he wants to talk off the record, we must ensure he says nothing with which he could incriminate himself, in the absence of his legal advisor. It will be very delicate. I'm happy to take the lead. Let me know the moment he arrives at the station.'

Ross arrived with two prison officers escorting him, handcuffed to one of them. He was taken into an interview room, where Ted and the Ice Queen soon joined them. Seeing her there, he immediately started to protest.

'I only want to talk to you,' he said to Ted, 'no one else.'

'Not possible, Mr Ross, that's not how it works. This is my senior officer, Superintendent Caldwell. Either she sits in or the interview is off.'

Reluctantly, Ross took a seat facing them when the prison officer had released him from the handcuffs.

'You two officers can go and get a coffee,' Ted told them. 'Just ask at the front desk, they'll show you where.'

The two hesitated, looking at one another. 'We're not supposed to leave him unattended, sir,' one of them said.

Ted smiled reassuringly. 'He's in a police station. I have black belts in four martial arts and believe me, the Superintendent is very fierce. I don't think he's likely to do a runner. If anything happens, I'll personally take full responsibility.'

Without further encouragement, the two men left and Ted turned his attention to Ross. 'Superintendent Caldwell is here to oversee this initial meeting. She will advise you if at any point we should caution you further and tape what you say.'

Ross nodded reluctantly. He had clearly envisaged a quiet chat between Ted and himself, but was going to have to settle for some sort of formality.

'Now, what was it you wanted to say to me, Mr Ross?'

Ross licked his lips nervously. 'I didn't have anything to do with that little boy getting killed,' he began. 'Yes, I touched him, to see if he was still alive, but I didn't kill him. I panicked, I got that halfwit Iosif to get rid of him and I shouldn't have. Then things very quickly got out of my control, because of the people who were involved. I can name names, I can tell you exactly what happened and who was involved. But I want protection. I've already had a taste of what it's like in prison for a nonce, and I'm only on remand. I'm not going down for it. But these people are ruthless, they will kill anybody to protect their own. You saw what happened to Iosif. I want to know that if I talk to you, I will be protected.'

The Ice Queen leaned on the table which separated them and looked directly at Ross. 'Mr Ross, I must stop you there. You are in danger of incriminating yourself, in the absence of your legal advisor.

'I understand that you are hoping for some sort of trade-off against whatever information you have. However, I must stress that any sort of deal is not something which can be arranged now, at this level. I would have to talk to other people to see what, if anything can be offered, and there are no promises. It also depends on the quality of the information you are proposing to give us.'

Ross made a noise like a snort. 'I can give you names right to the very top. If necessary, I would testify in court against them, but only if I could be sure I would be safe, on some sort of Witness Protection Programme, something like that. These people have a very long reach. I would need to be sure.'

'Very well, Mr Ross, leave it with me. Contact will be made with you if we can offer you something, but I must stress there are no guarantees. If and when that happens, we will begin this interview all over again, formally recorded on tape.'

As they saw Ross safely on his way between the two prison officers, the Ice Queen turned to Ted, one eyebrow arched, and something like a smile playing around her mouth. 'Four martial arts, Inspector? You certainly don't do things by half.'

Chapter Thirty-six

Ted was just getting ready to leave for work when his mobile rang and the caller display showed it was Willow. He snatched up the phone and said anxiously, 'Hello?'

'Don't panic, Ted,' Willow told him, hearing his tone. 'Trev asked me to phone you. He's fine, he's just gone to Berlin.'

'Berlin?' Ted asked incredulously.

'He's gone with Rupert. Rupe got a modelling job, big bikes, boys' toys, that sort of thing. Right up Trev's street so they've gone off together for a bit of a boys' jolly,' Willow told him. 'Are you free tonight? Since you and I are grass widows at the moment, I thought I could come round to keep you company. And see the lovely cats, of course.'

'I'd really like that,' Ted said, and meant it. 'Shall I cook?'

'I know you're busy at work at the moment, so why don't I just pick up a takeaway on the way over?' she asked. 'Is there anything you don't eat?'

'Not much,' Ted laughed. 'If you can buy it here, I'll eat it. Is seven thirty all right for you? I'll make sure I'm back by then.'

Willow agreed and rang off, leaving Ted to head off to the station. He bumped into the Ice Queen in the car park as she parked her immaculate BMW estate next to his decidedly shabby Renault.

'Ah, just the person I wanted to see,' she said ominously. 'Follow me into my office, will you?'

Ted took her at her word and followed dutifully behind her

tall and elegant figure. He found himself wondering if she ever relaxed, if spending time with her husband and sons ever saw her in jeans and wellingtons. He couldn't picture it somehow.

'Come in and sit down,' she said, switching on her coffee machine. She sat down at her desk facing Ted and started up her computer.

'I had a phone call last night from a contact of mine,' she told him. 'The Chief Superintendent we are interested in has, shall we say, come under some covert surveillance, or rather his computer use has. He clearly thinks he's rather clever, or quite well protected. He's been putting some fairly unpleasant images of himself in compromising positions with under age children into the cloud. He's clearly not aware of how easy it is for certain people to view what he has in storage. Either that or he thinks he's flame-proof.'

She was scrolling through her emails as she spoke and clearly found the one she was expecting as she continued, 'Ah, here it is. In the absence of much information to go on, I told my contact that if there was anything featuring four-poster beds I wanted it sending immediately, and he has done so.

'Now, I'm told that what he's sent here is comparatively mild, level one content, but it will nevertheless be difficult viewing, I have no doubt. I understand there is no real doubt over the identity of Chief Superintendent Danielson in the video footage he has sent, although the quality is not good. It looks like secret filming.

'The question is, Inspector, as you know the hotel that might appear in it, would you be willing to look at it and see if you recognise the background? As ever, with material like that, you are at liberty to refuse should you not feel up to it.'

Ted felt himself start to go hot all over, but fought the sensation and worked to control his breathing.

'That's fine, I'll take a look at it. It makes sense for me to do it. I've been in the hotel, I might recognise some of the fixtures.'

'If you're sure, I'll forward it to you now and you can deal with it and get back to me. It goes without saying that I don't want anyone else to see it at this stage, or to know of its existence.'

'Ma'am,' Ted said in agreement, before he went upstairs to talk to his team, and then face the ordeal ahead. He made himself a mug of tea before he sat down at the computer, loosening his tie. Level one was the lowest level of indecent images involving children. He still knew it was going to be harrowing to watch, especially for him.

As with the still shots he had seen, the quality was not good. Sometimes he could see only a part of the people involved, but there was sound with the film. The camera was obviously being operated remotely as it panned the room, trying to keep the face of the adult involved in shot as often as possible. The quality was completely different from the shots of Rory the Raver.

It was clearly Danielson, his face was visible several times, and his angular frame and stooped shoulders were unmistakable. He was naked. Ted had a shock when he saw the boy with him. It was Aiden Bradshaw, also naked. Aiden did not look particularly ill at ease, which Ted found strange.

Clearly the rumours on the website were true. To begin with, it seemed that all Danielson was interested in was administering not particularly severe corporal punishment. His flaccid penis hung resolutely between his legs, with no signs of a reaction.

Suddenly, he reached under a pillow and produced a pair of handcuffs. Ted heard Aiden's voice say loudly, 'Hey, I don't do no kinky stuff, that's not what you paid for,' but he was quickly overpowered by the tall man and soon had his hands attached to one of the bedposts.

Now Aiden was struggling hard, clearly getting frightened. Danielson put one hand over the boy's mouth to muffle the sounds he was making, while with the other hand he started to caress and fondle the boy's buttocks and between his legs.

Ted hit the pause button and closed his eyes, desperately taking himself away to the safe place in his head. Warm sun on his face, the sound of a nearby waterfall, birdsong above him, the soft feel of heather beneath his back. He just had to reach out with his hand and he could make contact with Trev's hand, close by.

Only this time Trev was not there. His reaching hand found no warmth of return contact, only the harsh stems of the heather. His breathing started to speed up. He felt the familiar sting of chlorine in his throat, the sensation of his lungs on the point of exploding. Panic was seizing him, he was going under for the third time.

Find a new safe place. Another memory, he desperately told himself. That fleeting moment when he had Green down on his back. The feeling of total control, at last. In his head he saw every move he had made, in slow motion, analysing every part of the tackle which had succeeded.

Slowly, he pulled back from the feeling of total panic and despair until he was in some degree of control of himself. He opened his eyes, swallowed his tea, and released the pause button.

There was not much more to see. Danielson's erection, when it finally appeared, was fleeting, far too short-lived to do anything with. He released the boy from the handcuffs and bundled him back into his clothes. He took a banknote out of his wallet to give to the boy, then all but pushed him out of the door. Then the film ended.

The room looked similar to the one Ted had seen, both in the stills he had looked at earlier and when he visited the hotel. He would need to look again to be absolutely sure, and to take stills of this film with him for comparison. But it seemed as if they had the first of their evidence to hook one of the bigger fish.

Ted was looking forward to spending time with Willow that evening. It would be nice to have some human contact, with Trev away. He hoped she could give him some advice on what he should do to get him back.

Willow arrived punctually, laden with Chinese takeaway bags containing a generous banquet for two. 'I hope you like Chinese,' she said, 'there's an awful lot of it.'

'Love it,' Ted assured her, helping her to unpack and producing plates and chopsticks. He was always amazed at how much Willow could eat. She was a model, tall, with impossibly long, slim legs. Her slender figure was sporty rather than skeletal, kept that way by her passion for badminton, tennis, swimming, riding, skiing, and lots of other outdoor activities. There was never any sign that she had to starve herself into shape.

Willow greeted each of the cats by name and was rewarded by a chorus of purrs. 'I was so sorry to hear about poor little John,' she said. 'I know Trev was absolutely devastated.'

'I let him down, didn't I?' Ted asked her, as they sat down and began to eat. 'I should have been here more for him. Will he come back?'

'Oh, Ted,' she said fondly, laying a hand on one of his. 'Of course he will, you silly man. He loves you. He's just finding it all a bit hard to cope with at the moment. He needs to go off and spread his wings a bit.

To his shame, Ted found his eyes filling with tears of relief at her words. To change the subject he said, 'I'm glad he's having some fun. He's travelled and lived abroad a lot, that's why he's so good at languages. His father's a senior diplomat, I don't know if you know that.'

Willow put her chopsticks aside for a moment and took his hand.

'Ted, Trev is the absolute soul of discretion. He would never talk about your work or your relationship or anything like that. The only thing he has mentioned is that you're having bad nightmares. I just wonder if perhaps you rely too much on him for support, and if you should think about getting some professional help for whatever it is that's troubling you.'

Ted's expression was anguished. He knew she was right. Trev had been his rock for the eleven years they had been together. His absence showed how much Ted needed him. No matter how desperately he wanted him back, Ted was still not sure he could find the courage to confront his demons with someone else.

Chapter Thirty-seven

As soon as he got a spare moment to himself at work the following morning, Ted got out his mobile to call his good friend and former boss, Jim Baker.

Jim answered on the second ring, his familiar voice growling, 'Morning, Darling.'

'Morning, Super,' Ted responded, their age-old joke working at last, now that Jim had finally climbed the career ladder to make Superintendent, after seeming to be stuck at DCI for years.

'I was just going to call you, Ted,' Jim told him, before Ted could speak. He gave a small laugh which sounded embarrassed. 'The thing is, I've started this online dating lark. I've met someone I quite like and I wanted to ask your advice on inviting her round here and, well, just on how to go on from there, basically.'

It was Ted's turn to laugh. 'You want to ask my advice on how to start a heterosexual relationship? Some mistake, surely?'

'You're just so good with people, though. Everyone likes and respects you. I just wanted to know your secret.'

Ted's short laugh this time was bitter. 'Not everyone, Jim. Trev's left me.'

'What?' Jim asked incredulously. 'Are you serious? But you two were always so solid.'

'I think the fashionable phrase is "taking time apart". What it amounts to is Trev's in Berlin and I'm here, and he's not returning my calls.'

'God, Ted, I'm so sorry. Is that what you wanted to talk to me about?'

'Partly,' Ted said hesitantly. 'It's just … I really need to talk about some stuff. I wondered if you would listen and maybe advise me?'

'Of course! Hell, you've listened to me crying on your shoulder often enough over the years. It's the least I can do, though I can't promise my advice will be any good. Do you want to come round tonight?'

'Can't tonight, it's the kids' self-defence club and my judo session. With Trev away, I can't let the kids down, now more than ever,' Ted told him. 'What about tomorrow?'

'Tomorrow's fine. I'll cook something. I'm practising, for this date. You can tell me honestly whether it's edible.'

'Could we perhaps …' again Ted hesitated. 'Do you fancy going for a walk?'

'A walk?' Jim sounded appalled at the prospect, as if it was an indecent proposal. 'I'm not much of a walker. If you want to be outdoors, we could perhaps go to a pub with a beer garden?'

'Too crowded. I'm just not very good at talking about this stuff anywhere, and I honestly can't do it indoors.'

'Sounds ominous. We could perhaps sit in the garden? ' Jim said tentatively. 'It's not overlooked and the neighbours won't hear anything. The old couple on one side are stone deaf and the young couple the other side are almost always out. If they're not, they have their music on so loud I sometimes have to go round there with my policeman's hat on, to get them to turn it down.'

They left it at that. Ted wondered if by tomorrow evening he would find the courage to talk. He had never spoken to anyone other than Trev about the horrors that he constantly tried to blot out of his mind. But he realised that Willow was right. He needed to get himself sorted out if ever Trev was to come back and their relationship was to survive.

He would usually have been able to work off the tensions at

his judo session, after the self-defence club. But there was no one at the club who could match him like Trev did, so any practice session would be tame by his usual standards. Only head coach Bernard could outclass him but he hardly ever took to the mat lately, except to referee, because of a back injury.

Ted needed to report to the Ice Queen about what he had seen on the video. He also wanted to remind her that he would be leaving in good time that evening because of the club. He was certainly not about to tell her that he and Trev were having difficulties, he just mentioned that his partner had gone to Berlin.

'So what's the plan now with the Chief Super?' he asked her.

'We just have a few more i's to dot and t's to cross and then I think we may be in a strong position to go down there and arrest him, at least on suspicion, on a number of serious charges. I take it you will want to come with me on that one?'

'I think the response to that, ma'am, would be, with respect, try and stop me,' Ted risked with a grin.

To his relief, the Ice Queen smiled back. Could there be a slight thawing in her attitude towards him?

'With four black belts to your name, Inspector? I wouldn't dare.'

Ted had phoned to tell Bernard that Trev was away tonight and to ask him if he could be there from the start for the junior session. Ted was perfectly capable of running the session by himself. However, anyone working with young people lately preferred always to have someone there as a witness, especially in sports where physical contact was unavoidable.

Flip was the first to ask where Trev was. Several of the other children were also concerned at the absence of the trainer they all adored. Ted did his best with them but he knew the sparkle was lacking when Trev was not on the mat with them.

When the kids had finished, Ted was just limbering up eagerly for his own training session when his mobile phone rang from inside his shoes, which he always left just inside the door of the gym. Ted was the only one allowed to disregard the phone ban in the dojo, as everyone from Bernard down knew he was theoretically always on call. He went across to answer the phone.

It was Kevin Turner. 'Ted, the Ice Queen wants us both in her office, now. I'm on my way to collect you. I know you're at the club and it's on my way.'

Ted sighed. 'Give me five minutes to shower and change,' he said.

'No can do. Her Majesty's orders were unequivocal. She wants us there now. I'm two minutes away, see you outside.'

Ted gave his apologies to Bernard and sprinted for the changing room. He was pleased he'd picked his boat shoes to walk down to the gym that evening, as he could simply slide his feet into them without undoing them. He just had time to drape his towel around his neck and pull on his leather jacket over his judogi, then stuff the rest of his clothes in his holdall.

Kevin was waiting outside with the car's engine still running.

'She's going to love that look,' he laughed, as he let out the clutch and headed at speed for the station. There was not a copper in the division who didn't know his car so he was in no danger of getting pulled over.

'I'm not even going to try getting dressed while you drive like a maniac,' Ted replied. 'She'll just have to take me as she finds me, if it really is as urgent as that.'

To his surprise the Ice Queen was also in civvies, although in her case they comprised impeccably tailored trousers and a soft cashmere sweater. She barely looked twice at Ted's attire. Her face was grim.

'To lose one witness is unlucky. To lose two, careless,' she began. 'Gentlemen, we are now in the position of having lost three on this one case. I had a call a short while ago. Anthony Ross was stabbed to death in prison earlier today.'

'How the hell did that happen?' Kevin asked. He had been kept up to speed with Ross's attempts to make a deal in exchange for information. 'Who knew that he was trying for a deal?'

'That's precisely what I wanted to ask both of you,' she replied, in a tone as icy as her nickname. 'It seems someone smuggled in a weapon, a sharpened piece of plastic so it passed through metal detectors. He was stabbed in the canteen at lunch time. They got him to hospital as fast as possible but he was dead on arrival. So the question, of course, is who knew enough about this whole affair to know what he was planning?'

'I'm assuming that whoever is at the top of this chain will have been twitchy about the possibility of him trying to buy his own freedom with a deal,' Ted said. 'Perhaps this was just precautionary?'

'The dateline is too coincidental for my liking,' she said.

'What about the prison guards who brought him here?' Kevin suggested. 'Could they be in the pay of someone?'

Like Ted, he didn't want to think that the leak had come from within their own nick.

'Ma'am, if my contact is right and we have Spooks sniffing round, then it's no real surprise that they know as much as we do about this whole case,' Ted told her. 'And how do we know that those spying on the bad guys are not also spying on us, the good guys? I hate to sound melodramatic, but is it time to think about our own systems being bugged?'

'I don't even want to have to think about that possibility,' she said firmly. 'I think, for now, we'll just have to put it down to the prison bush telegraph at its most efficient, or the well known fact that potential paedophiles are not everyone's favourite cell mates. Strange as it may seem, I think we now need to move forward as quickly as possible to bring Chief Superintendent Danielson into custody, for his own sake as much as that of the enquiry.'

Chapter Thirty-eight

Ted was on edge all the next day, fretting about the evening to come and wondering if he would find the courage to talk. He was even uncharacteristically sharp with his team members during the morning briefing, pulling them up short on normal, harmless banter, hating himself when he saw the crestfallen look on young Steve's face in particular.

He took himself off to his office for much of the time, to hide his growing anxiety and related bad mood. He promised himself he would make it up to the team but for now he was too anxious about the evening to come to be in the right frame of mind to do anything.

Jim Baker lived in a large Victorian semi-detached, set well back from a tree-lined road in Didsbury. He lived alone but Ted knew he had a cleaner who went in several times a week and the house was spotless and tidy. Ted could see that this was going to be a full dress rehearsal for the coming date. There were vases of fresh flowers everywhere and the table was laid with candles and a small floral arrangement as a centre piece.

Despite his own anxieties, Ted was keen to give encouragement so he smiled and said, 'That works for me. Yes, I will marry you.'

Jim laughed uncomfortably. He and Ted had been friends for years but he was still awkward with Ted's sense of humour at times.

'Would you like a drink? I haven't got any fresh limes but I've got dry ginger and some lime cordial left over from making snowballs at Christmas,' he said.

Ted was a non-drinker. His usual tipple was a Gunner, a mix of ginger beer and ginger ale with freshly squeezed lime juice. Jim did his best whenever he visited but never quite got the hang of providing for non-drinkers. Ted nodded his thanks.

'Do you want to eat first or talk first? Jim asked.

'Eat, definitely. I'm quite hungry and it smells good, whatever you've been cooking up.'

Jim had made a great effort with the meal. Ted reassured him it would be perfectly acceptable for a first date. He sincerely hoped his old friend might be on the brink of finding someone who would be the soul mate and companion who had been lacking in his life.

'All you have to do is be yourself, Jim,' Ted reassured him. 'Be honest, don't try to be what you're not. You're a nice man, and no, you're not my type. But seriously, if this woman can't see that, then you're wasting your time, frankly.'

They lingered at the table over coffee. Ted was dreading the moment when he was going to have to start talking. Despite being built like an American fridge, Jim was surprisingly sensitive. He could see Ted's discomfort and was quite happy to wait until he felt ready to talk. He'd left the French doors from the dining room to the garden open invitingly.

The garden was Jim's pride and joy and always looked lovely year-round. Living by himself, he spent a lot of time out there, tending the flowers and mowing the lawn. Ted's own gardening skills were confined to growing a few fragrant lilies in pots, safely fenced away from the cats, to whom they were potentially lethal.

When Ted was still hesitating, Jim picked up the coffee pot and suggested, ' Shall we go outside for a second cup? Might as well make the most of the nice weather.'

Ted followed him out but couldn't sit down, instead prowling round the small patio area, pretending to look at various flowers, but in fact his mind was far away. Jim gently took his cup and saucer away from him and set it on the table.

'Whenever you're ready, Ted,' he said quietly. 'No pressure.'

Ted perched on the edge of a garden chair, leaning forward, looking down. His feet were planted wide apart, clasped hands between his knees. He looked poised for flight at any moment.

'This case,' he began, clearing his throat. 'I've been finding it difficult. Having nightmares, flashbacks.'

Jim just sat quietly, letting him talk in his own time.

'I was raped. When I was a kid, when I first started secondary school,' Ted said finally, looking at the ground.

'God, Ted!' Jim exclaimed. 'I'm so sorry, I had no idea. Little boys can be such bloody monsters.'

Ted made a harsh noise which may have been a laugh. 'Not another boy,' he said. 'It was one of the masters. My swimming teacher, David Evans.'

Jim said nothing. He had no idea what he could possibly say. Now Ted had started to talk, he sensed it was best just to sit quietly and let him continue.

'It was about our second or third time at the baths. We'd just finished the lesson, had our showers, then gone back to our cubicles to change. Evans followed me into mine. He said I hadn't washed properly. He put his hand over my mouth, doubled me over, with my head rammed into a corner so I couldn't move, and raped me. It was brutal, but mercifully quick.

'I was shocked rigid. I barely managed to get dressed and on to the bus taking us back to school. I had no idea what to do.'

Ted seemed to have come to a halt, so Jim prompted gently, 'Did you tell anyone? Your family?'

'My mother had already walked out on us by this time. There was just me and my dad. He had so much to deal with, after he broke his back in the mining accident, and he'd started to drink by then. I didn't want to worry him. He was always so good to me. He paid for all the martial arts lessons so I would never be bullied. When I told him I was gay he just hugged me, told me he loved me and that was that.

'The next week at the baths, Evans tried the same trick again. He started to follow me into the cubicle. Then I remembered what all the martial arts lessons were about. I kicked him so hard he was off school for three days.

'After that he never tried anything with me in private, but he made my life a living hell in public. I wasn't a natural swimmer. I was always nervous of the water, so he took delight in throwing me in at the deep end, holding me under water till I thought I was drowning. Sometimes he'd pull off my trunks in the water so I had to run back to the changing rooms in the buff.'

'Did no one notice and do anything?' Jim asked.

Again the harsh laugh. 'You know what boys are like, Jim. The others just laughed and mocked, glad it was me getting the hard time and not them. And in those days, there was just him in there with us. It went on like that for two years, then Evans left the school in rather a hurry. I didn't find out why till much later on.

'I never learnt to swim at school. Trev taught me when we got together. It still scares me, but I'll swim if Trev is with me.'

'I remember Evans' trial, it was big news here. What was it, about ten years ago?'

'Just over eleven. I'd not long met Trev. I was in Firearms then,' Ted told him.

'Did you testify against him? I didn't know you then, of course, but I don't remember a copper giving evidence.'

There was a long pause as Ted continued to look down at the ground, as if fascinated by the intricate patterns of the crazy paving under his feet.

'Here's where we come to the part that's the most difficult for me. The part where I have to admit to myself, and to you, that I'm nothing but a coward. I didn't say a thing. I never came forward, never gave evidence, never told anyone. Trev is still the only person, apart from you now, who knows.'

'Bloody hell, Ted,' Jim exclaimed, and this time there was a hint of anger in his voice. 'No wonder Trev's taking a break. That's a hell of a thing to dump on him and only him. How old was he when you got together, eighteen?'

'Nineteen,' Ted's tone was slightly defensive.

' That's a shitload of baggage for someone who was still a boy to take on board. I'm surprised he hasn't needed to take a break before this. And now you're leading an enquiry which includes Evans as a suspect? I take it you've not told the Ice Queen? Have you any idea how serious this is? You could have compromised the entire investigation.'

Still not looking at him, Ted replied, 'If you're trying to make me feel bad about myself, Jim, you're on a hiding to nothing. I already loathe and despise myself. I should have come forward, spoken out, gone to court as a witness. My testimony, as a cop, would have carried a lot of weight. I persuaded myself there was enough evidence from the other boys who did come forward, men now, of course. Brave enough to speak out.

'There was me, a Firearms officer, a national long-range rifle champion, black belts in martial arts, and underneath it all I was still a scared little boy, clinging on for dear life to the hand rail in the shallow end.'

It was Jim's turn to stand up and march around, trying to regain control, but for different reasons. Finally he sat back down and said in a quieter tone, 'Ted, I'm telling you this not only as a good friend but also as a senior officer. You have to get professional help. You can't go on like this, and you certainly can't expect Trev to. And you have to tell the Ice Queen, no matter how hard it is. You need to cover your back and safeguard the enquiry.'

Ted was silent for a long moment. Then he slowly pulled out his mobile phone, looked for a number and dialled it. It was an answering service, as he expected. He needed to clear his throat a couple of times before he spoke.

'This is DI Ted Darling at Stockport. You've recently helped some of my team. I'm hoping you can now help me. Please would you call me so I can make an appointment?'

Chapter Thirty-nine

There was a timid knock on Ted's door the following morning but no one entered until he called out to them to come in. Young Steve's head appeared round the door hesitantly, as if he was about to enter the lion's den. Ted could have kicked himself to see the young TDC almost back to how wary he was of his boss when he first joined the team.

'Come in and sit down, Steve,' Ted said, in as encouraging a tone as he could manage. 'I'm really sorry about my grumpy mood yesterday, I just had a lot on my mind. Not that that's any excuse, but I hope it's an explanation.'

Steve took a seat, looking a bit more confident. 'I found something, or rather someone, I think you might be interested in, sir.'

He had a sheaf of computer print-outs with him. He spread them out on the desk in front of them for Ted to look at.

'I've started following someone on Twitter who sounds like he may possibly be able to help,' he began. 'He's not on Facebook, they've got very strict lately about real names only, and he uses a handle on Twitter.'

He'd already lost Ted at the mention of social media, something which was completely alien to him, but he tried to listen attentively.

'Anyway, I've started to tweet to him and try to find out a bit more about him. It seems he's an ex-Met officer who did some work on Operation Yewtree and on other ongoing child abuse enquiries. Thing is, sir, he's not much of a fan of the Met, he left them on bad terms, and he's been tweeting a lot of thinly veiled hints about a cover-up of paedos in high places.'

That part got Ted's full attention and he asked, 'Is he the PIEdpiper?'

'I don't think so, sir, although he may well supply that site with information. I just thought that perhaps if he could be persuaded to talk to you, he might have some useful leads to pass on.'

'Good work, Steve,' Ted said, and was relieved to see the young officer visibly start to relax as his boss seemed to be reverting to normal mode. 'Would he talk to us, do you think?'

'Erm, well, I've already been chatting with him, first by direct message on Twitter, more recently by email, when he got a bit more trusting of me,' Steve told him. 'I've been doing it from home, not on the work computer.'

'I hope you've not been putting yourself at risk?' Ted asked sternly. 'Remember what I said. I don't want you getting embroiled in anything that might put you in danger.'

'I think it's fine, sir,' Steve said with just a hint of defiance. 'In fact, it's possible that I'm even safer working from home than in here, with respect, given the leaks that seem to have been happening lately.'

Ted had to concede that he might be right. Word had quickly got out about what had happened to Ross after his visit to the station, and the team knew already about both the taxi driver and the waiter from the Sorrento.

'So where do we go from here?' Ted asked. 'It sounds as if I should try to meet this person. Ex- Met, you say?'

'Yes, sir, he was a sergeant, but it seems he had a lot of trouble, to do with what he was working on. Pressure was being put on him not to be quite so diligent. Shall I email him and say you'd be willing to go to London to meet with him, at a place of his choosing?'

'Yes, let's do it. See if he can make it the beginning of next week. The sooner I hear what he has to say, the sooner I'll know if it's of any help with our enquiry,' Ted told him.

'I could email him now, from my mobile, which is what I have been using. If he asks for your phone number, shall I give it to him?'

'Yes, no problem, let's try to get this fixed up. It may not get us anywhere but every lead is worth following up with this case. Well done, Steve, and sorry again about yesterday.'

It wasn't long before Ted's mobile phone rang. A voice said, 'I hear you want to talk to me.'

'I hear you might be able to help me with a current case,' Ted replied evenly.

'You do know I'm no longer serving? Anything I do tell you, if I choose to, is entirely off the record and I can't back it up with anything concrete.'

'At this stage of a difficult enquiry, I'll take anything I can get,' Ted told him honestly.

'Can you come to London on Monday? I could meet you and talk to you. It might not help you at all but at least it will show you that you're not the only who's come up against brick walls in this type of enquiry.'

'Where and what time?' Ted asked.

'Midday, Gladstone Park, NW10. Do you know it?'

'I can find it. How will I know you?'

'You won't. But I'll know you. Get a coffee when you arrive. Sit outside. I'll phone you and tell you where I am, once I'm happy no one is watching,' the man said.

'Can I at least know your name?'

The tone was scathing. 'You don't need to. We're not going on a date.'

Then the line went dead.

Ted decided he had better clear the trip with the Ice Queen, especially if he hoped to put the train fare on expenses. At least he had the feeling more and more that she listened to him, without dismissing his ideas out of hand.

'It sounds like a very long shot,' she said guardedly.

'I agree, ma'am, but some of the things he posts online are

very interesting. I'll get Steve to copy you in on everything he showed me. I think it's worth following up, and I think I'll get much more out of him face to face than either by email or over the phone. I should be there and back in the day, unless something completely unexpected happens.'

'Be careful, Inspector. You know what our loss rate is to date for witnesses. Let's not allow it to rise any further.'

'Just one more thing, ma'am,' Ted said hesitantly. 'I've decided to get a bit of help, personal help, with things from the past which this case has dredged up.'

He somehow couldn't bring himself to use the word counselling.

'I'm glad to hear that,' she said. 'Nobody should ever be afraid to seek help, it is never a sign of weakness.'

Ted had another call to make when he went back to his office. He dialled Willow's number and she answered almost immediately. He was itching to ask about Trev but he forced himself not to. She'd tell him if she had any further news.

'Sorry to bother you, I just wondered if you could perhaps help me out?' he asked. 'I have to go to London for the day on Monday. At least, I hope it will only be for the day. But just in case I get held up for any reason, I wondered if you could look in on the cats in the evening? Top up their food bowls and such?'

'I'd love to! You know how much I love the cats. Any excuse to come round and make a fuss of them,' she replied.

Willow adored animals, having grown up in the country surrounded by cats, dogs and horses. Her current lifestyle meant any kind of animal was out of the question, so Ted and Trev's cats were her surrogate pets.

'Do you still have a key?' Trev had given her one when she was getting over a bad relationship, before she met Rupert, so she would always have a bolt-hole if she needed one. 'If it's not too much trouble, are you free to pop round on Sunday evening, so I can show you what needs doing? The cats will all lie to you and demand too much food.'

She laughed. 'Not sure yet what I have on at the weekend but I'll phone you and let you know. The boys are fine, by the way,' she added, 'having fun, by the sound of it.'

Ted spent a lot of time at the weekend reading through all the stuff Steve had printed off for him, just to get an idea of what his mysterious contact might be able to tell him. He rewarded himself with some time out at his krav Maga Club, anxious to keep up with his recent training. The physical activity helped him stay focused more than anything else he had discovered.

Late on Sunday afternoon, as he was preparing food for the cats, he heard the front door open. He assumed it was Willow, letting herself in, but was surprised she had not telephoned him or rung the doorbell first. But it was Trev who came through into the kitchen and stood for a moment in the doorway looking at him, his expression neutral.

Ted didn't dare move or speak. He was so afraid of getting it wrong and seeing Trev go away again.

'Jim phoned me,' Trev told him. 'He told me about your conversation, and said you'd agreed to get help, at last. I thought perhaps you might need me to be around for that.'

'I'd really like that,' Ted told him. 'I didn't hear the bike when you arrived.'

'I left it outside.'

'Does that mean you're not staying?' Ted asked anxiously.

A slow smile spread over Trev's face, lighting up his blue eyes.

'I'm staying,' he said softly.

'Put the bike away first, so it doesn't get nicked,' Ted told him, his voice turning husky. 'Then let me show you how much I've missed you.'

Trev laughed aloud. 'Typical Ted! Always a copper first and a lover second. God, I've missed you.'

Chapter Forty

Ted caught the first train from Stockport to London in the morning. He had no idea who he was going to meet, so he wanted to be there in plenty of time to check out the meeting place for himself. He intended to get some sleep on the journey down as he'd not slept much the night before. First he took out his mobile to send a text to Jim Baker, saying simply, 'Trev home. Thanks.'

Ted would normally have walked the short distance from the station to the meeting point but he took a taxi to make sure that he arrived early. It was not a place he knew, and he wanted to check it out carefully with a trained police marksman's eye. He was not comfortable about meeting someone he did not know at all, not even by sight, but who clearly knew enough about him to be able to recognise him.

Away from the station, he had reverted to what Jim Baker always laughingly called his Mossad agent's uniform. A dark, soft cotton polo neck, black jeans, his old leather jacket - the colour of tobacco leaves - and his Doc Martens boots. He could blend in anywhere like that, and felt comfortable enough to move and to react to danger when necessary.

He found the café first and checked out the sight lines. He didn't like what he saw, but it would have to do as an initial point of contact. Then he went for a walk round to find what he considered a safer place to talk.

He returned to order a cappuccino and a Danish, then sat in the spring sunshine to enjoy his late breakfast. He chose a table where he could sit with his back to the wall and see everything that was going on in front of and to the sides of him.

He checked his watch occasionally. It was well past midday and still no call. He began to wonder if he had come on a wild goose chase. Then his mobile rang. An unknown caller. He picked up the call.

'Walk down to the duck pond, find an empty bench and wait for me there,' a voice told him.

Ted finished his breakfast first then got up, made his way down to the lake and sat on the nearest empty bench. He was consumed with curiosity but resisted the urge to keep looking around. Instead he simply sat, looking at the wildfowl on the water.

A jogger was coming towards him, a well-built black man in a track suit. As he got closer, he clutched at his hamstring and started to limp. He stopped at the end of the bench furthest from Ted and put his foot up on the back to do thigh stretches. He bent forward to take hold of his foot and pull it back towards him, as if easing a cramp.

Keeping his head down so no one could see he was talking, he said, 'You're the marksman and you've sussed the terrain. Where do you want to talk?'

Ted coughed and put his hand up to his mouth. 'Football pitch,' he said shortly, behind his hand then got up and walked away, not even looking at the man.

He didn't like much of the terrain, from a security point of view, but he'd picked out the playing fields as the most likely. As a specialised former firearms officer himself, he knew that it was the hardest part of the park in which to get off a shot with any degree of accuracy.

There was hardly anyone around. Nobody was playing on the fields at lunchtime on a Monday in school term time. The jogger caught him up and stood next to him. He was a lot taller than Ted, but then most men, especially police officers, were.

'So, what do you think I can help you with?' the man asked.

'My young TDC has been showing me the sort of posts you make. I'm investigating a paedophile ring on my patch, a young boy raped and strangled, and I think it goes high up, in terms of the people involved.'

'Steve's a TDC?' the man asked. 'I'm impressed. He's very bright. I can tell you now you're not likely to get far if you hope to go after those at the very top.'

'I think the Knave of Clubs may have been involved in this case,' Ted said.

To his surprise, the man laughed. 'Young boy raped and strangled? Wouldn't be the first time. He's known to get a bit carried away. But what makes you think you stand any chance of getting near him, when others have tried and failed?'

'You for one, I take it? Look, can I call you something, even if it's not your real name?'

The man shrugged. 'Call me Harry, if it makes you happier. And yes, I tried and failed. I was told from very high up not to stick my nose in where it didn't concern me. I took no notice, then the shit really hit the fan. If you think it's tough being a gay copper ...' he broke off at Ted's look. 'Oh yes, I checked you out very thoroughly before I agreed to a meeting. If you think that's hard, try being a black copper in the Met.

'They hit me with everything they had, even tried to do me for possessing indecent images of children. It was on my computer at work, evidence in a case I was working on. My house was broken into and ransacked several times. I had to move out and away from my family, for their safety.'

'I had a break-in too. They killed one of our cats, hanged him in the garden,' Ted told him.

'Just marking your card, showing you what they're capable of,' Harry said. 'In the end the force just paid me off and got rid of me. I'm still not sure why I didn't finish up under a bus, but maybe that's still to come. These people have eyes and ears everywhere and they all watch each other's backs. It goes high up within the police, too, that's half the problem.'

'We've currently got a high-ranking officer in our sights,' Ted told him.

'Let me guess. Simon the PIEman?'

'You're well informed.'

'Doesn't take a genius. I've been reading up everything I can find that's been happening on your patch, and I know he's not all that far away. You may get lucky, the ones at the top may throw you a few of the pond-life types lower down the chain,' Harry said. 'But you'll never get anywhere near the Knave, I can guarantee you that much.'

'Someone broke the news about the upcoming raid on Rory the Raver's place.'

'Not surprised. He was likely to squeal like a stuck pig once the noose closed around him,' Harry replied. 'They effectively silenced him forever. Where did he go, the Philippines, was it? He can never come back, so he doesn't need to do a deal with you. That means whatever he knows stays with him. You seem to have lost a few witnesses already, from what I've read and put together. I'd prepare yourself to lose a few more, to stop you getting at the truth.

'I'd be surprised if you were allowed to get near the PIEman, but there's always a first. He's in bed with his local MP. They scratch each other's backs. If you've got senior officers who will back you, you might have a sporting chance. Especially as you're not black and not in the Met.' There was dry humour in his voice.

'Shall we walk?' Ted suggested. 'We've been rather a long time in one spot for my liking.'

'You're the marksman, I'll go with your instincts on this one,' Harry said, as they started to move. As they walked, Harry told Ted more about the cases he'd worked on. From what he said it was clear he had been close on a few occasions to finding those higher up, but had been blocked at every turn. For perhaps the first time, it made Ted realise the finer points of the Ice Queen. At least she listened to him and had not yet tried to put a stop to any of his lines of enquiry.

The two men talked for almost two hours. A lot of it was useful to Ted in terms of what direction to go in. Harry refused the suggestion of coffee, preferring to keep out in the open and on the move. When it was time for Ted to leave, there was some warmth in the handshake.

'I have to keep on the move, I'm in and out of lodgings all the time these days, but I'll give you my mobile number so you can keep in touch. Bring down some of the big bastards, for me Ted, because I couldn't do it myself.'

'You've got my number, and if you ever need a safe house out of the city for a while, give me a call,' Ted told him as they parted, and he headed back to the station for the return train ride north.

Chapter Forty-one

Ted's team members were all grinning widely when they got together at the start of the next day. Ted hoped they had news of a breakthrough for him. They had not made much progress the previous week. They were two men down on the case. Sal and Virgil were both tied up with a serious assault and rape which had taken them out of the office on the previous Sunday, when Ted had been in.

Although Ted had come back feeling encouraged from his meeting with Harry in London, there was still nothing concrete he could offer as a result. He was looking forward to some good news. He nodded to Mike Hallam to start the briefing.

'We were on a roll yesterday, boss. The leads and breakthroughs just kept on coming. I'll let Sgt Reynolds kick things off.

'The missing lad, Brett Anderson, turned up and I got to talk to him at length,' she began. 'It seems Aiden Bradshaw was operating almost like a rent boy in his own right. He'd been abused so often in his life he'd started to see it as a way to make money, which can happen sometimes. He probably thought he was in control until the end, poor lad.

'Anyway, Brett went with him to the Sorrento one time. He didn't know the name of the place, but he identified it from photos I showed him. He said there was some sort of party going on, and he also talked about the ballroom with the wooden floor. He had a lot to drink and finished up in a room with David Evans. Evans gave him more alcohol. He doesn't remember any more until he woke up later the same night and

217

realised what had happened to him. He never went back.

'The very good news is that he immediately identified Evans from a photo. And, wait till you hear this, boss. I asked him about anyone else at the party. He told me there was a very tall man who looked like a vulture – his words. I showed him the photo of your Suspect A and he recognised him.'

On instructions from the Ice Queen, Ted had not yet released Danielson's name to his team, simply referring to him always as Suspect A. Only Steve knew who the man really was. Ted felt his hopes rising, sensing he now had Danielson in his sights, and Evans well and truly heading back to prison, hopefully this time for even longer.

Mike Hallam was still grinning like a Cheshire Cat.

'There's more good news, boss,' he said. 'We've started leaning hard on the hotel staff. I interviewed the receptionist, Chiara, yesterday, with Rob. She's obviously scared stiff, but it's clear she's not at all in favour of what's been happening at the hotel, and it's evident she was not aware of the full extent.

'She's agreed to talk, but only if she's fully protected. She has identified both Evans and Suspect A and says she would be willing to talk about other visitors to the hotel, but only if she's kept safe. She knows what happened to the waiter, of course.

'As you were out for the day, boss, I went to see the Ice …' Mike stopped himself just in time. Everyone in the station called her the Ice Queen behind her back but he knew Ted would never allow such disrespect in a team briefing, '… the Super, sir, and she's already had Chiara taken off to a safe house pending further questioning, which I thought you'd probably want to do.'

'Fantastic work, all of you, well done,' Ted said, pleased at so much progress.

Mike Hallam laughed. 'Oh, there's even more to come, boss,' he said. 'Steve and Sal have been busy tracking down who's behind the Sorrento Hotel. Sal?'

'Steve's done the donkey work on the computer, I've just

been chasing up the leads, with some help from Maurice. The actual owner is a man called Robert Smith, a convicted paedophile, who did twelve years for serious offences against young boys. He was the manager of a children's home, now moved to Sicily since his release and never sets foot in Britain, probably very wisely.

'There's a board of directors for the hotel and one of the names is a certain Miriam Danielson. The name meant something to young Steve, but I know he's been sworn to secrecy and he's said nothing. But I think that's good news for the enquiry.'

'The only reason I haven't told you all who Suspect A is at this stage is that it is a very delicate enquiry. While I hope you know I trust all of you implicitly, there have been leaks and we have lost witnesses, so I don't want to endanger any of you or take risks with the enquiry,' Ted told them.

'I'm going to talk to the Superintendent now about the possible arrest of a high ranking police officer, not in this division, as a result of what you've found out. So I think it had better be drinks on me after work for everyone. If we pull this off, this will be the highest ranking officer, to my knowledge, to be charged with offences of this nature.'

Before Ted went in search of the Ice Queen he made a quick phone call to Trev to ask if he wanted to join them for drinks that evening. Trev was popular with all of his team and often joined them at their usual watering hole, The Grapes, which a literary-minded graffiti artist had converted to The Grapes of Wrath on its pub sign.

The Ice Queen listened attentively to everything Ted had to report. His conversation with Harry the previous day had made him take a step back and consider his boss in a new light. He had to concede that she did always listen to him, even if she didn't agree with everything he said. So far, instead of putting him under pressure to ignore senior officers, she seemed to be doing all she could to help him catch the big fish. He'd finally believe it if and when Danielson was behind bars.

'It sounds as if you and your team now have enough to justify us going and bringing in the Chief Superintendent. I will sort out an arrest warrant and search warrants for his home, his computers and any other premises or property he has, then I think you and I should go and bring him in. I'll phone ahead on some pretext to make sure he's there. Shall we say tomorrow?'

Ted hesitated awkwardly. 'Er, ma'am, sorry, but I have my first appointment tomorrow,' he still found it difficult to use words like counselling or therapy. 'I could cancel it?'

'Absolutely not, out of the question,' she said firmly. 'I don't intend to pry at all into your reasons for needing help, but I strongly suspect you are someone who finds it hard to admit when you do need it. I imagine it's taken you some effort to build up to taking this step, so I don't want to do anything to delay your appointment.'

Ted couldn't hide a rueful grin. She certainly had his number.

'The Chief Super will keep until Thursday. It will give us more time to prepare thoroughly. Give me everything you have on him by the end of the day and I'll get warrants sorted,' she told him briskly. 'By the way, I must say you are looking better already than you have been of late. The first step is always the hardest. It goes on getting easier after that,' she said, in her most encouraging tone.

There was an air of optimism about the whole team that evening in the pub, and it was nice to see them all relaxing over a drink. Even better for Ted, now Trev was back at his side. Away from the office, Ted rid himself of his tie and unbuttoned his shirt collar so he, too, could relax.

The team were all making a big fuss of young Steve, much to his embarrassment. His computer skills had brought them on a lot with the case, especially the link to Suspect A through the Sorrento's board of directors. Danielson had probably thought himself clever in using his wife's name. Ted wondered if she actually knew anything at all about her husband's other life. From what he had seen on the video, he suspected there was no longer any intimacy in their relationship, and she might willingly turn a blind eye to what he got up to.

Ted wasn't feeling as apprehensive as he thought he would be about his first session of talking about his past on the next day. The Ice Queen was right. Taking the first step, talking to Jim, had been hard, but the hardest part of all had been picking up the phone to ask for help.

He looked fondly at Trev, who was laughing and talking with Sal and Rob, no doubt recounting his recent adventures in Berlin. He realised that getting help was something he should have done long ago. It had put an intolerable strain on their relationship, one which he now hugely regretted.

On an impulse, he moved across the room, took Trev by the elbow, excused himself to the others, and led him aside.

'Once this case is over, let's go away on a little holiday,' he said. 'We'll get someone in to look after the cats and we can go anywhere you like.'

It was rare for them to get away for much of a holiday, but Ted was determined that they should.

'Anywhere?' Trev asked with a laugh. He knew Ted didn't really share his love of travelling, especially by air, so he appreciated the offer. 'All right, then, deal. You catch the bad guys, I'll start planning where we should go.'

Chapter Forty-two

Ted took Jancis Reynolds with him to the safe house to interview the hotel receptionist, Chiara. Both he and the Ice Queen thought it would be safer to talk to her there, without risking her being seen going to the police station. She was being watched twenty-four hours a day by armed Close Protection Officers. The Ice Queen was determined not to lose another potentially valuable witness.

They took with them the means to record and film the conversation, together with photos for the witness to look through. To those of other known sex offenders on their patch, Ted had added a few still shots of Rory the Raver, David Evans, Simon Danielson and, just on the off chance, one of the Knave of Clubs.

It was clear from the outset that the woman was extremely scared. Ted was at pains to reassure her that she was not currently under suspicion of any crime. He was also anxious to point out to her how completely her life would change if she did testify, and was placed under the Witness Protection Programme.

'I don't care if I have to leave this place and never see it again. I honestly had no real idea of what was going on at the hotel,' she told him. 'I knew there were sometimes children hanging around, but I swear I didn't know how bad it was. We were all told to keep our mouths shut about anything we saw. I thought it was just because some of the guests were celebrities and VIPs.'

'Celebrities like him?' Ted asked, showing her a picture of

Rory the Raver.

'Oh yes, he came a few times. But he wasn't there the night the little boy died, I'm sure of that,' she said.

'Are any of these faces familiar?' Ted asked, spreading out a few more photos, mostly local sex offenders, including David Evans, but with a few stock photos in there to test her powers of observation. They included some of people who were long dead. If she picked any of those, he would know her testimony was not infallible.

Her hand went unerringly to the shot of David Evans. 'He's been a few times too, I recognise him, but none of the others.'

'What about any of these?' This time his selection included Simon Danielson and, on a long shot, the MP for Danielson's local constituency.

'Oh I know him,' she said immediately, pointing to Danielson. 'Hard to miss him, or forget him. He's very tall and used to lurk around looking like a vulture waiting for the lions to finish. Him, too, although not often,' she said, indicating the MP.

Ted risked an exchanged glance with Jancis. Full score so far. He decided to go for broke. 'Anyone here?' he asked, spreading out a random assortment of photos which included a snapshot of the Knave of Clubs.

This time she hesitated slightly, poring over the pictures, pulling some closer to study in more detail, pushing others aside. Finally she put a finger on the one of the Knave of Clubs.

'This one, I think. I'm pretty certain I've seen him at the hotel, only once, I think, but quite recently.'

'Could you be more specific about a date?' Ted pressed.

'He was there at the same time as The Vulture, I'm pretty certain of that, as I think I remember them exchanging a few words. I don't know who this one is but I think he must be another celebrity, because he had a couple of men with him who seemed to be like bodyguards,' she said.

'Can you tell me what happened on the night Aiden Bradshaw died?'

'There was a block booking for a firm, Parish's Pies. They've been before. It's like their works dinner dance, that sort of thing. They had a meal but they mostly went off to bed early. I was on the reception desk till midnight,;it's not manned through the night.

'Just as I was getting ready to leave, someone came downstairs looking for Mr Rossi. Then there was a lot of commotion, a bit of a sense of panic really. I thought perhaps something had been stolen in one of the guests' rooms. Mr Rossi came back down looking very worried, but he told me to go, practically bundled me out of the door, and said he would deal with whatever it was.

'I heard the next day, of course, about a little boy's body being found not far away, but even then I didn't really connect it to the hotel, I honestly didn't. And I had more things on my mind. The whole computer system was down. Mr Rossi said it had crashed but he was getting it sorted. But everything was wiped, we lost all the hotel records, everything. The men who came to fix it seemed to make it worse, if anything.'

'What about the waiter, Iosif? Was he there that night?'

'He was on duty, yes, but that was the last time I saw him,' she said. 'Poor Iosif, he was a kind man but not at all bright. We were all shocked when we heard what had happened to him. Shocked, and terrified. We were starting to wonder what we were mixed up in, but Mr Rossi kept telling us to keep our mouths shut and we would be fine.'

Ted started to gather up the photos. 'Thank you, you've been a great help to us.'

'Enough to keep me safe?' she asked anxiously.

'We are doing everything we can to protect you, hence the armed officers with you twenty-four hours a day,' Ted reassured her. 'I know it's not easy for you, being cut off from friends and family like this, and I'd like to thank you for being brave enough to speak up.'

'I have no family,' she said, 'that's why I came to England for a new start. But perhaps it's time for me to start all over again, somewhere else. I swear to God I knew nothing of what was really going on. I like to think I'd have been brave enough not to stand by and let that happen to children without doing something.'

'Bingo, boss,' Jancis said as they walked back to the car. 'She seems like a very credible witness.'

'As long as we can keep her safe until she testifies, if she's willing to,' he replied.

Ted had deliberately chosen a Wednesday afternoon for the first of his counselling sessions. He suspected he might be in the mood to let off steam afterwards and it was his day for the dojo after work. He'd also left himself time to nip home and change into his casual clothes before turning up for his appointment. He knew he was going to find it hard enough to sit indoors and talk about himself to a virtual stranger, without feeling he was being strangled by his shirt and tie at the same time.

Countless times during the day he considered picking up his phone and cancelling, not sure he could go through with it. But he knew he owed it to Trev to get some professional help at last, and he also knew both Jim and the Ice Queen would be on his case if he failed to attend.

Just in case he found it even harder than he expected, he put a bag of Fisherman's Friend in his pocket as he left the house.

He arrived promptly for his appointment and obeyed the sign on the door telling him to ring the bell and enter. The waiting room was decorated in soft creams and sages, intended to create a calming ambience, with pastel water colour prints as focal points. There was no one else there so Ted hoped he wouldn't have long to wait or he feared he would simply turn tail and run. He was too on edge to sit down.

The door to an inner room opened and a pleasantly smiling woman emerged, hand outstretched to shake his. 'It's nice to be able to put a face to the voice on the phone, finally,' she said. 'Why don't you come in and sit down. Then in your own time you can tell me how I can help you.'

It felt to Ted like the longest half-hour he had ever spent, and he didn't manage to say very much. When he got home, Trev was waiting anxiously to hear how it had gone. He had the kettle on ready and was making Ted's green tea when he walked through the door.

Seeing Ted's despondent look, he didn't say anything, just folded him in a hug and held him.

Eventually Ted spoke, his voice muffled against Trev's chest. 'I felt so stupid. I just couldn't start to speak. I sat there like a lemon most of the time, although she kept telling me that was fine.'

'Of course it was fine,' Trev said reassuringly, 'it was the first time and it was a big step. Next time will be better, and every time after that. Come on, drink your tea and let's go and equip some more kids for the big wide world.'

Ted was unusually quiet on the walk down to the gym, and even Trev's efforts to cheer him up were falling short. Hopefully a hard training session would lift his sombre mood.

Flip was the first of the children to arrive for the training session, again with his foster mother in tow, and he ran across the gym in obvious delight to see Trev back. But it was always to Ted he turned, and this time he did so beaming with pride.

'Look Ted, me foster mam's bought me a judogi,' he grinned. The judo outfit was slightly too big for him. Ted had suggested they leave him a bit of room to grow into it. 'Is me belt tied right?' he asked anxiously.

He was wearing his red sixth kyu belt, the starting grade. Ted bent down to check it for him. 'Perfect, Flip, well done,' he told him. 'You look great.'

Trev was watching him, a smile on his face. 'That kid thinks the sun shines out of you. And it's nice to see he has the power to cheer you up,' he said when Flip went off to start his warm up exercises.

'I see a bit of me at that age in him,' Ted admitted, before calling the juniors to order and getting the session under way.

Flip was on his best form, so proud now that he was wearing the right outfit, and clearly dying to show off to his foster mother. After the session she came closer to the mat to speak to Ted.

'Flip wanted to know if we could stay to watch you and Trev training,' she told him. 'And he wants to find out about signing up for junior judo classes. I've said he can.'

'I'm sure that will be all right, Mrs Atkinson, I'll just check with Bernard,' Ted told her.

'Flip, you go and get changed now, then we can watch together,' Flip's foster mother told him.

Flip's face fell. 'Can't I keep me judogi on a bit longer?' he asked hopefully.

'You'll get cold, not good for your muscles after working hard,' Ted explained, so the boy trotted off obediently to the changing rooms.

'He has a serious case of hero worship for you,' Mrs Atkinson said, but she was smiling indulgently. 'He says he's going to join the police when he's old enough. Oh, and I haven't said too much to him yet because there's still a long way to go, but my husband and I are hoping to adopt him officially.'

Ted smiled in delight. 'That is possibly the best news I've had all day.'

Chapter Forty-three

Ted and the Ice Queen set off in good time the next morning. Their journey should take them no more than an hour and a half but they took an area car so they could use blues and twos to get them through any dense traffic so they would arrive on time.

The Ice Queen drove and Ted was not surprised to discover that she was an excellent driver. She had phoned ahead to make an appointment with the Chief Superintendent, on a pretext. He hopefully had no idea they were in fact going to arrive with a warrant for his arrest.

There was a secretary sitting protectively at her desk outside Danielson's office when they arrived. The Ice Queen was at her most formidable as she swept past the woman saying, 'There's no need to announce us, the Chief is expecting us.'

After a peremptory knock at the door, she strode in, Ted trailing in her majestic wake. Danielson half rose to his feet, his vulture's face darkening with anger at the abrupt intrusion. Ted noticed he was quick to close the lid of his laptop as they came in.

'It's customary to wait for an invitation to enter before barging in, Superintendent,' he said coldly.

'Ordinarily I would agree, sir,' she said levelly, 'but this is not a social call. I have to tell you that DI Darling and I are here with a warrant for your arrest under the Sexual Offences Act. You do not have to say anything. But it may harm your defence if you do not mention when questioned something you later rely on in court. Anything you say may be given in evidence.'

Danielson glared at her. 'If this is a joke, it is in extremely poor taste. I will be reporting this matter to your superiors.'

'No joke, sir, and I can assure you that I am here with their full knowledge and support. Now, in deference to your senior rank, I am happy to keep your exit as low key as possible, if you would be kind enough to co-operate.'

He gave a harsh bark which may have been laughter.

'I am going nowhere until I phone my solicitor. This is outrageous!'

'No, sir, it is standard police procedure in a serious enquiry. You will, of course, be allowed to telephone your solicitor as soon as we arrive at Stockport. For now I am asking you to come quietly and keep this as civil as possible.'

There was a timid knock on the door and the secretary bravely put her head round.

'Is everything all right, Chief?' she asked anxiously.

'Yes, yes, fine, Mrs Harris, please don't worry,' he waved her away with one hand. 'I'm just having to go up to Stockport with these officers to clear up some sort of mix-up. You have my solicitor's number, please phone him and ask him to contact me on my mobile number, urgently. And please cancel my appointments for the rest of the day. I'm not sure what time I will be back.'

When she withdrew from the office, Danielson turned back to lock eyes with the Ice Queen, his face contorting with fury.

'You are making a very serious mistake, both of you. One which is going to cost you both your careers. I'll have the two of you back on the beat, if you even survive in the force at all.'

'Please don't attempt to threaten or intimidate either myself or DI Darling, sir. It won't work on either of us and it's merely a fruitless time-wasting exercise. I would strongly advise you simply to accompany us quietly out of the building. Once we arrive at Stockport, you will of course be allowed to call your solicitor.'

His lips curled in contempt.

'You have absolutely no idea what you are venturing into,' he sneered. 'You are going to regret this. It will take my solicitor some time to get to Stockport.'

'And of course no questioning will commence until he is present. I really do urge you strongly to come quietly now, sir,' the Ice Queen persisted, completely unruffled by the threats. Ted was impressed. 'If this really can all be sorted out to your benefit, then the sooner we do so, the better.'

Still muttering angrily, the Chief Superintendent grabbed his tunic and put it on as they headed for the door. His office was on the second floor. As the three of them made their way down the stairs, doors opened and heads looked out in curiosity at the sight of the station's most senior officer being escorted away by a uniformed superintendent and a short, insignificant-looking man in plain clothes.

The car they had come in was parked as close to the main entrance as possible. As they started across the car park, they heard the sound of running feet behind them. With his finely tuned self-defence instincts, Ted whirled on the balls of his feet, ready to face whatever threat they might represent.

A voice was shouting, 'Ma'am, excuse me, I need to speak to you.'

A uniformed inspector was hurrying towards them clutching a fat, over-stuffed file, which he thrust towards the Ice Queen.

'If someone is finally arresting the Chief Super, you'll want to take a look at this on his friend, our illustrious MP. I've been trying to get him to act on it for months and he's been ordering me to bury it.'

The Ice Queen had never yet had chance to see Ted in action. Afterwards she was quite incapable of accurately reporting the sequence of events, it all happened so quickly. They had to rely on CCTV footage from the front of the station to confirm what took place.

The uniformed inspector seemed to lose control at the same time as Danielson did. Clark, they later discovered his name was, launched himself in fury at the suspect, fists flying, as the Chief Super first tried to block his attack then started aiming blows at Ted so he could make a break for it.

Ted went straight into action. A carefully controlled kick to the solar plexus took Clark down to his knees and left him gasping for air, unable to move. In the next instant, the Chief Superintendent was face down across the car bonnet, one hand behind his back, completely immobilised but seemingly unharmed.

'Perhaps you could lend me your handcuffs, ma'am, just as a precaution?' Ted asked, not even out of breath.

'With pleasure, Inspector,' she said, as she cuffed Danielson and carefully installed him in the back seat of the area car. 'Which of your four martial arts was that?'

Ted grinned. 'That was what in musical terms I think they call a mash-up.'

He moved over to where Clark was slowly regaining his breath and squatted down beside him.

'Are you all right?' he asked anxiously. 'I pulled the kick as much as I dared but I had to stop you. You can imagine what his solicitor would have done with a police brutality allegation as we were arresting him.'

Clark nodded and got warily to his feet.

'Yes, sorry, I just lost it for a moment there. We all know the rumours about him and his pals. Several of us have been trying for ages to bring them down. Looks like you might be about to succeed. Thanks,' he said and shook Ted's hand.

Ted took off his jacket and said to the Ice Queen, 'Ma'am, you'll have to excuse me being in shirt sleeves. It seems this suit was not made with martial arts in mind, surprisingly. The

seam at the shoulder has gone right round the sleeve and
halfway down it on both sides.'

'Give me your jacket and you drive,' she ordered. 'I have a
repair kit in my bag. It won't be invisible mending, in a moving
vehicle, but you will at least be decent by the time we get
back.'

Ted laughed as he got into the driver's seat and pulled it
forward to accommodate his shorter legs. He was somehow not
surprised. She was the sort who probably travelled with
everything she might need for all eventualities.

She worked meticulously all the way, clearly a
perfectionist. It was not easy, even though Ted tried to drive as
carefully as possible. Danielson kept up a continuous barrage
of threats and complaints all the way, but they largely ignored
him. Ted noticed there had been no phone call from his
solicitor.

The Ice Queen was just putting the finishing touches to her
needlework as Ted swung the car into the car park in front of
the station, where he said under his breath, 'Houston, we have
a problem.'

She looked up immediately. There were reporters and
cameras swarming all over the front of the station. However
they had got wind of who was being brought in, the press
clearly had heard and swung rapidly into action.

'Drive round the back, the last thing we want is a media
circus,' the Ice Queen ordered. Pulling out her mobile she
phoned Kevin Turner to get him to stall the press pack while
they brought Danielson in through the back entrance. 'Perhaps
you would be kind enough to lend your jacket to stop the
suspect's face from appearing on tonight's news, Inspector.
And as soon as we get in, I want to know just how this leak has
happened.'

'If I might make an educated guess, ma'am,' Ted said as he
manoeuvred the car back out into the traffic to head for the rear
entrance, 'I would say that the Chief Super is not exactly top of

the popularity polls in his own station, and his officers have already started throwing him to the wolves.'

Ted's comment brought a further stream of vitriol from their suspect, which told him he was probably on the button.

Chapter Forty-four

The Ice Queen herself was going to question Danielson, with Ted sitting in. They followed the rules to the letter to get him booked in, carefully reminding him he was still under caution. The first thing was to allow him his one phone call to his solicitor, as he had not heard from him on the journey to Stockport.

They had installed him in an interview room, with a uniformed officer just by the door, and made sure he had been offered refreshment. Neither of them was taking any chances at all.

'Would you like us to leave the room while you call your solicitor, sir?' the Ice Queen asked politely, removing his handcuffs.

'There is no need for that,' he snarled. 'I want you two cretins to realise from the start what a serious error of judgement you are making.'

He took out his mobile phone, found the number he required and dialled it. The call was answered quickly.

'Michael? It's Simon. You obviously didn't get my message ... ' he broke off, clearly being interrupted at the other end.

'Yes, but ... ' again he was cut short.

He listened for a moment, his face draining of colour. Then he said stiffly, 'I see,' and ended the call.

He cleared his throat and said, 'Unfortunately my solicitor is, er, on another case, out of the area, and can't get here.'

'No problem at all, sir, would you like me to arrange a

local one for you?' the Ice Queen offered. Danielson nodded curtly.

'Very well. Inspector Darling and I will take a short break whilst that is arranged. I would just remind you that you are under arrest, therefore you are not free to leave. An officer will be posted with you at all times. As you have now made your one permitted phone call, I must ask you to give me your mobile phone. Its contents come under the terms of the search warrant I have, a copy of which I will give you shortly. As soon as a solicitor arrives for you, Inspector Darling and I will return to begin the interview.'

'Your inspector is nothing but a thug,' Danielson snarled. 'I shall be pursuing a claim against him for excessive force,' he gingerly touched the side of his face. 'My cheekbone is very painful from where he slammed my head against the car, without justification.'

'In that case, I will arrange a visit from the police surgeon to assess the extent of your injuries, sir. I will also telephone your own station and request tape from the CCTV cameras, which I notice you have conveniently covering the access to the building and part of the car park. They will, of course, be made available to you, should you so wish. And indeed to me, as I shall be adding a charge against you of assault on a constable in the execution of his duty, contrary to section 89(1) of the Police Act 1996.'

She marched off down the corridor issuing a short, 'Follow me,' order over her shoulder to Ted. She paused to tap on Inspector Turner's door and put her head round when he answered.

'If I find out it was anyone in this station who tipped off the press to the arrival of the Chief Super, I will personally have their guts for garters. And if anyone at all says so much as one word to those jackals outside, even if it's only hello, the consequences will be dire. Do I make myself clear, Inspector?' she asked him.

'Crystal, ma'am,' Kevin replied.

'And make sure that a solicitor is found for Mr Danielson as soon as possible, please. Let me know when one arrives. Get him checked out by the police surgeon, too. He is complaining of pain in his cheek from when Inspector Darling was obliged to restrain him,' she added, then said to Ted, 'Come to my office. I want to see if there is anything on the national news about this already. It's really the last thing we need.'

She opened a twenty-four news channel on her computer. She and Ted watched as a journalist did a piece to camera in front of the unmistakable façade of their own station.

'We have no confirmation at this stage and no statement has been issued yet, but sources tell us a high-ranking police officer may be in custody here at Stockport, in connection with an ongoing enquiry into alleged child sex abuse.'

'Damn,' she said, to Ted's surprise, as she muted the sound but left the channel running. 'That is not what we want happening on our doorstep right now.'

The phone on her desk rang and she said to Ted, 'No prizes for guessing who this will be,' as she picked up the call.

Ted was not sure whether to leave the office or not, opting to lurk by the window so he could at least look out at passing traffic. The Ice Queen was not able to say very much other than 'yes, sir, no sir,' in the brief pauses in what was clearly a tirade from an executive officer.

She hung up the call and grimaced at Ted in an almost conspiratorial way.

'As you can imagine, the top brass are not amused, to say the least. Sit down. Would you like coffee?'

He nodded and thanked her. For the first time in their working relationship to date, he felt she might almost be glad of his company.

'So, are we going to snatch defeat from the jaws of victory or can we still turn this around and get some convictions, do you think?' she asked.

'We've done everything by the book. The only person in this station except for us and Kevin Turner who knew the identity of this suspect is TDC Ellis. I would bet a year's salary that he hasn't spoken to anyone. I wouldn't have known about Danielson if Steve hadn't found details of him on the website. He will want him convicted so he wouldn't take any risks of compromising the enquiry.'

'Your loyalty to your team is commendable. However, we must recognise the fact that there have been several leaks of information. We need to make sure going forward that we can get a solid case again him. I've put things in motion for the search of his property. Once we find out what else he has lurking on his computer, we should have a watertight case against him. Any theories as to why his high-powered brief seems to have dropped him like a hot potato?'

She served them both coffee as she was speaking. Ted realised they had just had a conversation without her constantly calling him Inspector or him calling her ma'am.

'They must surely be worried that he'll start to name names in an attempt to do a deal, if we have too much on him,' he said.

'If we succeed in getting him remanded in custody, and I see no reason why we shouldn't, I am going to make sure he is kept in solitary confinement and on twenty-four-hour suicide watch. I am not letting any more suspects or witnesses slip through our fingers.

'We should probably both quickly grab something to eat so we're ready as soon as the solicitor arrives to continue the questioning. I intend now to show Danielson some of the photographs we have so far, just to let him know he is not as clever as he thinks he is.

'But first I must go and issue a very brief statement to our friends from the press pack outside, which should, I hope, have been forwarded to me,' she was scanning her emails as she spoke. 'I take it you would prefer not to be involved in that side of things?'

'Quite happy to leave it up to you, ma'am, I'm sure you're far better at it than I am,' Ted told her, as he went off in search of food. He had taken the precaution of bringing a sandwich with him, not knowing what time he would get to have dinner in a potentially busy day. He had enough time to eat it, drink his tea and polish off a date and cashew bar for an energy boost, before he was summoned to go with the Ice Queen to start interviewing the Chief Super.

He sat back to watch his new boss at work. It was the first time he had seen her in action and he was impressed. She was icily polite at all times, economical with words yet relentless. She laid out for Danielson the case they had against him so far. As she spoke, she started to place still shots of the naked officer in a hotel room, with Aiden Bradshaw, on the table in front of him. The man's face slowly turned a deathly pale and his hands were visibly shaking as she did so.

The solicitor who had come was a local man, Ian Barnes, thoroughly professional though pedestrian. He was certainly not at all of the calibre of the one Danielson had no doubt expected to appear to represent him. Barnes had been visibly shaken to find his new client wearing the pip and crown of a chief superintendent, but quickly regained an impassive expression. He quietly and repeatedly advised his client to say nothing at this stage.

'Mr Danielson,' the Ice Queen began, deliberately dropping his rank now that he was nothing more than a common suspect. 'As you know, you have already been cautioned prior to interview about several offences under the Sexual Offences Act. Now we come to something rather more serious.

'I have reason to believe that the adult in these pictures, which were taken from a video retrieved from your cloud storage, is you. It is my belief that the location in which the film was shot is the Hotel Sorrento, here in Stockport. The child in the tape and photos has already been identified as

Aiden Bradshaw.

'Aiden was murdered on a date after these particular films were taken, and we have an eye witness who places you at the hotel on the date he died. We will require a sample of your DNA in order to continue our investigations into this young boy's death.

'Because of your connection to this boy, it is my intention now to charge you with an additional offence of conspiracy to murder. You will be held here for up to ninety-six hours, and we will apply for extensions as necessary. You will then appear before magistrates to be further remanded. We will be opposing any application for bail on the grounds of the serious nature of the charges.

'You will now be handed over to the custody sergeant who will take charge of all your personal possessions, for which you will of course receive a receipt. Do you understand, sir?'

'You really do not know who you are going up against, Superintendent. You are going to regret your actions for a very long time.'

Chapter Forty-five

Ted's office phone was ringing before he got through the door the next morning. He picked it up quickly and a voice asked, 'Is that Ted Darling?'

'It is,' he said rather warily, as he didn't immediately recognise the voice.

'It's Bob Clark, we met yesterday. I was on the receiving end of a pretty impressive karate kick.'

The voice was totally without rancour so Ted chuckled and said, 'Yes, sorry about that. How are you today?'

'I have a colourful bruise forming,' came the rueful response. 'If that was you pulling a kick, I hope I never meet you when you're in the mood to cause serious injury. Anyway, that's not why I called. This news hasn't broken yet and I thought you'd want to be one of the first to hear it.

'I imagine you were probably too busy yesterday to look at the file I gave you on our perverted MP? Well, I have an update for you. I'm just back from his place and he's dead. Found hanging early this morning by the cleaner, who didn't expect him to be there. He should have been at his London flat and sitting in the House today.'

Ted let out a low whistle.

'Shit,' he said. 'I suppose it's definitely a suicide? No chance someone strung him up?'

'Doubt it, you know as well as I do how rare murder by hanging is,' Clark replied. 'My guess is that he heard you had his friend, our Chief, in custody and didn't want to take the risk of what, and especially who, he might start talking about to cut himself a deal.'

At that moment there was a brief knock on Ted's door and the Ice Queen swept in, not looking best pleased. Ted immediately sprang to his feet and said into the phone, 'I have to go now, Bob, thanks for putting me in the picture. I hope we'll meet again one day soon, I feel I owe you a drink or two.'

'You've heard, then?' the Ice Queen asked, sitting down in response to Ted's gesture.

Ted nodded. 'That was Bob Clark on the phone, just filling me in. Would you like a cup of green tea, ma'am?'

'Why not?' she said, her tone slightly weary. 'We're clearly going to need something calming to get us through the day. Thank you.'

She had with her the thick file Bob Clark had handed her the day before, which she now put on Ted's desk.

'Is it such a bad thing, though?' Ted asked, putting a mug of tea in front of her. 'It might make Danielson's tongue a bit looser, when he knows another of his friends in high places is no longer there for him. I take it we are going to tell him what's happened?'

'I think we are morally obliged to, if nothing else. It does narrow his options considerably if he was thinking of offering us some names in exchange for a deal, once he realises no one is going to come to his rescue, and yet another of the names is no longer around.'

'Would he offer up the Knave of Clubs?' Ted asked. 'I've already got a fairly strong ID on him from the receptionist at the hotel, and her witness statement about him seeming to know Danielson.'

She sipped her tea and said, 'I think we have to take a reality check at this stage. Despite all our best efforts and desire to do so, we may possibly need to accept that our chances of taking down even a very minor member of the extended royal family are slight. As you have said yourself, some of the events in this enquiry have all the hallmarks of our friends from the Security Services.'

'Surely we have to try, at least? Shouldn't someone try, for all the kids like Aiden out there?'

'I agree, in principle, but let's not forget the collateral damage. Two key witnesses shot, one about to turn Queen's evidence stabbed to death in prison. And I include your poor little cat in the tally. In view of all that's happened, I'm inclined to agree with you that its killing was no coincidence. So who might be next? You? A member of your team?'

She could see the frustration on Ted's face and shared it.

'Why not spend some time today going through this file on the MP, see if there are any links in there you could exploit. But please take extreme care. We are clearly in dangerous waters. What I might be able to do is to get the MP's DNA cross-checked against Aiden Bradshaw's, to see if there was any contact there, just so that we know, at least.'

She finished her tea and rose to go. 'Thank you for the tea. I'd just like a few words with your team. They've done excellent work, it's only right that I tell them so.'

Ted followed her into the outer office. His team members were all at their desks working and waiting on him for the morning briefing. Seeing the Ice Queen in their territory, they all shot to their feet except for Steve. His nose was, as usual, buried in his computer so he was totally unaware of what was going on around him. Eventually, Maurice, who sat nearest to him, hissed a warning. Steve looked up, saw the Superintendent looking at him and leapt up so quickly his chair flew back and almost tipped over.

'I just wanted to say that you have all done extremely good work in difficult circumstances. I also wanted to tell you, before the news breaks officially, that the man we have in custody is Chief Superintendent Simon Danielson. His identity must remain strictly confidential until his first appearance before magistrates, the date and time of which has not yet been decided.

'Very few people know who he is, so were it to become known by the press at this stage, each and every one of you would come under suspicion of having leaked the information. I would take an extremely dim view of that. Thank you again.'

She turned back to Ted. 'Shall we say ten o'clock to resume our interview of Mr Danielson? I will tell Inspector Turner to arrange for his solicitor to get here by then.'

Ted had the file on the MP in his hand. He set it down in front of Maurice. 'Maurice, I want you and Steve to work on this all day. Go through every lead Inspector Clark had found. In particular, I want you to try and trace any time when either Danielson or the MP were at any event at the same time as the Knave of Clubs. I assume Steve will be able to find that out with his usual computer wizardry. I just have to make a phone call, then I can probably give you some dates when there were similar cases to Aiden's in and around London, the Knave's regular hunting ground, I presume.'

Ted went back to his office to make the call on his mobile. It was answered on the first ring.

'Morning, Ted. I hear you have a big fish on the end of your line.'

'Morning, Harry. We have him, and we are hopefully about to net him,' Ted told his new contact. 'But it's still not a big enough fish for my taste, so I wondered if you could help me?'

'Try me.'

'You mentioned deaths in connection with the Knave of Clubs. Are there any dates or details you could let me have in that respect? I want to cross check his movements with some of our suspects.'

'Remember that anything I could give you is not official, and you certainly didn't get it from me,' Harry replied. 'But I'll try and get something to you today, before the weekend. Shall I email it to your young Steve?'

Ted agreed, thanked him and rang off. His desk phone rang almost immediately. This time it was a familiar voice, one he detested, the oily, sycophantic tones of a local newspaper reporter. Ted had no time for the press. He found this one particularly hard to stomach because of his disconcerting habit of playing 'pocket billiards' the whole time, which was distracting face to face.

'DI Darling, what can you tell me about the police officer you have in custody?' came the wheedling voice.

'Nothing at all, Alastair, you're wasting your time,' Ted replied brusquely. 'You'll find out everything there is to know if and when there's a remand hearing in court.'

'Can you at least tell me when that's likely to be?'

'No,' Ted snapped shortly and rang off, then headed downstairs to find the Ice Queen so they could have another crack at Danielson.

The Chief Superintendent had clearly not spent a comfortable night in police custody. His once immaculate uniform shirt was crumpled, his trousers creased. He looked haggard and drawn but most of all his expression, as Ted and the Ice Queen sat down opposite him and his solicitor in the interview room, was one of raw fury.

'You have made a serious error of judgement, Superintendent,' he began, his eyes flashing. 'I have friends in high places. They are not going to be at all pleased to hear of your actions against me.'

'I am sorry to be the bearer of bad news, sir,' she replied levelly, 'but I am afraid you have one friend fewer than before. I have to tell you that your MP, also a personal friend, I believe, Richard Morgan, was found dead at his home early this morning. The enquiry is not yet complete but it would appear that he took his own life. Perhaps you may be able to help with that enquiry? Are you aware of anything which may currently have been troubling Mr Morgan?'

Ted saw a number of emotions flash across Danielson's face. The most striking one was probably fear when he realised the safety net he thought was in place was rapidly unravelling.

The Ice Queen's questions were relentless and probing but, partly on his solicitor's advice and also on his own initiative, Danielson was saying nothing.

Eventually his solicitor spoke up.

'Look, Superintendent, you have already charged my client with a number of offences, now you really must put him before magistrates for remand. Time is getting short, with the weekend nearly upon us. I shall, of course, be applying in the strongest possible terms for bail for my client.'

'Which I will be resisting in equally strong terms,' she countered smoothly. 'And you are right, we need to take decisive action now. I will arrange for a special remand hearing later this afternoon after which I very much hope, Mr Danielson, you will enjoy a comfortable weekend in prison.'

'This is outrageous!' Danielson said, his voice rising. 'You cannot remand me in custody, you know perfectly well what happens to police officers in prison.'

He half rose from his seat. Ted was on his feet in an instant, calm and in control, but the message was clear. Although Danielson towered above him, the man already knew there was nothing he could do physically against Ted. So far his threats and bullying had proved ineffectual against either of them.

'Please sit down, sir, until the Superintendent has finished speaking to you,' Ted said politely.

The remand hearing was a formality. Bail was refused and Danielson was led away to a prison van, to enjoy his first taste of what it was like to be behind bars.

Ted was keen to share the news of some success with his team before they broke for the weekend. It would be a good morale booster in a difficult case.

'Have a good weekend, all of you. Who's on duty this weekend?'

'Me and Virgil, boss,' Mike Hallam told him.

'You again, Virgil? Weren't you on last weekend?'

'I volunteered, boss. I'm in dead lumber with the missus yet again and she was threatening to take me shopping,' Virgil grinned.

'Right, well, enjoy yourselves, whatever you're up to, see you all on Monday. And Steve, try to take a break from the computer, for once!'

Chapter Forty-six

Ted had enjoyed a great weekend with some time off. He and Trev had been hill walking in the Peak District and enjoyed a meal out, which always put him in good spirits. He felt more relaxed and in control than he had for some time. He hoped the rest of his team were also feeling recharged.

Unusually, there was no sign of Steve when they were just starting the morning catch-up.

'Anyone heard from him, or know where he is?' Ted asked, but no one had any idea where he might be. 'Does he have a girlfriend, someone he's seeing, who may have distracted him?'

'No girlfriend, boss, Steve's in love with his computer,' Virgil said quickly, amidst some laughter.

Mike Hallam tried phoning his mobile number but the call went straight to voice-mail. He left a brief message, asking Steve to call in.

'It's not like him,' Ted said, a note of concern in his voice. 'If we haven't heard anything by late morning, I think a couple of you ought to go round, just to check on him. Maurice, can you sort that and keep me posted? I don't like that we've not heard anything, not even a phone call.'

There was still no word by lunch time, so Maurice asked Rob to go with him to check out Steve's address. Rob immediately volunteered to drive and take his own car. Since his divorce, Maurice fought a constant battle between trying to stop smoking and binge eating sticky buns to deal with the nicotine cravings. His car famously smelled like an old ash tray and was full of crumbs and food wrappers.

Steve rented a poky basement flat in a house on the edge of town which had known better days. Maurice and Rob picked their way down the exterior stone steps, carefully edging round empty chip papers and takeaway wrappings. The curtains were closed and there was no sign of life.

Maurice knocked loudly, both on the door and on the window but no one opened up. There was a letter box in the door which he tried shouting through.

'Doesn't look as if he's here,' Rob said, turning to go back up the steps.

'Hang on, listen a minute,' Maurice told him, his ear to the open letter flap. 'There's someone in there, I can hear a noise.' He put his mouth back to the flap and called, 'Steve? Steve, lad, are you in there? It's Maurice.'

He listened again then turned to Rob. 'It sounds like someone groaning.'

He stepped back from the door and lifted a foot.

'What are you doing?' Rob asked. 'You can't just kick the door in.'

'Got a better idea?' Maurice asked as his foot crashed into the flimsy door, which yielded immediately, bursting back against the inside wall.

They stepped straight into a small kitchen, a sink and units against the left wall, a small cooker and a couple of cupboards in front of them, with an open doorway leading to a room behind. The place looked like a bomb had hit it, but neither Maurice nor Rob knew Steve well enough to tell if that was the way he normally lived.

Maurice led the way through the doorway into a bed-sitting room. There was a cheap desk against the right-hand wall, with what had clearly been an expensive, top of the range computer sitting on it, now smashed almost beyond recognition. Clothing and possessions were strewn all over the floor.

In a narrow bed, pushed up against the left-hand wall, a

huddled form lay under a heap of bedclothes, groaning quietly. Maurice approached the bed cautiously and gently pulled back the covers at the head end.

Steve's face, what they could see of it as he lay huddled on his side facing the wall, was swollen, battered and bloody. They could both now clearly hear that he was moaning to himself and crying.

Gently, Maurice perched on the bed beside him. 'Steve, lad, whatever happened to you?'

Then he looked at Rob and said, 'Phone an ambulance, then get on the blower to the boss and tell him to send SOCO.'

At his words, Steve tried to stir and caught hold of Maurice's sleeve with his left hand. Maurice could see that the right hand was bloodied, black and blue. Steve tried to keep his voice quiet so only Maurice would hear him.

'No ambulance, please, I don't want anyone seeing me like this. I've wet myself,' he said pleadingly.

'Don't worry about that, bonny lad,' Maurice said soothingly. 'That's just normal, nothing they haven't seen before.'

'Please,' Steve said again, his face anguished. His whole body was now trembling violently. Maurice very gently put an arm round him and soothed him, as he would have done with his own children.

'It's all right, Steve, we're here now, everything's going to be all right. We'll take care of everything, you've nothing to be worried about. I'll help you get cleaned up.'

'You can't move him,' Rob said warningly. 'There may be internal injuries.'

'I did the first aid course, remember,' Maurice said, still holding on to Steve. 'I only went as a bit of a skive but I did pass, don't worry. I'll help Steve get dressed then I'll take him to casualty, but I'll need your car. You stay here and see to SOCO. Make sure the boss knows there's no need for him to come,' Maurice made his tone heavy with meaning. He knew

Steve wouldn't want his boss to see him in such a state.

'We'll get you cleaned up and into fresh jim-jams, Steve, then I'll take you to hospital. I think they'll probably want to keep you in at least overnight.'

I don't have any pyjamas,' Steve wailed.

'Eh, Steve, lad, what are we going to do with you? Don't worry, everything will be fine. I'll help you. We'll find you something clean to wear. We'll get it all sorted.'

Again, Maurice turned to speak to Rob. 'You'll probably get better mobile reception if you go back up the steps,' he said meaningfully.

Rob nodded his understanding and went out, walking back up to street level. He was glad of an excuse to slip out. Seeing Steve like that had really upset him. But what he found was making him well up was Maurice's unexpected gentleness, the tender way he was helping Steve. Rob could see why, despite a disastrous marriage, Maurice was still allowed unrestricted access to his children. He was clearly a brilliant father, something Rob had never known.

Maurice realised that he and Rob should have gloved up before entering what was clearly a crime scene, but his main concern had been for Steve's welfare. If he got his backside kicked by Forensics, so be it. His main priority was to get Steve cleaned up and dressed, with as much dignity and as little damage as possible.

'How long have you been here like this?' he asked, carefully helping Steve to sit up and swing his legs out of bed, completely ignoring the smell of stale urine.

'Saturday,' Steve told him, clearly finding it difficult to talk through pulped lips and broken teeth.

'And your mobile phone?'

Steve shook his head carefully, then Maurice spotted it on the floor, also thoroughly smashed to pieces.

When he finally got Steve to hospital, Maurice shamelessly waved his warrant card until they were seen. Steve was taken away to be examined and Maurice was left to wait anxiously. Ted and Rob turned up not long afterwards.

'Rob needed his car so I brought him in,' Ted explained as Maurice handed over the car keys and Rob left. 'Is there any news? Can we see him?'

'Still waiting to hear the full extent of the damage, boss, but they will be keeping him in overnight. He's seriously dehydrated, for one thing. I don't think he'll be up to seeing anyone this evening, give him a bit of time, eh? Poor lad, he was there since Saturday night with no way of contacting us. I should have gone round this morning, it was so unlike him not to turn up without a word.'

'We were all guilty of that, Maurice,' Ted told him, 'me included. But blaming ourselves doesn't help now. Let's just hope there's not too much damage to Steve. From what Rob told me on the way over, his computer's a total write-off.'

'The whole place, and Steve, have had a thoroughly professional going over, boss. Computer and his mobile smashed to pieces. Is this because of the case? Something to do with one of the
suspects?'

'Looks that way, but I don't know for sure.'

Maurice went to find a machine and brought back hot chocolate while they waited for news. A doctor finally came to find them. He and Ted knew one another by sight, having played badminton in the same club once or twice.

'He's been quite lucky. It's just as well you found him when you did. We've got him on a drip for the dehydration, and he has some concussion but he should be fine. He has four broken ribs, a broken cheekbone and several bones in his hand are broken, but nothing that requires anything more than rest and a plaster cast to put right. Oh, but he will require some extensive dental work. Everything else is just bad bruising, painful but not serious. He certainly had a fairly thorough going over.'

'Thank you, doctor. Keep him as long as you need to, don't let him tell you I'm an ogre who's demanding his early return. Please tell him that from me.'

Ted offered to drop Maurice off as they headed back to his car.

'As soon as they let him out, he can come and stay with me for a bit, until he gets back on his feet,' Maurice said, then, seeing Ted's look, he laughed. 'Don't worry, boss, my car may be like a shit heap but my house is surprisingly homely. I don't smoke in the house, because of the kids visiting. Just what Steve needs till he's back on his feet.'

Chapter Forty-seven

Ted was home late that evening. He'd found the time to send a quick text to Trev warning him that he would be, then went from the hospital straight back to the station. The Ice Queen was waiting for him, to hear his report on what had happened with Steve.

It led to a long and at times heated discussion. For perhaps the first time in their working relationship, Ted felt he was being treated like an equal, his opinions being valued and weighed up.

'I'm not saying we give up altogether on pursuing the Knave of Clubs,' she said, as she brewed a second pot of coffee. 'I just think that for now, we content ourselves with Evans and Danielson, get a cast-iron case built against them and secure their convictions, then regroup and decide where we go next.'

'In the meantime, others might be at risk of the same fate as Aiden,' Ted protested. 'Steve was looking into some information I got from Harry, the ex-Met officer, into dates of other similar offences in their area.'

'Was he working on it at home?' she asked sharply.

'He was under strict orders not to but he may have got carried away. If someone was watching his online activity, it would explain how this happened. In fact, Steve said he thought his own system may have been safer to use than the one here. Is it time to consider checking for bugs?'

'Isn't that getting a bit into the realms of fantasy? Someone breaks into a police station to bug our system?' She lifted the coffee jug to offer him a refill but Ted shook his head. He was already sure he wouldn't sleep after the amount he had drunk this late in the day.

'But this was very clearly a serious warning. The question is, what happens next if we continue to ignore it and forge ahead with the enquiry?'

Ted sighed, aware that her point was valid.

'Will Danielson offer a deal now, do you think? Names in exchange for a lighter sentence and a cushy ride inside?'

'Between you and me, and I can't stress that enough, the top brass are not prepared to do a deal with him, no matter whose head he offers up on a plate,' she told him. 'They think any such suggestion would be enormously damaging to the public perception of the force's integrity. They want him hung out to dry to restore public confidence, and to show that they will take decisive action against their own when necessary. The only deal on offer would be to drop the conspiracy to murder charge, as frankly it was not going to stick anyway.'

'He's not going to like that,' Ted said dryly. 'He thought he was untouchable.'

'Nobody is above the law, and that's the message we need to get out there.'

'Not unless you're royalty,' Ted said sharply.

'I do understand your frustration. Sometimes we just have to play the long game, which I imagine is not your preferred tactic.

'Now, I have a suggestion. We still need to resolve how we go forward with this case, without endangering anyone. I think you and I should get together on another day, away from the office. I'm aware you're not entirely comfortable indoors in a suit and tie, but as I've said before, I'm not your enemy. I want us to work well together,' she said, to Ted's surprise.

'I don't know the patch all that well yet, so could you suggest somewhere we could meet up, somewhere quiet, out in the open, where we could perhaps have a coffee, go for a walk, throw some ideas around?'

Ted couldn't have been more surprised if she'd suggested they spend a dirty weekend in Blackpool together. He decided to treat it as the olive branch it clearly was. His personal preference for walking was always the Peak District, but that was special to him and Trev so he didn't feel inclined to share it with the Ice Queen.

'Lyme Park isn't far,' he said. 'There are plenty of places to walk, moorland, formal gardens, and there's a good café for tea and scones. When did you have in mind?'

'What about Friday afternoon?' she asked. 'Start our weekend early. We'll both need to go home and change first, so shall we say two o'clock? Where should we meet?'

'The main car park, I'd say. I doubt it will be crowded on a Friday at this time of year.'

'Right, that's settled then. I will, of course, see you daily before then, but put that in your diary for the end of the week.'

Ted puzzled over it on his short drive home. It seemed so out of character for what he knew of the Ice Queen so far. He looked forward to perhaps seeing a different side to her, one which might help their working relationship.

He was tired by the time he got home, despite all the coffee. It had been a long and rather draining day. He was looking forward to something to eat, something mindless on television and, above all, enjoying Trev's company now he was back home.

Trev was at the kitchen table, looking at his laptop. 'Long day?' he asked, without looking up. 'There's some supper for you, keeping warm. I didn't know if you would be hungry.'

'Tired, hungry and above all a little puzzled,' Ted said, planting a kiss on top of Trev's silky black curls. 'The Ice Queen has asked me out.'

'Really?' Trev turned and looked up at him. 'Does she not know you're spoken for?'

'She suggested we go somewhere away from the office to

255

discuss the latest case. We're going to Lyme Park on Friday afternoon.' He looked over Trev's shoulder at the laptop. 'What are you looking at?'

'Choosing this holiday you're going to take me on,' Trev said, his blue eyes sparkling. 'There are some fantastic ones to choose from. Just look at these tropical islands! Little huts on stilts over the ocean. Miles of white sand. Just lazing about in the sunshine.' He was flicking through the pictures as he spoke.

Ted's mind was busy calculating how many hours flying from Manchester these places were and wondering how, if he survived the flight, he could keep from going mad at the inactivity. But he'd promised Trev whatever holiday he wanted and he knew he had a lot of making up to do so he said, 'Fabulous. Just choose the one you want and book it. Stick it on my card.'

Trev looked at him, grinning widely. Then the grin turned to a chuckle and before long he was laughing hard.

'Oh Ted,' he said fondly, 'sometimes, for a copper, you are so easy to wind up! I know you'd go mad on the first day and it's not my thing either. Look, this is what I've actually been looking at for us – glamping in Italy.'

'Glamping?' Ted asked suspiciously, not sure if he was still being made fun of.

'It's a bit like camping only more luxurious. Just look at this, a cute little wooden hut in the Apennines. No other guests, miles of hill walking, wildlife, wine for me, good food. We could take the bike, see a bit of France on the way over. What do you think?'

'Do they have ginger beer in Italy?' Ted tried to sound unenthusiastic but failed.

It looked perfect, just what they both needed to repair the ravages of such a hard case.

Trev laughed again. 'I'm sure we'll find you something to drink. And look,' he toggled to another site. 'We can get Animal Aunts to babysit the cats so we won't have to worry about them.'

He got up from the table and served Ted's food, then sat down opposite him with a glass of wine.

'Hard day today?' he asked.

'Up there with the worst. Steve got badly beaten up and he's in hospital.'

'Oh God, Ted, I'm so sorry,' Trev reached over and put a hand on Ted's arm. 'And here's me prattling on and clowning around. Poor Steve. Is he going to be all right?'

'Physically he'll mend, if he finds a good dentist. Trouble is, the emotional scars of something like this can sometimes take the longest time to heal. This is delicious, by the way, thank you.'

Trev smiled. 'Yeah, I know you missed my cooking while I was away.'

'Not just your cooking,' Ted said with feeling. 'I'm so sorry I drove you away. I thought I could handle things on my own. But now I've started counselling, I hope things should be a little easier for you from now on. And I am going to make it up to you.'

'Wow, you said the C-word,' Trev smiled. 'That's progress in itself.'

'"I should have done it long ago, instead of letting it put me at risk of losing you.'

'You never lost me,' Trev told him. 'You were just in too dark a place for me to handle. But it was never you I left, just the ghosts from the past.'

'Did you have a good time while you were away?' Ted asked.

They hadn't really talked much about Trev's time in Germany. Ted had been almost afraid to ask how it had gone. 'I know how much you liked living in Berlin when you were there with your parents. Don't you miss the lifestyle you used to have?'

'I had a brilliant time. I got proposed to in a nightclub, and

I was offered modelling work,' Trev told him, grinning. 'The trouble is, I missed you, and the cats. Tell me how the case is going. Have you caught the bad guys?'

'Some, not all of them. I'm not sure if we ever will catch them all. Maybe I'll know better after my date with the Ice Queen on Friday.'

Chapter Forty-eight

Steve was kept in overnight for observation. When Maurice rang the hospital first thing, he was told he would be allowed out after morning rounds, once his medication was sorted and a doctor had signed his discharge papers. Maurice promised to go and collect him, then went to talk to the boss.

'I'll have to bring him in here, boss, poor lad is too afraid to stay anywhere on his own.'

Ted shook his head. 'You know he can't come back to work without a certificate to say he's fit, and he's not likely to get one of those just yet.'

'We can't just abandon him, boss, he has no family. We're his family. What harm can it do if he just comes in and sits quietly, as long as he's not working?'

'You know that's not how it works, Maurice,' Ted said patiently. ' This isn't a kindergarten. It would be breaking all kinds of rules.'

Maurice was nothing if not stubborn. 'So what am I supposed to do with him? Leave him shut up alone at my place, scared out of his wits? This is our Steve we're talking about, boss, injured in the line of duty, most probably. Can't you square it with the Ice Queen?'

'Superintendent Caldwell to you, Constable,' Ted growled, trying to sound fierce but falling short. 'All right, bring him in, I'll take full responsibility. But he does not so much as touch a computer, or any files. Make sure he understands that or I'll have to handcuff him.'

'Thanks, boss,' Maurice grinned. 'By the way, I doubt

Steve's computer was insured for this type of loss, so I wondered about having a whip-round, at least help him on his way to a new one?'

'Good idea. Let me know how much you want. You're a kind man, Maurice.'

Maurice shrugged. 'He's a good lad, is our Steve.'

After Maurice went off to collect Steve, Ted called Harry's mobile number. Once again it was quickly answered.

'Mind-reader, Ted. I was just about to call you to see if that stuff I sent was of any use, and to fill you in on further developments.'

'Dynamite, I'd say. Young Steve was working on it. Someone broke into his flat at the weekend, smashed his computer beyond repair and beat the crap out of him.'

'Sorry to hear that. Your Steve seems very switched on, although if he was working on any of this stuff from his own address, he was running one hell of a risk.'

'These people could trace him that easily?' Ted asked, with not much of a clue how such things worked.

'These people know which side of the bed you and your partner sleep on. You'd do well to remember that.' Harry's tone had a warning edge. 'Right, new developments, on our patch. A young boy, twelve, seriously sexually assaulted and semi-strangled. He's alive, just, but I hear he may well have brain damage. Rumour has it our friend the Knave was involved. He was certainly in the area at the right time.'

'How can he keep getting away with it?'

'Can you seriously imagine the repercussions if it got out? Not just his actions but the extent of the cover-up there's been all along.' Harry said. 'The more they cover up, the more they need to. One day someone will bring him down, though, somehow.'

'Is this where you expect me to saddle up my white charger and ride into battle?' Ted asked. 'I've only been on a horse once and then I fell off it. But I do think my Super has integrity. She's also the mother of two boys. If anyone tries to take him on, she might. I'll go and talk to her now and keep you posted.'

The Ice Queen listened in silence while Ted spoke. He mentioned in passing that he was allowing Steve into the office as his flat was now a crime scene and he needed somewhere to feel safe. Then he outlined what Harry had told him, asking again if there was not some way they could at least begin a formal investigation of the Knave of Clubs.

'I don't even know where the protocol would begin,' she told him honestly. 'I'd have to go much higher up the chain of command to find out and I would need a very strong file to back up any such request. Do you have such a file?'

'Honestly, ma'am? No, I don't. I just have a lot of speculation and possible coincidence. Apart from the eye witness account of the receptionist at the Sorrento Hotel placing him there, possibly on the night Aiden Bradshaw was killed. My contact in London sent some details to Steve, which is presumably what led to him being targeted.

'Although his own computer was smashed, I'm assuming Steve still has the means to access his emails, which I will get him to do once he's certified fit to work.'

'Leave it with me, Inspector. I will give it my full attention and see what, if anything, we can do at this stage. I would certainly hope to have some definite news for you before the weekend. As I said, and as I firmly believe, no one is above the law.'

'Speaking of Steve's computer, ma'am, Maurice Brown is organising a whip-round to give him a helping hand towards replacing it. I didn't know if you would want to contribute?'

'Absolutely,' she said emphatically. 'Put me down for whatever seems reasonable. I won't come up and frighten him, but do please pass on my best wishes. For some reason, I seem to intimidate him.'

Ted smiled to himself and thought that Steve was not the only one, but said nothing and went back to his office.

Maurice had told him that he would personally interview Steve about what exactly happened at his flat, as he knew the TDC would find it hard to talk about. Maurice seemed to have taken him under his wing which was probably a good thing for both of them.

Everyone available on the team was working flat out on the files against Evans and Danielson, pulling together witness statements and interview transcripts. Ted was determined that neither man could get off on a technicality because of sloppy paperwork. Their job was to make the bullets for CPS to fire. All of them particularly wanted to see Danielson go down for as long as possible. Nobody liked a bent cop at the best of times but one carrying out sex offences on children was beyond contempt.

There was a spontaneous round of applause from the team when Steve made his slow and painful way up the stairs and into the main office, helped by Maurice. Ted went out to see him. He looked rough and in a lot of pain, but he was smiling in evident pleasure, although with difficulty, to be back amongst the team-mates he clearly thought of as friends and family. His swollen right hand was in a cast and an elevated sling, his face puffy and discoloured, eyes half closed, and he was clearly relieved to be able to sit down after climbing the stairs.

'It's good to see you, Steve. Now, you're sitting at your desk but you're not on duty and you are not to do any work at all until I have a certificate passing you as fit,' Ted told him.

'Sir, I want to do something to help,' Steve said determinedly. 'I'm part of the team, I want to be involved. If I don't do it myself, but I show Maurice how to retrieve the file from Harry I was looking at, that wouldn't really count as me working, would it?'

Ted shook his head, but he was smiling. 'You're determined to get me into trouble, aren't you?'

'No sir,' Steve said earnestly. 'I'm determined to help you catch whoever killed young Aiden.'

Chapter Forty-nine

Ted was early for his meeting with the Ice Queen at Lyme Park on Friday afternoon. There were not many vehicles there and he picked a parking space from where he could watch any car which approached. He was keeping an eye out for her sleek BMW.

While he was waiting, a red motorbike drove into the car park. Living with Trev, Ted now knew enough to know it was a Ducati. As it parked nearby, he could see it was a 999. He watched as the rider got off and removed their helmet. As they shook out long, sleek black hair, he realised to his surprise that it was the Ice Queen herself, dressed in black leathers.

She was smiling at his surprise.

'This is my guilty little secret,' she told him. 'The BMW is fine for work but when I go out to play, this is my chosen means of transport. I know, the 999 is unbelievably kitsch and a total cliché, but it's just my sense of humour.' She looked around her then said, 'Shall we walk first and have coffee later? I've never been here so I'm relying on you to show me the sights.

'This afternoon we're going to do a bit of bonding, you and I. I keep telling you I'm not your enemy but I sense I have not yet truly convinced you. We're both off duty, so for now, and only now, I shall call you Ted and you may call me Debs. So, where do we begin?'

'If we walk up to the Cage, there's a nice view from up there. It's an old hunting lodge,' Ted said, leading the way.

'I must bring the boys here. They'd love it, plenty of room

to roam around.'

It was not a long walk. They chatted inconsequentially as they went. From the top, they could look out over the surrounding parkland, hundreds of acres of it. A herd of red deer grazed peacefully in the distance, totally unperturbed by the occasional passing car or walker.

'This is very nice, a good suggestion, Ted.'

She looked at the deer and raised an imaginary rifle, sighting on the herd.

'I don't like hunting or killing animals but, hypothetically, which ones could you pick off from up here?'

As if sensing their interest, even from a distance, a magnificent stag, furthest away from them, raised his head and looked towards them.

Ted looked at the distance and angles.

'About the same as you, I would imagine, although I'm out of practice. And you were always a better shot than me, especially with a handgun, even if I did beat you once with a long-range rifle.'

'You beat me twice,' she said. 'Thank you for being gallant and pretending not to remember. Do you miss firearms?'

The Ice Queen sat down in the grass to watch the deer, long legs stretched out in front of her. Ted sat down a short distance from her. He was still finding it hard to be totally relaxed in her company, although he was making the effort.

'Not really. I gave it up when I knew it was serious with Trev. It worried him too much.'

'I gave it up because of the boys,' she said. 'I still keep my hand in on the ranges when I can, as I expect you do.'

There was a long silence between them, then she said, 'I've been making enquiries, as I said I would. I don't know if we can get any further forward. But sometimes, these things have a way of working themselves out, even if it's not exactly the result we were looking for.'

Ted was taken aback. Her words were so like those of

Green, sitting on top of the Brecon Beacons. He was still not sure what they meant.

The next silence was protracted, so much so that Ted felt obliged to fill it. He surprised himself by suddenly saying, 'I was one of David Evans' victims. When I was a kid. He raped me.'

She said nothing, just remained sitting quietly beside him, her eyes on the herd of deer. He found that her silence gave him the strength to continue. He knew he had to tell her, knew he should have done so from the outset. Out here in the open, with both of them relaxed, it suddenly became, if not easy, then possible.

'I never testified, I couldn't face it. But I haven't compromised the enquiry in any way, I've kept out of it.'

'I would never think for a moment that you would, Ted. You're an excellent officer. Perhaps a little old-fashioned and sometimes naïve, but your work is beyond reproach. You also have an uncanny way of getting people to like you, even when you are karate kicking them. Thank you for telling me.'

She didn't tell him that she had already deduced as much. She'd seen Evans' file, knew which schools he'd taught at. She'd also read Ted's CV and knew where he was educated.

'It must have made this case particularly difficult for you. I'm glad we've got enough of a case against Evans and the Chief Super to have them more or less in the bag. I wish I could promise you more, but I assure you I am doing everything I can.'

She left a pause for the words to sink in, then sprang to her feet. 'Where now? Can we look at the hall? I might as well do the whole tourist thing.'

Ted smiled, seeing her in a completely different light. She looked a lot younger, out of uniform, much more human without her brittle work veneer.

'They filmed Pride and Prejudice here, you know. I can show you the lake where the famous scene with Mr Darcy getting his clothes wet was filmed if you like.'

They walked across to the hall. Ted led her round to the rear, for the view of the imposing building from the far side of its famous lake. To his surprise, the Ice Queen got out her phone and said, 'Selfies! Come on, Ted, we have to do this.'

She had to bend down a little to get her head at his level, moving in close and laughing into the camera as she said, 'That's an immortal moment. Two of the force's finest marksmen, shot with a single camera.'

She checked the image on the screen and said, 'That's really nice. I'll send it to your mobile, as a souvenir. Hopefully it will help you to remember that the Ice Queen is not quite as frosty as you think.'

Seeing his look, she laughed and said, 'Oh yes, I'm well aware of what everyone calls me, of course. It's not entirely justified. I hope today will show you that I am a human being, and you can talk to me.'

Ted's mobile pinged as he received the photo. He looked at it on his phone. The afternoon had certainly given him a whole new perspective on the Ice Queen. He would probably never feel entirely comfortable in her presence, as he had done with Jim Baker, but he had seen a new, warmer and more relaxed side to her.

'The sunken gardens are rather fine,' Ted said, aware he sounded like a tour guide. 'Italian. We could walk through them, then on down to the Timber Yard for coffee?'

Chatting over coffee and cakes, Ted finally started to feel at ease in her company. When he caught sight of the clock in the tea room, he was surprised how late it had become. Trev would be home from work, probably starting to cook as they had not made plans to go out.

He and the Ice Queen walked back to the car park together. As she took her helmet out of the top-box on the bike, she turned to him, her tone reverting to its usual formality, and said, 'Well, Inspector, thank you for showing me this lovely place, and for your time. I hope now we can move forward as colleagues with a better understanding of one another.'

With that, she mounted her bike and roared off across the car park, leaving Ted still feeling a bit bemused by his afternoon.

Trev was sitting in front of the television when Ted got home, with it tuned to a news channel. He was leaning forward on the sofa, his eyes glued to the screen.

'Have you heard this?' he asked, barely glancing at Ted. 'I heard it on the radio so put the news on for an update. Someone shot a royal.'

Ted absent-mindedly scooped up cats so he could sit down next to Trev. His knees suddenly felt weak. He watched the running news-feed scrolling across the bottom of the screen which confirmed that the Knave of Clubs had been shot dead whilst on an official engagement.

A news reporter was delivering her piece to camera. 'Early indications are that the shot which killed the royal visitor, here to open a sports facility, came from one of those tall buildings in the background.'

The camera panned away to show where she was talking about.

'Unconfirmed reports say there was a single shot to the head. A doctor and paramedics arrived within minutes, but he was pronounced dead at the scene.'

The camera cut back to her. The background scene showed police, many of them armed, swarming all around. Ted also spotted several grim-looking men in suits, and wearing earpieces. Police tape had gone up, cordoning off the scene, and there were area cars parked everywhere, lights flashing.

Ted looked again towards the background, the buildings which had been indicated. To take a man down from that distance and angle was the work of a highly proficient sniper. To do it with a single head shot was beyond the capabilities of most but an elite few. He knew that at his peak, he could have done it, and so could the Ice Queen, but there were not many others capable of it.

Slowly he took his mobile phone out of his pocket and opened it up to the date-stamped photo she had taken of the two of them together, remembering her words.

'Two of the force's finest marksmen, shot with a single camera.'

The End